# THE LAST REFUGE

# THE LAST REFUGE

A Hannah Ives mystery

## Marcia Talley

This first world edition published 2012
in Great Britain and in the USA by
SEVERN HOUSE PUBLISHERS LTD of
9–15 High Street, Sutton, Surrey, England, SM1 1DF.
Trade paperback edition first published
in Great Britain and the USA 2012 by
SEVERN HOUSE PUBLISHERS LTD

British Library Cataloguing in Publication Data

Talley, Marcia Dutton, 1943-
   The last refuge. -- (The Hannah Ives mysteries series)
   1. Ives, Hannah (Fictitious character)--Fiction.
   2. Detective and mystery stories.
   I. Title II. Series
   813.6-dc23

ISBN-13: 978-0-7278-8153-3 (cased)
ISBN-13: 978-1-84751-418-9 (trade paper)

*All Severn House titles are printed on acid-free paper.*

Severn House Publishers support The Forest Stewardship Council [FSC],
the leading international forest certification organisation. All our titles that
are printed on Greenpeace-approved FSC-certified paper carry the FSC logo.

FSC
www.fsc.org
MIX
Paper from
responsible sources
FSC® C018575

Typeset by Palimpsest Book Production Ltd.,
Falkirk, Stirlingshire, Scotland.
Printed and bound in Great Britain by
MPG Books Ltd., Bodmin, Cornwall.

*For Barry*

# ACKNOWLEDGMENTS

Writing is a solitary business, yet it takes a team to put a novel into the hands of readers. With thanks to my incredible team:

My husband, Barry Talley, who turns down the TV and slips thin food under my office door whenever I'm on deadline.

My editor, Sara Porter, my can-do publicist, Michelle Duff, publisher Edwin Buckhalter and everyone else at Severn House who makes it such an incredibly supportive place for a mystery writer to be.

Historic Annapolis Foundation and the staff of the William Paca House for allowing my imaginary LynxE production team and cast to move in, particularly Alexandra Deutsch, Curator (2004–2008); Glenn Campbell, Historian; and Scotti Preston, Living History/ Special Projects Coordinator.

Joseph Gagliardi, M.A., M.D. who practices medicine both in the past (as Doctor A. Dobbs) and in the present as Medical Director of the Detox Center of Central Maryland, in Columbia, Maryland.

Lt Paul Wood, USN, for . . . well, if I told you, he'd have to kill me.

And once again, my fellow travelers at various stations on the road to publication, the Annapolis Writers Group: Ray Flynt, Lynda Hill, Mary Ellen Hughes, Debbi Mack, Sherriel Mattingley, and Bonnie Settle for tough love.

To Kate Charles and Deborah Crombie who are always there to help out whenever the muse takes a vacation.

And, of course, to Vicky Bijur.

*'Patriotism is the last refuge of a scoundrel.'*

Samuel Johnson (1709–1784)
James Boswell, *Life of Johnson,*
entry for Friday, April 7, 1775

# ONE

*'As I faced my own mortality, I asked myself: "If not now, when?"'*

Hannah Ives

Hollywood legend has it that Lana Turner was discovered while perched on a fountain stool at Schwab's drugstore. Not true, according to Wikipedia. The sixteen-year-old truant was sneaking a Coca-Cola at Tops Café at the corner of Sunset and McCadden, but it just goes to show that when you think you know what you're doing, life pitches you a curve.

I'll never fill out a sweater the way Lana did, Lord knows, but my introduction to show business was similarly mundane: I was cleaning out my fridge. Sink full of soapy water, arms submerged up to the elbows, mold-stained plastic containers bobbing like derelict boats among the suds, Barbra Streisand and I belting out *People Who Need People* at the top of our lungs, when I thought I heard the telephone ring. Using my elbow, I punched the power/off button on the Sirius radio and listened. When the telephone rang again, I stripped off my rubber gloves and answered it.

'Hannah? Hannah Ives?' The voice at the other end of the line sounded familiar, but I couldn't place it immediately.

'Yes?'

'It's Jud, Mrs Ives. Jud Wilson.'

The last time I'd seen Jud, a young production assistant at Lynx News, we'd been sitting in a studio at network headquarters in Washington, D.C., reviewing Library of Congress security camera footage he'd pulled strings to lay hands on for me. I still owed him. Big.

'Jud! How the heck are you? Still with Lynx News?'

'In a manner of speaking,' the young man told me. 'After John Chandler went over to CNN, I hung around for a while working for the anchorman who replaced him, but when a job came up at Lynx Entertainment, I jumped at it.'

I'm a sucker for those make-over shows on the House and Garden Network, but LynxE wasn't one of the channels I made a habit of watching. The network had inflicted such must-sees on the American viewing public as *Stranded* and *Take My Wife, Please!* and *Carpool Confidential*. 'Don't tell me you're responsible for *CEO Kids*,' I said, naming one of LynxE's most popular summer shows where child protégées were installed in senior positions in some of America's largest companies, including ExxonMobil and Bank of America. When one budding genius managed to lose half a million dollars in an hour of trading for Merrill-Lynch, the show's ratings had shot into the stratosphere.

Jud laughed. 'Not one of your faves, I take it.'

I snorted.

'You're probably wondering why I'm calling, Hannah.'

'The thought crossed my mind, yes.'

'The truth is, I'm kind of in a bind, and I'm hoping you can help me out.'

'You know I will,' I said, remembering how he'd stuck his neck out for me. Then I added cautiously, 'If I can. Would you care to elaborate?'

'It's too complicated to go into over the phone. Are you free right now?'

I considered the disaster that was my refrigerator – door yawning open, plastic tubs full of the colorful, furry remains of God-knows-what littering the countertop awaiting triage – garbage disposal or trash? – and said, 'Sure. Where and when?'

'I'm in Annapolis, so how about now?'

'As good a time as any. Where are you calling from, Jud?'

'Look out your window.'

I wandered through the dining room, into the living room that spanned the front of our Prince George Street home and drew the curtain aside. Jud Wilson stood outside, running shoes firmly planted on the uneven brick sidewalk, his cell phone pressed to his ear. He sported the same fashionably layered do with a fringe of bangs as the time I'd last seen him, but had replaced the chinos, white dress shirt and tie that had been his uniform at Lynx News with a black T-shirt tucked and belted into a pair of neatly pressed blue jeans. When Jud saw me peering out, he waggled his fingers.

'Silly boy,' I chided over the phone. 'Why didn't you simply ring the doorbell?'

On the other side of the window, Jud shrugged.

'What the heck are you doing out there?'

'I was in the neighborhood,' Jud said, as if that explained everything. He pointed east down Prince George Street in the direction of the William Paca House, a colonial mansion built in the mid 1760s by Maryland patriot William Henry Paca, a signer of the Declaration of Independence. Fully restored to its 1770s splendor, the house was now a popular tourist attraction. I could see a Lynx News truck parked in front of the house, partially blocking traffic on the narrow, one-way street. A VW Jetta was easing carefully around it, one wheel kissing the opposite curb.

I stifled a gasp. 'A news truck? Why? What's happened?'

Jud raised a hand. 'Don't worry, no problem. It's for a show I'm producing.'

In the past several days, I'd noticed moving vans coming and going, workers wearing overalls and white gloves lugging furniture out of the historic home. There'd been much speculation about it in the neighborhood, but I'd reached an over-the-fence consensus with my next-door neighbor, Brad Perry, that renovations must be going on and that the furniture – some of it original to the house – was being removed for safekeeping.

Brad and I were right, but we were also wrong.

'We're shooting a TV show at Paca House,' Jud explained, gesturing at me through the window. 'It's called *Patriot House, 1774.*'

'Ah.' I thought I could predict where this conversation was going. Jud was in cahoots with my daughter, Emily, who'd been his college friend. Somehow he'd learned that we had three empty bedrooms. 'Let me guess,' I continued. 'The hotels are all full and you're looking for places to put up your staff.'

'No.' He chuckled. 'Kind of the other way around.'

I was puzzled, and curious. 'Look, Jud, we can talk to each other through the window all day, I suppose, but wouldn't it be more comfortable if you came inside?'

Jud nodded in agreement, and pocketed his phone. Five seconds later, I'd laid my own phone down on the entrance-hall table and was greeting him at the front door. 'Something to drink?' I asked as I signaled for him to follow me into the kitchen.

'How 'bout a shot of whiskey to wash down a Tylenol?'

I turned. 'You're kidding.'

'Just barely. *Patriot House* has been a headache from day one, but we're too far down the road to cancel the show now.'

I apologized to Jud for the mess, then fixed him a tall glass of iced tea. 'Lemon?' When he nodded, I dropped a wedge into the glass and handed it to him. 'No whiskey, I'm afraid, but the tea's the right color. Use your imagination,' I joked, waving the young man into a chair and pointing out the sweetener, in case he needed it.

Jud raised the glass and drank half of it down, straight. 'Ah.' He sighed. 'Nothing better than iced tea on a hot August day.'

I poured a glass of tea for myself, then joined him at the table. 'So, tell me. How can a documentary be trouble?'

'Not a documentary. A reality show.'

'A reality show? Here in Annapolis?'

'You know those PBS shows where they take a dozen or so modern people and see how they cope with everyday life in another time and place?'

I nodded. 'I remember watching *Manor House* about ten years ago, and I thought *Texas Ranch House* was a hoot, especially when the "Indians,"' I drew quote marks in the air, 'turned into cattle rustlers.'

Jud laughed. '110 degrees! 200 cows! 47,000 acres and fifteen people! Who could forget it?'

'I don't watch a lot of TV,' I confessed, 'but haven't living history shows gone a teeny bit out of fashion?'

'Tell that to LynxE. These days, the suits are calling them experiential history shows.' Jud grinned. 'With TV, what goes around comes around, like bell-bottomed pants.' He paused to take another long, slow swallow of tea.

'So, what's the problem?'

'Can I tell you a little bit about the show first?' When I nodded, he continued on in a rush, as if reading a teaser from a listing in *TV Guide*. As the show's producer, though, I figured he'd pitched it a thousand times. 'The Donovans are a real, upper-middle-class family. John and Katherine, and their two kids, are playing the well-to-do owners of the Paca House. For three months, they'll be sharing the house with a cast that includes an African-American cook and her son, a tutor and a lady's maid, assisted by a housemaid, valet, gardener, groom and a visiting dancing master. There's a camera team on site ten hours each day taping the participants as they dress, eat, work, play and worship just as the home's original occupants did more than two hundred years ago, with all the modern conveniences of, well, 1774. There's no electricity, no running water, no telephone and the "necessaries" are way out back.'

'Privies? What fun,' I deadpanned.

'We had everyone in place; they're down in Williamsburg, Virginia for orientation right now, in fact. But three days ago, Katherine Donovan, who's playing the mistress of the house, had to quit the cast.' He ran a hand through his hair. 'Just what I need! We start filming in two weeks.'

'She quit? Why?'

'That's one of the reasons I thought of you. She's been diagnosed with breast cancer. Kat's about to have the surgery, but she'll have to undergo chemotherapy, like you had to. There's no chance of her getting back on her feet in time to participate in the show.'

I was a survivor, too. I knew what it was like to have your life turned upside down by a diagnosis of cancer. I felt sympathy for this woman – been there, done that – but had no idea what her unfortunate situation might have to do with me . . . unless. 'Do you want me to talk to her, Jud? Reassure her? If so, I'd be happy to.'

'That would be gracious of you, Hannah, but that's not exactly what I'm after. I need to find a replacement for Kat, and I don't have much time.'

'But don't you spend months and months auditioning people

for those shows? Surely there's someone waiting in the wings, an understudy, champing at the bit.'

'Ordinarily, yes. You wouldn't believe how desperate some people were to participate. We had applicants from all fifty states and at least twelve foreign countries, including Thailand. One woman sent in samples of her needlepoint. Others sent videos of themselves shoeing horses or milking cows.' Jud raised a hand, palm out, as if taking an oath. 'One guy, I swear to God, wrote his application on parchment in ye olde letters with a quill pen.'

I had to laugh. 'So, pick one. It can't be that hard.'

'I already have.'

'So, why the Tylenol?'

'I haven't asked her yet.'

I gave him a look. 'Well?'

The tips of Jud's ears turned pink. 'Hannah, I'm hoping you'll agree to take Katherine Donovan's place.'

When I could breathe again, I sputtered, 'No way!'

Jud nodded, his face as solemn as a priest at a funeral. 'We'd like you to play Jack Donovan's sister-in-law, recently arrived in Annapolis to be mistress of his house and mother to his kids. We'll pretend his wife died of smallpox or something. Things like that happened back then.'

'And my name would be?'

'Hannah Ives. Everyone's keeping their real names.'

I raised a hand. 'Wait a minute. Don't you have to vet your people? Do background checks and so on? Make sure they aren't publicity seekers? Psychotics? Axe murderers? Whatever?'

'That's another reason your name leaped to the top of my list.'

'Now I *am* confused.'

'When you poked your nose into Lynx News headquarters last year asking all those questions about John Chandler? I ordered a background check on you.'

I felt my face grow hot. 'I passed, I take it?'

'Squeaky clean.'

'But . . .' I closed my eyes and tried to work out the time-line. 'Three months is a long time!'

'We'll pay you fifteen thousand dollars.'

'That beats selling candy bars outside the Safeway, but still . . .' I thought ahead to my calendar which held the usual stuff – lunches with friends, charity work, running the occasional carpool for my grandchildren, babysitting. The semester had already started so my husband, Paul, would be teaching math full time to undergraduates at the United States Naval Academy, a few short blocks from our house. He could certainly manage without me using a combination of daily lunches at the Officers and Faculty Club and dinners from the hot food bar at Whole Foods, Galway Bay or by mooching off our daughter, Emily. Emily had to cook for five anyway – including her husband, Dante Shemansky, and my three darling grandchildren – so setting another place at the table was rarely a problem. Still, three months under virtual house arrest with a bunch of people I didn't even know seemed like a tall order, even with a check for fifteen thousand dollars at the end of it.

My mind raced ahead. No electricity, no modern plumbing, and grande cappuccinos from Starbucks wouldn't have been invented yet.

Jud looked so young, so enthusiastic, so hopeful, I hated to disappoint him. 'I'm not sure I'm the woman for the job, Jud. Everything I know about living during Revolutionary War times comes from watching the *John Adams* series on HBO.' I paused, ticking the items off on my fingers. 'Let me get this straight. No running water, no heat, privies way out back . . .'

'Right. And no Internet or cell phones, either.'

'You make it sound so attractive!'

Jud flashed me a mischievous, schoolboy grin and I felt myself weakening. He stood up, looked around for a coaster – a properly brought-up lad – and set his empty glass down on it. 'Before you make up your mind, there's something I'd like to show you.'

Despite the many negatives, my interest was piqued. 'Lead on,' I said, and before I knew it, I was picking up my iPhone, following him out the front door, and walking into history.

# TWO

*'You want to see my stays? They're worn over this shift
which doubles as a nightgown, and they've got boning
from the bust to below the waist, sort of like the corset
that Scarlett O'Hara wore in* Gone With the Wind, *you
know, but not nearly so tight. There's really not room for
my bust in this thing, but shit! Check out my cleavage!'*

Amy Cornell, lady's maid

**W**illiam Paca's five-part, Palladian-style Georgian
mansion towers over its neighbors from its perch
on an embankment several feet above street
level. The three-story, five-bay central house is flanked by
symmetrical two-story pavilions – one a former office, the
other a kitchen – each connected to the main house by short,
one-and-a-half-story hyphens, or passages. Perfectly balanced.
Out back, a two-acre formal garden steps gently down to a
wall that borders King George Street, a garden that was (and
still is) the most elegant in Annapolis. In 1965, exactly 200
years after it was built, the house – which had been converted
into a hotel – was scheduled for demolition, but after an
eight-year struggle by a group of tenacious Annapolitans, the
building and its terraced gardens had been saved and lovingly
restored.

'Paca House fits our needs perfectly,' Jud said as we paused
on the sidewalk to admire the impressive façade, which was
built of brick laid in the Flemish bond style – narrow end of
the brick out – so Paca could show off his wealth.

Jud pronounced the name 'Pack-ah,' and I had to correct him.
'It's Pay-kah. According to a rhyming couplet Paca wrote
himself in 1771, it rhymes with "take a."'

'Is it Paca Street in Baltimore, too?' he asked, correcting
his pronunciation.

'Nope. Pack-ah. Go figure.' I stepped aside to allow a

workman carrying a large wooden crate to pass. 'When I saw all the to-ing and fro-ing, I thought they'd closed the house for repairs.'

'That's what we asked Historic Annapolis to say,' Jud informed me. 'Actually, we're replacing all the antique furnishing with high-quality reproductions specifically made for us in Wilson, North Carolina.'

'I can't imagine the expense.'

Jud grinned. 'Our sponsor has deep pockets.'

'Sponsor?'

'The show is being underwritten by Maddingly and Flynt.' I must have looked puzzled because he continued: 'Paints. They specialize in recreating historical colors. Some of them are pretty vibrant, like Ripe Pear and Presidential Blue.'

'I remember a bit of hoo-hah when historians bored through all the paint layers at Mount Vernon and discovered that George and Martha Washington favored gaudy, Easter-egg colors. Their dining room is green, as in emerald green.'

Jud grinned. 'At Paca House, I understand researchers used an electron microscope and discovered more than twenty layers of paint, all the way down to the brilliant peacock blue you see on the walls of the main floor rooms today.'

'I'm familiar with it,' I said. I'd toured the house often, in fact, whenever we had out-of-town visitors, and we'd attended the occasional garden wedding there, too.

Jud and I detoured around the moving van where two burly guys, sweating profusely in the noonday sun, were struggling with an eighteenth-century sideboard, and continued down Prince George Street past the house.

'Historic Annapolis – affectionately nicknamed Hysterical Annapolis by some of us locals – isn't generally noted for their flexibility. How on earth did you get them to agree to closing the place to tourists for three whole months?' I asked.

Jud paused to look at me, and tapped his temple with his index finger. 'Ah, that's where we had to get creative. Technically, the house *is* getting some renovations done, but at Lynx network expense. The roof needed to be replaced, for example, and the cypress shingles set us back nearly a quarter of a million. And as a gesture that we weren't going to eat and run, so to speak, we've set up an endowment that should pay for the services of a professional gardener, pretty much in perpetuity, thanks to another sponsor, Hughes Horticultural. We've repointed the brick on the façade – a minor expense compared to the roof – and there were things we had to remove, of course, so we could return the house to some of its eighteenth-century functionality. We uncapped all the chimneys and had the flues checked to make sure the fireplaces could be used without burning the house down. Took out the storm windows, too; otherwise nobody would be able to open the windows.

'I'm hoping the weather stays temperate so we don't have to use the fireplaces that often,' he continued, 'but the fireplace in the kitchen will be going pretty much twenty-four seven.'

We were making our way down a narrow alleyway sand-wiched between the Paca House and a private residence that eventually led to a parking lot tucked behind Brice House, another Georgian masterpiece that now served as the head-quarters of the International Masonry Institute. Normally, there would have been half-a-dozen cars in the lot, but through some Lynx magic, the cars had been made to disappear – probably to assigned spaces in the Hillman parking garage off nearby Main Street – and the lot was now occupied by two aluminum-sided trailers, their doors standing open in the late August sun. Cables snaked from the Paca garden, through the hedge, along the ground and into the trailer marked 'Production,' outside of which several well-tamed coils of wire were connected to a giraffe-like stalk antenna. The second trailer was marked 'Wardrobe.'

Jud bounced up the fold-down steps that led into 'Wardrobe,' poked his head out the door and motioned me inside. 'In here.'

It took a few seconds for my eyes to adjust to the low light inside the trailer, but once inside, I noticed a woman sitting behind a table, head bent over her work which was spotlighted by an anglepoise lamp. When we entered, she looked up, dress pins studding her lips, paused in the act of sewing lace onto something that looked like a collar. She considered me over the top of a pair of half-glasses perched precariously at the tip of her nose.

Jud introduced us. 'Alisha, this is Hannah Ives. I'm twisting her arm, hoping she'll agree to fill in for Katherine Donovan. Can you show her Katherine's costumes?'

Alisha laid her work down on the narrow table in front of her, spit the pins out into a glass dish and stood. 'Sure.' She led me down a long aisle toward the back of the trailer.

Rich costumes hung along both sides of the aisle like the seventy-per-cent-off sales at Macy's, if Macy's had been unloading merchandise that had been hanging around since 1780-something, that is. Groups of costumes were bundled loosely together, labeled with signs hand-lettered in felt-tip marker: Karen Gibbs, Dexter Gibbs, John Donovan, Melody Donovan and a dozen or so others. Katherine Donovan's wardrobe hung on padded hangers in a section just past her daughter's.

'Here you go.' Alisha shoved the hangers along the pole to make maneuvering room then, to the accompaniment of a soft rustle of silk, pulled out one of the most beautiful gowns I had ever seen. Holding the hanger in one hand, she draped the exquisite garment over her extended forearm. It was a pale peach confection, with gold, dark rose and deep blue flowers embroidered all over. 'This is a ball gown,' Alisha said. 'Hey, Jud, hold this for me a minute, will ya?'

As Jud took charge of the hanger, I fingered the fabric, imagining myself waltzing around in the gown, like Cinderella at the prince's ball. After a moment, Alisha called my attention to the other garments on the rack. 'This pale blue linen is for everyday wear, of course . . .' She shoved it aside. 'And this thing that looks like a nightgown is called a shift. Colonials wore them pretty much day and night.'

I thought about all the clothes in my closet at home – if I stopped shopping at Chico's, the company would have to declare Chapter 11. 'Only two dresses?' I asked.

Alisha chuckled, tucked a stray strand of wiry brown hair back into the untidy knot at the back of her head. 'Lord, no. The Donovans are supposed to be wealthy. If you sign on, you'll have several more made during the course of the show, and your fancy ball gown, of course.'

I couldn't think of anything more appropriate for a ball than the gorgeous gown she'd already showed me. 'Ball?'

'At the State House – the show finale. Every VIP in Annapolis will be attending it. The governor, the mayor, the superintendent of the Naval Academy, senators, congressmen. Your husband will be invited, too . . . you've got a husband?'

I nodded. 'Will everyone be in costume?'

'Of course. The ball is the climax of the show.' Alisha stared dreamily up at the ceiling. 'Candlelight, music, tables groaning with food.' Suddenly she snapped out of it. She grabbed the hanger from Jud's outstretched hand. 'This is something special, all right. You gotta try it on.'

I stood rooted to the floor, mouth slightly ajar. 'Are you making *all* the costumes?'

'Just for the principals,' Jud commented from behind me. 'For the special events, we've arranged rentals from A.T. Jones up in Baltimore for the invited guests.'

'Back here,' Alisha ordered in a time-is-money sort of way, indicating the rear of the trailer with an impatient jerk of her head. She hustled me into a cubicle separated from the front of the trailer by a thin blue and white gingham curtain and, once I was inside, ordered me to strip. When I got down to my bra and panties, she waved an impatient hand. 'Everything's gotta come off, sweetie.'

'Everything?' I felt like I was back at the doctor's office, preparing for my annual physical exam.

'Well, you can keep the panties on for now,' she relented, 'although they didn't wear panties back then, you know – but the bra's got to go.' I turned my back, unhooked, and slipped out of my bra. Although the reconstructive surgeon had worked wonders after the mastectomy that had separated me from my breast, it still wasn't ready for prime time. Alisha, bless her, didn't seem to notice, or care. She thrust the nightgown-like shift in my direction. 'Put this on first.'

I slipped the garment over my head, smoothing the fabric down over my hips. Before I could even turn around, she wrapped a corset around my waist, adjusted it under my breasts and ordered me to stand still while she laced it up the back like an old-fashioned tennis shoe. 'I feel like a sausage,' I said, sucking in my gut as she tightened the laces.

Next came an under-petticoat that tied around my waist

with a drawstring, followed by a delicately embroidered silk petticoat in the same soft peach as the gown.

I now saw that the gown itself was in two parts – an ankle-length robe, open at the front so the petticoat would show through, and a triangular-shaped piece that served as the bodice. 'It's called a stomacher,' Alisha explained as she clapped it to my chest and pinned me into it. 'And you'll be wearing pocket hoops – sometimes called a farthingale – but we're not going to bother with them now. There's not enough room to swing a cat in here as it is. Shoes, too, but frankly, dancing slippers haven't changed much in two hundred years. You could probably get away with Capezios from Zappo dot-com.'

Alisha seemed to be assuming that I'd already agreed to participate in the *Patriot House, 1774* experience. I was simply trying on costumes, though, not committing myself to anything. '*If* I sign on,' I reminded her.

Alisha squinted at me, her head tilted, ignoring my remark, then drew the dressing-room curtain aside. 'Take a look, Jud. Perfect fit. Don't think we'll need to do any alterations at all.'

Jud studied me critically. 'Jesus, you take my breath away.'

I felt my face redden. Jud was young enough to be my son, but the compliment pleased me enormously. 'Is there a mirror somewhere?'

Alisha tugged on a rolling clothes rack and when it gained momentum, wheeled it to one side, revealing a full-length mirror mounted on the inside of a door that led to a pocket toilet. 'Who *is* that?' I gasped when I saw my reflection.

I certainly wasn't what anybody would call fat, but the woman in the mirror had a waist the size of a mayonnaise jar and – Oh. My. God! – a pair of round, plump breasts and a goodly amount of cleavage. I tucked my chin down for a closer view. 'Wherever did *those* come from?' I asked of nobody in particular.

'You can thank the corset,' Alisha replied. 'Good for back support, too,' she continued, flexing her knees in way of illustration. 'You'll probably be doing a lot of heavy lifting.'

'Won't there be servants for that?' I mused, turning to check myself out in the mirror, back, front and sideways.

Jud and Alisha exchanged a knowing glance. 'You've decided to do it then?' Jud prodded.

I whirled around to face them, petticoats sweeping the dark green linoleum. 'Not so fast, young man! I've got a million questions. I'm curious about the Donovans, for one thing. When Kat Donovan had to withdraw from the show, how come her family decided to stay? There's no way that Paul would have left me to deal with my cancer treatments all alone.'

'LynxE was set to send all of the Donovans packing and go with another family,' Jud explained, 'but it was Katherine Donovan herself who insisted that her husband and children be allowed to stay on.'

'Why would LynxE agree to that?' I asked.

'It's purely a practical matter,' Jud explained. 'The Donovans were halfway through the orientation, for one thing. For another, the wardrobe is a huge expense. We'd have to remake *four* sets of costumes, instead of just one. So, with the Donovan family's full concurrence, we decided simply to replace Kat.'

'But why *me*?' I asked as Alisha began to help me undress.

Jud shot me a crooked grin. 'Lady of the House number two was a size fourteen, at least. As for Lady of the House number three? We would have had to use a shoehorn to get that woman into the dress that you're wearing now. So that's why we cooked up the sister-in-law scenario, and why I thought of you.'

'Just like Cinderella. Her foot fit the glass slipper, and she got the prince. I fit the dress and if I want to, I get to be a television star.'

'You'll do it, then?'

Barefoot, stripped down to the shift, I stared at him for a moment, considering my options. Jud was still grinning boyishly, sucking up to me big-time, the rascal. 'I like to think I'll try anything once, but . . . gosh, Jud, I feel like a fish out of water. A beautifully dressed fish, to be sure . . .'

'Tell me you'll consider it seriously, Hannah.'

'It'll take a lot more than beautiful dresses and sweet talk, Jud. Do you have some sort of prospectus with details about the show? And I imagine there's a contract you expect cast members to sign.'

'If you have time to accompany me to the production room, I'll see that you get a contract.' He did an about-face, threw Alisha a kiss, and said, 'Thanks, doll.' Then, to me: 'Get changed and we'll tour the house. That should answer some of your questions. I'll wait for you outside.'

After I dressed, Jud escorted me through the Paca House garden where workmen were busily assembling an old-fashioned wooden well. 'Colonials had to be careful about drinking the water,' he explained, 'but we're connecting this well up to the city water supply. Coming down with cholera would be just a bit too real, you know?'

I had to agree.

We passed through the spacious kitchen and walked down a narrow hallway that led into a bright English basement situated directly under the main house. Jud paused in front of a door that was secured by a combination lock, its keypad resembling the face of a telephone. 'Ordinarily, this is a conference room,' Jud told me as he punched four numbers into the lock and twisted the knob. 'But we'll be using it as an on-site staging and storage area.' Jud pushed the door open and held it aside, waiting for me to pass through. 'We'll keep the camera equipment in here, use it as a break area for the crew, et cetera, but as far as the cast is concerned, the room will be strictly off limits.'

A half-dozen plastic filing crates lined the long, walnut conference table that dominated the room. Jud rummaged through one of the crates, extracted a fat sheaf of papers secured with a paper clamp. From another cube he took a manila envelope.

'Here's the contract,' he said, handing it to me. While he scribbled something on the outside of the envelope in black felt tip marker, I scanned the contract quickly. Although the print was minuscule, a phrase on the first page practically jumped out and slapped me in the face: *You will be required to wear a microphone twenty-four seven.*

'Jud, what's this about wearing a microphone all the time? I mean, my God, even in the privy?'

Jud capped the marker, eased the contract out of my hand and stuffed it into the envelope. 'Sorry about that. It's a

boilerplate contract we borrowed from another show.' He
hauled a cell phone out of his pocket and tapped in a memo.
'Just reminding myself to have the lawyers modify that clause.
We have microphones, of course, but due to the wonders of
modern technology, cast members won't be wearing them.
Follow me. I'll show you something amazing.'

Jud tucked the envelope containing my contract under his
arm, then pulled the door shut behind us, jiggling the knob to
make sure it was securely locked. I followed him back towards
the kitchen and up a short flight of stairs into Paca House's
spacious entrance hall, where Jud pointed to a flat disk about
the size of a dinner plate mounted high on the far wall.

'That's it?' I asked. 'The microphone? It looks like a mini-
UFO, or a fancy shower head.'

Jud grinned. 'It's called a SelectoZoomMini. The technology
was originally designed for sporting events, a much larger
version, of course. They would install SelectoZooms high
above stadiums, and a wide-angle camera would look down
on the scene from the center of the disk. All an operator has
to do is pinpoint a spot on the field using his monitor, and the
SelectoZoom can zoom in on that spot and pick up the audio.
It's so sensitive that it can actually hear somebody popping
their chewing gum.'

'That must have kept the censors busy,' I joked, 'bleeping
out all the cussing.'

Jud laughed. 'I imagine so.'

He led me into a spacious room just to the right of the
massive front door, where a workman was assembling a
wooden bookcase. The worker glanced up curiously, then went
back to leveling a shelf. 'We're setting this room up as a
library. We've installed SelectoZoomMinis here and in all the
main rooms of the house,' Jud continued, 'including the kitchen
and the schoolroom, and there's one in the upstairs hallway,
too. There will be a couple of Steadicam operators on hand
to film close-ups, and to accompany you to places and events
outside the house, of course. But when you're in the house,
you won't need to worry about wearing microphones.'

'Do you have mics in the bedrooms, too?'

Jud snorted. 'No way. We're not *that* kind of network. If

we decide we need to film you dressing or bathing – although they didn't do much bathing in 1774 – we'll give you fair warning and, I assure you, we'll do it tastefully.'

'What's that, then?' I asked a few minutes later as we descended the staircase that led back to the kitchen. I was pointing to a wooden box about the size of a bird house that sat on a deep window sill to my right.

'That's a diary cam. There are four of them – one here, as you see, one in the library, one in the storeroom just off the kitchen, and one out in the summer house at the foot of the garden. Patriot House participants will be able to use the diary cams at any time to record their private thoughts or register their concerns. The diary cams are monitored, and someone on the production staff will collect the tapes daily.'

He opened a little door on the box, stepped aside with a slight bow and a wave of his hand. 'Take a look.'

Inside the box was a video camera, straight off the shelves of Circuit City or Best Buy. A simple control was mounted just above it with two big buttons, one red and one green. 'Push the green button, wait for the red eye on the camera to start flashing, then say anything you want.'

I followed Jud's instructions, and when the red eye began winking at me, I said, 'Hello, my name is Hannah Ives, and I am out of my freaking mind.' I pushed the red button to stop the recording (I'm a quick study) and said, 'There you go. A comment that millions of viewers will soon be programming their TiVos to hear, I'm quite sure.'

'I honestly hope so.'

'Which reminds me,' I said as we headed into the kitchen. 'When will *Patriot House* actually air?'

'We start taping on Labor Day and wrap up with the State House Ball, just before Thanksgiving. Throughout December, we'll be editing the show. The first of eight episodes will air on January the third.'

Labor Day was less than two weeks away. If I signed on to the show, I'd miss the family's annual end of summer cookout, but it wasn't my year to play hostess, so perhaps they would forgive me. 'Is the show scripted?' I wondered.

Jud paused beside a long oak table covered with iron utensils and stacks of crockery. 'Lord, no. We've provided cast members with customized orientation packets, of course, tailored to their specific roles in Patriot House. Some of the cast have taken advantage of the library of eighteenth-century reference material we've made available down in Williamsburg, but otherwise . . .' Jud shrugged. 'Founding Father will assign certain tasks – a formal dinner, or a shopping trip, for example – but the whole point is to see how the cast naturally reacts, how they work as a team to accomplish those tasks.'

'Founding Father?' I laughed out loud. 'Sort of like Big Brother?'

'You got it, but with broader vocabulary and posher grammar.'

'By my faith, sir, methinks 'tis vain so to primp and preen before the looking glass,' I improvised. 'Like that?'

'Forsooth, methinks not,' Jud said with a laugh. 'We expect the cast to speak in plain, twenty-first century English, otherwise nobody'd understand them.'

'Thank you, Jesus,' I said.

Back in the garden, on a path overlooking the herb beds, Jud handed me the envelope. 'Go over the contract carefully, Hannah. Have your attorney take a look at it. How soon can you get back to me?'

'I'll want to discuss it with my husband, of course.'

Jud sucked in his lips. 'Of course. That goes without saying.'

Paul's attorney, Murray Simon, dealt with big issues, like bailing me out when I was mistakenly arrested by the FBI. When I wasn't getting into trouble, Jim Cheevers was our lawyer of choice, but I knew he was on holiday in Costa Rica. Nearing retirement age, Jim was shopping for a villa in Tamarindo.

Jim's secretary would have happily handed me over to Jim's second-in-command, but we already had a lawyer in the family, my brother-in-law, Gaylord Hutchinson – nicknamed 'Hutch' – who was married to my older sister, Ruth, so I made up my mind to consult him first, even though I knew that the majority of his business had to do with real property, trusts and estates. 'I know you're slammed, Jud, but can you give me a couple of days?'

'Slammed doesn't begin to describe it,' Jud complained as we strolled past the herb garden and out gate that led back into Martin Street. 'Try back against the wall, puffing my last cigarette with a dozen M-16s aimed at my chest.'

I touched his arm. 'I guess I'd better be quick about it, then. I wouldn't want your execution on my conscience.'

'Thanks, Hannah. Much appreciated.'

As we strolled down Martin Street, Jud pointed out the greenhouses where the gardener had been at work for several months growing the vegetables needed to sustain the Patriot House cast over the course of the program.

Further on, another parking lot was being transformed. Straw had been strewn over the gravel and, as I watched, workmen began to erect a log-like structure – half barn, half lean-to – where, Jud informed me, our horse stall, cow shed, chicken coop and rabbit pens were going to go. Milk and eggs I could deal with, but I tried not to think of chicken and dumplings or rabbit stew.

As Jud walked me home, the great circle route via King George Street and Maryland Avenue, I continued to worry aloud about being thrown into the mix so late, but when we arrived back on my doorstep, Jud pinned me with a disarming grin and said, 'It's reality TV, Hannah. If the missus had been kidnapped by Indians, or died of smallpox or something – God forbid – it would be natural to expect Jack Donovan to send for a female relative to help run his household. That's how it was done.'

Not much different from today, I mused, remembering how my two sisters, Ruth and Georgina, had rallied to take care of Paul while I was undergoing chemo and feeling like crap. 'Well, I certainly trust that Paul won't be busily lining up wife number two just to keep him in clean laundry and freshly-baked bread while I'm away – if I decide to come on board, that is.'

Jud grinned, and raised a pale eyebrow. 'By Sunday, then? You'll let me know?'

I reached out and shook his hand. 'Today's Thursday, so yes, by Sunday. One way or the other. Promise.'

# THREE

*'I own a car dealership in Texas, so I'm not exactly up to speed on entertainment law, but there is the darndest clause in the contract I signed in order to be on this show. It gives the producers – hold on a minute, I had to write it down – it gives them rights "in perpetuity and throughout the universe and for any and all forms of expression whether now existing or hereafter devised." As far as I can tell, the only loophole in that clause is if I suddenly slipped through a wormhole into a parallel universe.'*

Jack Donovan, Patriot

All the way home, floating several inches above the sidewalk, still caught up in the fairy-tale world Jud had painted for me, I'd been wondering how I'd break the news to Paul. When that thought rose to the surface, I realized that I'd half decided to do it.

Back in my cluttered kitchen, I checked the calendar I keep stuck to the fridge with a magnet, and decided that I'd have to reschedule a mammogram and a bone scan, but they were routine; waiting another couple of months shouldn't be a problem. I had a few lunches with girlfriends, but they'd understand – maybe even be green with envy. My daughter, Emily, would be totally cool with 'My mother, the TV star,' even if she'd have to make alternate arrangements for carpool on Tuesdays and Thursdays.

But Paul? My husband, the mathematician, was a financial wizard. I imagined he'd apply the same intense scrutiny to the contract Jud wanted me to sign as he did to his quarterly investment reports, so I figured that before he got home that evening, I'd better get my ducks in a row.

I fingered the manila envelope holding the contract that I'd laid on the kitchen table, hefted it, and decided I'd need a cup of hot tea to help me deal with actually looking inside. While the tea bag was steeping in the cup, I slid the contract out of the envelope and flipped through – all thirty-two pages of it – and began to read, but by the time I got to page four of the teeny-tiny print, my eyes had glazed over and, in spite of all the caffeine in the tea, I was in danger of slipping into a coma.

I checked my watch. Just two o'clock. I picked up the telephone and called Hutch.

Maurice Gaylord Hutchinson, Esquire, is a prominent Annapolis attorney, married to my older sister, Ruth. Sometimes when I telephone I get my sister, who fills in when the secretary is away, but that day Megan answered and put me straight through.

'Hannah!' Hutch sounded genuinely pleased to hear from me. 'I've been meaning to thank you for that fabulous dinner party you put together last week, but when I got back to the office the next morning, things kind of got away from me.'

'You brought the wine, Hutch. That was thanks enough. Look, I apologize for calling during office hours, but I have something strange and rather important I need to talk to you about.'

'Yes?'

'Can I come and see you? Ordinarily I wouldn't dream of bothering you, especially as I know you're super busy, but it's a contract I need someone with brains to look over, and it's time critical.'

'Now?' I could hear papers rustling in the background. I held my breath, hoping Hutch was checking his calendar. 'I have a three thirty, so if you come right away . . .'

'Thanks!' I said, before he could even finish the sentence. I wasn't planning on wasting a second of my brother-in-law's valuable time.

Hutch's office is on Main Street – several doors up from his wife's eclectic, New Age boutique, 'Mother Earth' – on the second floor of a building that houses an upscale leather bootery.

I hustled up Prince George Street and down Maryland

Avenue toward the State House, taking a path through the alley near the Maryland Federation of Art that cut between State Circle and Main Street. I bopped into Hutch's office just seven minutes after I hung up the phone.

Megan, Hutch's secretary, glanced up from her keyboard. 'Good to see you, Hannah. He's expecting you. He'll join you in a moment in the conference room.'

The last time I'd been in Hutch's conference room was when we were arranging a home equity loan to help cover Emily's Bryn Mawr College tuition. Hutch wasn't there yet, so I sat down at the head of the table and made myself comfortable, admiring an oil painting on the wall of a sailboat under sail, its red, blue and yellow spinnaker billowing.

When Hutch breezed into the room I looked up and barely recognized him. His floppy, neatly trimmed hair style – so very *GQ* – had been replaced by a buzz cut. 'My goodness,' I chirped. 'What on earth did you do to your hair? Were the U.S. Marines looking for a few good men?'

Hutch rubbed a hand briskly over the pale stubble. 'Ruth and I have taken up dancing again, so I figured I needed something a bit more wash and wear.'

I considered his new do with a critical eye. 'Too bad. The Leonardo di Caprio look had your younger clients swooning. The older ladies, too, come to think of it.' I winked, so he'd know I was teasing.

'I don't need clients to swoon over me, Hannah. I need them to pay attention, and do what I say.' His eyes flicked from my face to the clock on the wall, then down to the manila envelope I'd placed on the table in front of me. 'So, what have we here?' he asked, pulling up a chair and sitting down next to me. He laid a hand lightly on the envelope.

Hutch is one of the most unflappable guys I know. You'd have to be, married to the superannuated flower child that is my sister. Ruth had actually *been* at Woodstock in 1969. She'd *inhaled*. She'd *enjoyed* it. I watched Hutch's green eyes widen as I explained about *Patriot House, 1774* and my potential role in it.

When I ran out of steam, he asked, 'What does Paul have to say about this?'

I shrugged. 'I haven't mentioned it to him yet.'

An eyebrow shot up, but before Hutch could say what he was probably thinking, I added: 'I wanted you to look over the contract first. There's no point in getting Paul all spun up over nothing. If you think it's OK, and I decide to sign on the dotted line, *then* I'll tell Paul about it.'

'I see,' he said in a tone of voice that suggested he thoroughly disapproved of my proposal. 'Well, I'd better have a look at it, then.'

I watched, practically holding my breath, as Hutch shook the contract out of the envelope and onto the table, picked it up, licked a thumb and used it to rifle through the pages. After a few minutes he whacked the pages on the edge of the table and said, 'Shit, Hannah. It's thirty-two fricking pages! I have multimillionaire clients whose wills take up fewer pages than this.'

'Are you saying that it's unusually long?'

'I'm saying that I'm a real estate attorney. I don't have much experience with entertainment law.'

'But you studied entertainment law at Georgetown, right? You know *something* about it.'

Hutch's eyes were on scan, reviewing the first page. Without glancing up, he said, 'But that was a long time ago, back in the good old days before reality TV was invented, when we watched scripted shows like *M\*A\*S\*H* and *Archie Bunker*.'

'Please, just tell me what you think, Hutch. I'll be happy to pay you for your time.'

'Don't be ridiculous.' He flipped from page two to page three, scowling. A few excruciatingly long minutes later he looked up and said, 'You realize that if you're accepted as a participant in this series, you're agreeing to allow them, and I quote, "to videotape, film, portray and photograph me and my actions and record my voice and other sound effects in connection with the production of the series on an up to a twenty-four-hour-a-day, seven-days-a-week basis, whether I am clothed, partially clothed or naked, whether I am aware or unaware of such videotaping, filming or recording, and by requiring me to wear a microphone at all times."'

I thought about the costume I'd just tried on, about the shift,

the corset, layer upon layer of petticoats before I even got
to the dress and had to laugh. 'This is 1774,' I reminded him,
'not *Survivor*.'

'Still . . .' He read on.

'They're going to pay me fifteen thousand dollars,' I added.

'I see that. And I'm sure you're thinking that a salary of
five thousand dollars a month is pretty tempting, but remember,
you're going to be working' – he drew quote marks in the air
– 'twenty-four seven. And furthermore . . .' He flipped forward
a few pages, searching for something. 'Ah, here it is. You
won't even be able to profit from any of the spin-offs.'

'Ha ha,' I said. 'As if everyone in the world is going to
want to own a Hannah Ives bobblehead doll.'

'Seriously, Hannah. Residuals and product tie-ins are major
income producers. If you sign this, you're agreeing that they
can use your image in any way they want – websites based
on the series, video games, pasted all over the sides of the
Goodyear blimp for all I know. It goes way beyond T-shirts,
coffee mugs and bobblehead dolls.' He shot his sleeve to check
his watch, looked up at me and smiled his best reassuring
smile. 'Look, why don't you go for a walk and come back in
an hour. By that time I'll have given this *doorstop* a closer
look and be better able to advise you.'

Sitting in an air-conditioned room watching somebody else
read a bunch of fine print was about as interesting as watching
the U.S. Open on television, so I readily agreed. 'Thanks,
Hutch. I really appreciate it.'

Still frowning over the pages, Hutch tipped an imaginary
hat as I left the room.

One hour, fifteen minutes and a double-scoop of rum raisin
ice cream from Storm Brothers Ice Cream Factory at City
Dock later, I was back. Hutch was waiting for me in his office.

'Hannah, I didn't trust myself to advise you on this, so I
consulted with a colleague in D.C. who represents Sonic Ice
Cream Junkies, Gurlz-N-Boyz, and one of the contestants on
the twenty-first season of *Survivor*.'

'Sonic Ice Cream Junkies?' I asked.

'It's a rock group. Go figure.'

I snorted. 'Sorry, go on.'

'Max emailed me a PDF of one of the boilerplate contracts in his files. I compared them and we agreed that what you have here is industry standard. In spite of the length, it's pretty straightforward,' my brother-in-law explained from across his desk. 'I don't know who the attorneys who drafted this document are, but it's tight as a tick. Basically, you agree to give them three months of your time in exchange for fifteen thousand dollars. They've thought of everything you could possibly sue them for, then added an additional clause that pretty much says if you can think of something to sue them for that they haven't mentioned herein, you can't sue them for that either.'

That actually made me laugh. 'What could possibly happen in an eighteenth-century house with cameras following you around twenty-four seven?'

'I don't know. But if an asteroid slams through the atmosphere and lands on you while you're picking green beans in the Paca garden, don't expect Paul to get any money out of it.'

'Thanks, Hutch. I'll remember that.'

'In addition, you're prohibited from writing a book about the show, and during the course of the show, you can't grant interviews, have a personal website or blog; nor can you post about the show on Facebook or Twitter.'

'I don't have a personal website, and since we'll be living in 1774, I don't believe there'll be any Internet, so Facebook and Twitter are definitely out. Seriously,' I said after a moment, 'if you have any specific concerns, isn't there any place we can modify the contract?'

'It's pretty much take it or leave it, Hannah. In my opinion, this contract contains much more than a producer could possibly need, but it'd be next to impossible to push back, since they could always put somebody else on the show.'

I thought about how Kat Donovan's costumes fit me like a glove, and about Jud's desire to stay on schedule and within his budget, and thought that wasn't very likely.

'And Paul has to sign something called "An Immediate Family Release,"' Hutch added, shoving another sheaf of papers that I had obviously overlooked across his desk.

I simply stared at it for a moment, paralyzed by the number of pages in the supplemental agreement. 'You mean I have to have Paul's *permission* to be on the show? That's positively Victorian.'

His upper lip twitched. 'You don't need Paul's permission, no. But, he has to agree not to hold LynxE liable for anything bad that might happen to you, nor can he profit from any interviews, books, films – blah-de-blah-de-blah – that concern the show without their approval either before, during or after. Basically, Paul will have to agree that in terms of *Patriot House, 1774*, his life, like yours, will be an open book with LynxE pulling the strings, food for their publicity mill.'

Hutch pushed back his chair and rose to his feet. He laid a gentle hand on my shoulder, squeezed. 'Think hard about this, Hannah. Is this something you *really* want to do?'

Still seated, I smiled up at him. 'I have to confess that I'm torn. I'm an incurable romantic, you know. When I was in high school, I devoured books by Victoria Holt and Georgette Heyer.' I pressed a hand to my chest. '"*You may have married her, but she is mine. Do you think I shall let you take her? She may be ten times your wife, but, by God, you shall never have her!*"' I quoted, batting my eyelashes furiously. 'That's from *The Devil's Cub*, one of Heyer's early Georgian romances. I've probably read it a hundred times.'

'Playing damsel in distress seems like a pretty lame reason for giving up three months of your life,' Hutch said reasonably. 'The novelty of wearing fancy frocks will wear off fairly quickly, I should imagine, approximately two minutes after you make your first middle-of-the-night run to the outhouse.'

I had to laugh. 'That's why chamber pots were invented, silly.'

'And if you decide to leave the show in midstream,' Hutch continued, his face serious, 'you not only lose the fifteen-thousand dollars, but you open yourself up to a million-dollar lawsuit.'

'Jesus! Really?'

'It's in the contract.'

'Damn.'

'Exactly.' I must have looked stricken because Hutch

continued, 'There are exceptions for serious illness or injury, of course. But if you simply walk out . . .' Hutch drummed his fingers on the tabletop and hummed the first few bars of Chopin's 'Marche Funèbre.' 'In Max's experience such a clause has never been enforced, but it could end up costing a lot of money if you pull out and their legal people decide to go after you.'

'I went through six months of chemotherapy, so I figure I can soldier through anything, as long as I can see light at the end of the tunnel,' I said. 'But based on what you've told me . . .' I tapped the contract where it lay on the desk between us. '. . . I'd hate to put my hard-earned retirement account at risk.' I sighed. 'So I guess I won't be flouncing around Paca House issuing orders to the servants any time soon.'

'Wise decision.' Hutch grabbed my hand, raised it to his lips and kissed it. 'Well, it's been fascinating, truly fascinating, but Milady will need to excuse me, or I'll be late for my next client,' he drawled, before bowing slightly at the waist and leaving the room.

'My hero!' I shouted after him.

'Bullshit!' he replied.

I gathered up the scattered pages, tapped them together and slipped the contracts back into the envelope Jud had given me. I stared for a long time at the LynxE logo in the upper left-hand corner of the envelope, pondering my next move. Then I took a deep breath, dug my iPhone out of my bag, found Jud's number under 'Recents' and punched it in.

Jud answered on the second ring. 'Hannah! You got me on the Washington beltway. What's the good word?'

I didn't realize I'd been holding my breath until I let it out slowly and said, 'I've just met with my attorney and much as I'd really like to do the show, I've got to say no.'

Jud didn't answer, and I thought we might have lost the connection. 'Jud?'

'I'm here, just trying to stay alive while some idiot is changing lanes. Asshole! OK, I can talk now.'

'I'm really sorry, Jud, but in the cold light of day, I realized I was being seduced by the fifteen thousand dollars, my romantic nature and some pretty amazing cleavage.'

A few seconds went by before Jud replied. 'Look, what would it take to get you to say yes?'

I thought for a moment. 'It's not about the money.'

'Try me.'

An idea sprang to mind, an idea so outrageous even I was amazed at my audacity. It was an offer I figured Jud would *have* to refuse. 'A seventy-five-thousand-dollar donation to Komen for the Cure,' I said, naming my favorite charity, 'earmarked for breast cancer research.'

On the other end of the line I heard a truck rumble past Jud's car, the impatient *toot-toot* of a horn. 'OK.'

I sucked in air. 'You will? Guaranteed?'

'Yes. One of the sponsors might have a coronary, but don't worry, I'll sort it out.'

'Written into my contract?'

'Of course. Have your attorney contact me ASAP. We'll make it happen.'

*Hoist on your own petard, Hannah. Now it's time to fish or cut bait.* I took a deep breath. 'Then I'll do it,' I told him.

His 'thanks' came at the end of a long sigh of relief. 'You won't be sorry, Hannah. I promise.'

After arranging an overnight delivery of a packet of materials about the program and a schedule of the training sessions I'd be attending at the orientation in Colonial Williamsburg, Jud bid me a grateful goodbye.

Now I was back at square one, sitting in my brother-in-law's comfortable office, wondering what Paul would have to say when I told him what I'd just promised to do. After the steak dinner I planned to prepare for him, of course, accompanied by a fine red wine.

Because if I couldn't persuade Paul to sign that stupid Immediate Family Release, no matter what commitment I'd made to Jud, I figured I was pretty well screwed.

# FOUR

*'I miss my boyfriend back in Texas real bad! I didn't get a letter from Tim this week, so I worry that he's hooking up with that little slut from driver's ed, Stacie Green. She better keep her hands to herself or I'll scratch her eyes out, I swear. Are you listening to this, Tim?'*

Melody Donovan, daughter

My famous grilled rib-eye, twice-baked potatoes and fresh green salad worked their usual wonders. Paul dabbed sour cream off his chin, folded his napkin, then leaned back in his chair. 'I'm overwhelmed,' he said, rubbing his stomach like a contented Buddha.

When I told him about *Patriot House, 1774*, however, it's fair to say he was pretty underwhelmed. As I began to plead my case, I figured my Cinderella at the Ball routine wouldn't cut much ice with my uber-practical husband, so I focused on the financial perks of the job.

As usual, Paul performed the calculations without counting on his fingers. 'Twenty-four hours a day times ninety days, divided into fifteen thousand dollars, that's around seven dollars an hour. Minimum wage in Maryland is $7.25 an hour. Shit, Hannah. Emily pays her *babysitters* more than that.'

That was a sobering thought. 'But,' I countered, playing a practical card of my own, 'I'll earn *zero* dollars per hour by staying at home.' I raised my wine glass in a toast. 'Better than a sharp stick in the eye, as Mother would have said.'

'Hannah, can't you ever be serious?'

'I *am* being serious.' I leaned my elbows against the table and, holding the glass between both hands, swirling the liquid around from time to time, I continued to sip my wine. 'We could start college funds for the grandchildren. Five thousand each.'

'That'll go far in this wretched economy,' Paul harrumphed.

'But wait! There's more,' I said, and explained about the seventy-five thousand dollars that would go to Komen for the Cure if I managed to stay the course.

'I see,' my husband said, fixing me with his serious, dark-chocolate eyes, and I could tell that he did.

I watched Paul pick up the wine bottle and top off his glass. I steeled my nerves and trotted out my best Lady Di sideways-through-the-eyelashes glance. 'Uh, there's this form you have to sign.' I set my glass down on the tablecloth and retrieved the envelope from the floor under my chair. I laid it on the table between us.

'Why do *I* need to sign anything, Hannah? *You're* the one who wants to take part in this cockamamie adventure, not me.' Paul slid the envelope from beneath my fingers and extracted the form.

'They want you to agree never to blog, Facebook or Tweet about this, or grant interviews or write a bestselling tell-all about your life as the husband of a reality show participant. Unless LynxE arranges for it, of course.'

His eyes scanned the first page. Without looking up he said, 'So, if I don't sign this you can't go on?'

'More or less.' I had to force myself to breathe. The pen lay, silent, like an exclamation point on the table between us.

'You really want to do this, Hannah?'

'Call me crazy, but I do. And I'm doing it for charity, too, don't forget.'

Paul shrugged, picked up the pen, and signed the form with a flourish. 'I know better than to argue with you when you've already made up your mind,' he said, holding the form out to me. 'So, tell me, is there any way I'll be able to get in touch with you while you're away?'

'Letters, Jud says. Once every week to a post office box in Annapolis, but I'm pretty sure they'll be monitored.' I took the agreement from his outstretched fingers and slipped it back into the envelope next to the fatter contract that had to be revised before I would be able to sign. 'They're probably delivering them by pony express.'

Paul sniffed. 'No cell phones, I presume.'

'Ha ha ha. If there'd been cell phones back then, Paul Revere would have Tweeted that the British were coming. "1 F by C."'

He didn't crack a smile. 'So, what if I need to contact you, like in an emergency?'

'There'll be a number to the production team that you can call. Wait a minute! I'll give you Jud's cell. He called me, so the number's still on my iPhone.'

Paul didn't look entirely convinced. 'And if you need to talk to *me*?'

I shrugged. I hadn't thought that one through. 'Jud will contact you if there's an emergency. Otherwise, red petticoat hung out to dry on the clothesline? Notes in a hollow tree?'

Paul reached for my hand. 'You are a devious wench, but I love you. And I'm going to miss you like crazy.'

'It's only three months, Paul. I was out of it for six months when I was undergoing chemo.'

'I know, but at least then I could see you, touch you, hold you.'

'How about this, then? I'll write you in code.'

'Ah, there you go, guilt-tripping me again. But, I could use the lonely hours to work on my book.'

Paul and his colleague, Brent Morris, had a friendly academic rivalry going on. Brent had surged ahead, having recently published a paperback called *The Math of Card Shuffling*, while Paul's book, *Famous Unsolved Codes and Ciphers*, still languished in a Word file on his computer. It had been a copy-edit away from being ready to go, then somebody had conclusively solved the Dorabella Cipher – sent by composer Edward Elgar to a young Dora Penny – and the project had stalled.

'There's one thing that concerns me,' I said, reaching out for his hand, kicking myself for being so self-centered that I hadn't considered this before. 'I'm afraid Lynx'll take this agreement as an invitation to invade *your* privacy, whenever they want to.'

I had nightmare visions of cameramen and reporters ambushing the poor man the minute he walked out our front door, dogging his tail all the way to his office at the Naval Academy. They'd barge in, interview his students, disrupt his classes. When I voiced my concerns to Paul, however, he waved them away. 'You don't need to worry about that, Hannah. They've signed an agreement with *me*, not the United States government. They'd never get past the Marines guarding the Academy gates. And the Marines have guns.'

Since 9/11, security at all government installations, including the Naval Academy, had been beefed up. Bancroft Hall, the largest single dormitory in the world, is home to four thousand midshipmen who call it affectionately 'Mother B.' With 1,700 rooms, 4.8 miles of corridors and thirty-three acres of floor space it was a target-rich environment, well worth protecting.

I had to smile, though, when Paul pouted pitifully and said, 'But, you'll miss our anniversary.'

That missing our anniversary mattered really surprised me. Paul and I had been married on October the tenth, but it was a rare year when he got the date right, usually over- or under-shooting by a day or two, if he remembered it at all. One year, he had invited me on an outing to the county dump. I was thrilled: a surprise party in the offing! I went along, helped him offload a trunk full of old computer components, then went home to bathe and read a good book when it was clear he'd completely forgotten our special day. 'We'll have other anniversaries,' I stated with confidence. 'Our thirty-fifth will be coming up in a few years. We can do something really special then.'

He frowned. 'I'm not sure I can manage three months without you.'

'Oh, for heaven's sake, I'll be half a block down the street!'

'Might as well be the other side of the world,' he grumbled. 'Security will be as tight as Fort Knox, if only to keep out the paparazzi.'

'It's not like we had any special plans, is it?' I said.

Paul gave me a poor, big-eyed orphan sort of pout. 'Not really. And I know that I'll be tied up with teaching, but still . . .'

I got up from the dining table, stood behind his chair and wrapped my arms around his neck. With my lips close to his ear, and the lingering smell of his aftershave teasing my nose, I whispered, 'I really, really want to do this, Paul.'

Paul grabbed both of my hands and held them tightly. 'You said Hutch has looked over the contracts?'

I nodded, Paul's five o'clock shadow gently scratching my cheek. 'He did.'

'And he's OK with it?'

'Not OK, exactly. He consulted with a colleague and they agreed it was typical of such contracts, and there were no surprises.'

Paul sighed deeply. 'Seven dollars an hour. Christ! Cashiers at the checkout counters of Safeway make more than seven dollars an hour!'

'I know, darling. But they don't get to wear fabulous silk ball gowns with hoop skirts while they're ringing up my extra virgin olive oil and coffee beans.

'You'll get to attend the final ball at the State House,' I hastened to add. 'Everyone who's anyone is going to be there. The governor, the mayor, the supe . . .' I went through the list of dignitaries as I remembered it. 'I can't wait to see you in panty hose and a powdered wig, Professor Ives.'

'I'm going to miss you, Hannah Ives.' He kissed each of my palms in turn, then pulled me around to sit on his lap. 'Be sure to spend time in the summer house, and I'll blow kisses to you over the King George Street wall. When do you start?'

'Once the revised contract has been signed, immediately, I should think. The rest of the cast has been down in Colonial Williamsburg for a week already getting orientation training.'

'So, Sunday? Monday?'

'Probably. I won't need to pack much.'

'And you'll be back in Annapolis when?'

'Taping starts on Labor Day.'

'I wonder if they'll keep Patriot House locked up at night?' Paul, it seemed, was already planning a midnight expedition over the Paca House garden wall.

'It's my understanding that as mistress of the house *I'll* have all the keys.'

'Ah, ha. In that case, madam, would you prefer a roger or a flourish?' he whispered, nibbling gently on my ear lobe.

I pulled away from his embrace and looked directly into

his luminous, dark-chocolate eyes. 'What the hell are you talking about?'

'You think you're the only one who reads historical fiction, my dear?' He tapped my nose affectionately with his index finger. '"Roger" and "flourish" don't seem to be defined in *my* edition of Webster's Collegiate Dictionary, but from extensive reading of seventeenth- and eighteenth-century diaries – some of them written in code – I've been able to deduce that a flourish is properly done while in bed. A roger, on the other hand, is accomplished while the couple is standing up, preferably after a chase round the billiard table.'

I laced my fingers with his. 'Unfortunately, we don't own a billiard table.'

'Improvise, improvise, improvise,' my husband said.

A few minutes later, in my own twenty-first century dining room, I got rogered, good and proper.

# FIVE

*'I've been wearing the same dress for a week and, look at it! It's a road map of kitchen disasters. This grease spot was yesterday's roast and this crusty one over here is where I slopped egg yolks all over it. There's burn marks from practically falling into the fireplace, and I can't tell you how many times I wiped my face with the hem. I stink to high heaven! I would kill for a hot shower.'*

Karen Gibbs, cook

I t actually took until Wednesday before all the paperwork was in order and I found myself and my overnight bag of toiletries being whisked away from Annapolis in the back seat of a black Lincoln Town Car, heading south to Williamsburg, Virginia where I'd meet the rest of my television family.

After a four-hour slog down Interstate 95 – a nightmare commute, no matter what the hour, but at least *I* wasn't driving – the chauffeur dropped me off at Providence Hall Guest Houses on South England Street, one of Williamsburg's finer hotels in the heart of the historic district, directly adjacent to the posh Colonial Williamsburg Inn.

As part of the orientation packet Jud had promised, I'd been given a handout from Colonial Williamsburg entitled 'Daily Schedule for an Urban Gentry Housewife' which I'd read in the limo on the way down. I was relieved to have it confirmed in writing what Jud had told me earlier: that the Donovans were well-to-do. I'd have domestics – both indentured servants and slaves – to perform the grunt work around the house, although I'd be expected to supervise their efforts. In the days to come, Jud's memo said, I'd be taken in hand by re-enactors and given crash courses in cooking, cleaning, gardening and dairying, eighteenth-century style.

Also in the packet were several sheets of 8-1/2 x 11 with

color photographs of the cast, their names and ages underneath
their headshots; a kind of *Who's Who* of *Patriot House*. The
cover sheet was stamped 'Confidential: Not for Dissemination'
and I could understand why. It'd been thrown together in a
hurry. I'd seen more flattering photographs on Most Wanted
posters.

Arranged in four rows of three like a high school yearbook
– but without the autographs and scrawled endearments – were
my TV family. John 'Jack' Donovan, Patriot, his red hair as
abundant and perfectly coifed as the Nightly News anchor on
WFXM. Jack's children, sixteen-year-old Melody – looking
like she'd rather be anywhere else – and nine-year-old Gabriel,
eyes full of mischief and cute as a button. Katherine Donovan
was included, too, with an 'X' over her photo, one black line
marring the perfection of her pale Irish skin. *Harsh.* I hoped
her children hadn't seen this; it seemed a touch insensitive, to
say the least. The list continued: Amy, Gwendolyn and Karen,
Michael, Alex and Dex. Jeffrey Wiley, too, eyes huge behind
his glasses, with a toothbrush-style moustache – think Adolf
Hitler as geek. Over the next three months, I'd get to know
them all, and their roles, very well indeed.

I'd checked into the hotel, found my room and was pressing
a hot washcloth to my face when Jud knocked on the door
armed with my schedule for the next four days. A few minutes
later, with cursory introductions all around, he inserted me
into a late-afternoon training session on colonial games and
pastimes, already in progress, before rushing off on some
important errand.

Sprawled in an armchair in one corner of the hotel lounge,
a girl who looked about fifteen or sixteen was scowling over
a piece of embroidery. Embroidery cottons, each color
wrapped around an hourglass-shaped bit of cardboard, were
lined up on the arm of her chair like soldiers. A strand of her
stick-straight black hair – a stark contrast to the girl's pale
skin – hung over her left cheek as she worked. She swiped
it away impatiently, revealing a multi-studded and be-ringed
earlobe. This had to be Melody Donovan, my 'niece.'
Eventually somebody would have to tell Melody that the
earrings – and the stud that presently decorated her

nose – would have to go. I'd dealt with sullen teenagers before – my daughter, Emily, had been a worrisome handful at that age – but I hoped it wouldn't end up being me.

At a table to my right, a bespectacled youth was playing checkers with a boy who, judging from his black hair, had to be Gabriel, Melody's little brother. As I stood stupidly in the doorway of the room where Jud had abandoned me, Gabriel – playing black – jumped three of his older partner's pieces and snatched them triumphantly off the board. 'Woot, woot!'

At a square table in the center of the room, four people sat playing cards. 'Here. Sit,' one of them said, leaping to his feet. 'We're about to start another hand. You can partner with Amy.'

I started to object, but he flapped a hand. 'No, no. It's fine. I have to work with Melody on her dance steps anyway,' he said, glancing toward the girl in the armchair. 'She can probably use a break from, well, whatever it is she's doing over there.'

The dancing master, then. What the heck was his name? Alex something. That meant that the guy playing checkers had to be Michael Rainey, the children's tutor.

The trio remaining at the table looked up from their cards, expressionless, almost as if they resented the interruption. I squared my shoulders and pasted on my friendliest smile. 'Hi,' I said, directly addressing the only male at the table, a stout, forty-something fellow whose pale red hair, already long, had been pulled back into a neat ponytail at the nape of his neck. 'I guess I'm your sister-in-law. What are you playing, then?'

John 'Jack' Donovan, Patriot, smiled at me, revealing a row of teeth as white and even as George Washington's famous ivory choppers. 'Whist,' he said as he shuffled the cards for the next hand.

I sat down in the chair Alex had just vacated. 'I've never played whist,' I said. 'Is it difficult to learn?'

'Easy peasey.' Amy Cornell, lady's maid, smiled at me then, and her face was transformed from a mask of indifference into a face of such natural, youthful beauty that it belonged on the cover of *Cosmopolitan*. Her honey-blond hair was cut in a stylish, fuss-free shag with a fringe of bangs that almost hid her gray eyes. 'It's like bridge,' she informed me. 'Except there's no dummy. You play bridge?'

'My husband and I used to, but we had so many arguments over it that we decided to quit. He's a mathematician,' I explained as Jack began to deal. 'He can remember every card that's been played, and who played it.' I picked up my hand and fanned the cards, sorting them into suits as I went. 'For me, bridge was just a game. So what if I trumped his ace? To Paul, though, it was a blood sport.'

'I hear you,' the woman on my right said as she picked up her hand. 'Like I always say: there are three kinds of people in this world. Those who are good at math, and those who aren't. I'm Gwendolyn Fry, by the way, but people call me "French."'

It took a moment for all that to sink in, but when it did, I laughed out loud. 'French Fry? You're kidding.'

French shrugged. 'Anything's better than Gwendolyn.'

Jack dealt the last card, face up, in front of him. The seven of diamonds. 'Diamonds are trump,' he announced. Amy, on his left, immediately played a four of diamonds and I smiled, knowing I held the king. French played a two, and when Jack laid his seven next to my king, Amy and I took the trick.

All the while we were playing, I kept one eye on Melody and Alex and the dancing lessons going on over in the corner. 'One, two, three, curtsey . . . four, five, six . . . hand up, now turn, turn, turn . . .' I recognized the minuet, and realized that the dancing lessons I'd taken prior to Ruth and Hutch's wedding – where we learned the waltz, tango and foxtrot – were probably not going to be relevant to my new life in the past. It was a good thing that dancing lessons had been blocked in on my schedule, for two o'clock the following day.

A sudden movement caught my eye. A dark shape seemed to materialize from the shadows on the wall next to a highboy. I gasped, then relaxed as I realized it was only a cameraman, clad in black from head to toe, like a ninja, wearing a Steadicam strapped to his chest. As the cameraman passed behind me, I pounded my chest to jump start my heart and said, 'Gosh, you scared me!'

'That's Derek,' Amy said calmly, slapping a ten of clubs

down on Jack's nine. 'Chad's around somewhere, too. They don't talk. You'll get used to them eventually.'

'I didn't think they'd be filming us quite so soon,' I commented before taking the trick with my queen to end the game. 'Considering the contracts we signed, that was probably a naïve assumption.'

'We call them Thing One and Thing Two,' French said. 'From *Cat in the Hat*,' she added, just in case I didn't get the reference.

'What role are you playing at Patriot House?' I asked French as Amy began to deal the next hand.

'I'm the housemaid,' she said. 'One of the indentured servants, supposedly from Scotland. I finished up early over at the Wythe House today. Sweeping, mopping, turning the mattresses – all good preparation. When I got back, Jud cornered me, saying they needed a fourth for whist. Not that I'll be playing cards with any of you upstairs types, mind.'

Four hands later, Amy and I were ahead by two points and the beginner in me was feeling rather smug.

Jack was shuffling the deck, preparing to deal again, when a woman rushed in. She paused for a moment in the doorway, one hand clutching the door frame, the other pressed to the small of her back. She was dressed as a household slave in brown homespun, and her gray apron was dusted with flour. Her head was wrapped, turban-like, in a white scarf from which a few dark curls had managed to escape, bobbing like tiny springs over her forehead. Her mahogany skin glistened with sweat.

'You better finish up in here if you're gonna want time to freshen up before dinner,' she drawled. 'They said to let you know that they start serving in twenty minutes. Me? I'm for the shower.' And she disappeared as quickly as she had come.

'That's Karen Gibbs,' Amy told me before I even had time to ask. 'She's our cook. They've had her working over in the Raleigh Tavern Bakery for a couple of days. Her boy's with her, too. Cute kid named Dexter. Dex. Nine or ten, I should think.'

'What's Dex going to do?' I wondered aloud. 'Chop wood? Pump water? Build fires?'

'Whatever a little slave boy would do in 1774,' Jack muttered without taking his eyes off his cards. 'Empty the chamber pots, too, I imagine. Wouldn't want *my* boy saddled with that. Don't know what the woman can be thinking.'

Amy's eyes blazed. 'Karen's got a PhD, Jack. She graduated from Oberlin College and has been teaching sociology there for ten years. That's more than most of the rest of us can say.'

I had graduated from Oberlin College, too, but quite a few years before Karen, I suspected. When Oberlin opened its doors in 1833, it never occurred to the founders not to admit blacks or women. The college had a long association with progressive causes. It had been one of the breeding grounds of abolitionism and a key stop along the Underground Railroad. When I visited the campus in 1965, in fact, Martin Luther King had been the commencement speaker.

'Oh, I'm not questioning the woman's intelligence,' Jack hastened to add. 'I'm sure she has her reasons.'

'As a black woman and a sociologist, this experiment must have seemed a unique opportunity for Karen to understand her own history by actually living it,' I commented. 'I'm not sure I would have involved my son, either, Jack. Dex seems a little young to really understand what slavery was all about.'

'I don't think she had a choice,' French said as she slapped an ace of hearts on the table and took the trick. 'She didn't have anyone at home to leave him with.'

'She's not married?'

French shook her head. 'Never has been.'

I knew about Jack's marital situation, of course, but was curious about the others. 'I've got a husband waiting for me at home, probably wondering where his next meal is coming from about now. How about you two?'

'I'm engaged to an investment banker in Boston,' French said. She glanced quickly at Amy who was studying her cards intently, silently. 'Amy's a widow.'

Amy, who I guessed to be in her mid to late twenties, looked too young to be a widow. A look of such sadness passed over her face that I could have kicked myself for bringing the subject up. 'I'm so sorry, Amy.'

She glanced up, eyes glistening with unshed tears. 'It's OK, really. Drew was a Navy SEAL. We both knew the risks when I married him.'

I stared at her pale face and shuddered. During our long association with the Naval Academy, Paul and I knew a number of midshipmen who'd gone into Special Ops after graduation, but we'd not lost any of them . . . yet. 'Was he an Academy grad?' I asked.

'No. UVA.'

I was about to comment on the high quality of naval officers coming out of the NROTC program at the University of Virginia when Jack took control of the conversation and made a U-turn. 'I went by the bakery this afternoon. The apple pies looked fantastic. Seems like our Karen can actually cook.'

'Speaking of Karen,' I said, laying down my cards and rising to my feet, 'I'm going to take her suggestion and go freshen up. See you at dinner?'

As I left the parlor, Derek disengaged himself from the dance lesson. He and his Steadicam shadowed me out of the room, down the hall and onto the elevator, a red light near the camera lens indicating that he was filming me the whole way. As I slotted the key card into my door, I turned and waggled my fingers at the camera before slipping inside and closing the door in his face.

'Cameras already dogging my tail,' I texted to Paul on my iPhone from the bathroom a few minutes later. 'Apparently I'm today's fresh meat.'

Dinner that night was a buffet affair – mixed green 'salat,' sliced roast of beef, and an oven-roasted potato and vegetable combo, all set out in very twenty-first-century chafing dishes on a dark oak sideboard in one of the hotel's private dining rooms. Cast members, some already in costume, continued to arrive in dribs and drabs as they finished their training at various locations throughout the 'plantation.'

My costume consisted of the same jeans and T-shirt I'd ridden down in, although I had washed my face, put on a bit of eyeliner and a smear of lipstick.

I loaded up my plate, snagged a brandy-spiked bread pudding from a side table and sat down opposite Jack Donovan, who was already tucking into his beef. His daughter, Melody, sat to his right, her plate heaped with vegetables, but she was having the bread pudding as an appetizer. At sixteen her baby fat was not likely to go away without a bit of push-back-from-the-table discipline, I thought. Fortunately, the mistress of Patriot House (me!) was not planning to serve quarter-pounders with cheese in 1774, so perhaps she'd make some headway when we got back to Annapolis.

Melody's little brother, Gabriel or 'Gabe,' as he was more commonly known, and to whom I'd been introduced in the game room, had finished his meal and from the sound effects leaking out of his iPod Touch, I gathered he was playing Angry Birds. Since discovering my role in the cast, he was pointedly ignoring me, as if holding me responsible for his mother's absence.

'How's your wife doing?' I asked Jack Donovan, genuinely concerned.

Jack swallowed the morsel of steak he'd been chewing, looking surprised that I asked. 'The prognosis is good. She still needs the chemo, but we are all optimistic.'

'It must be hard for her back in . . . sorry, I forget where you're from,' I babbled.

'Texas,' he said simply.

I paused, a fork loaded with potatoes halfway to my mouth. 'Texas is a big state.'

He sawed off another chunk of steak. 'A little town north of Dallas. McKinney. You've probably never heard of it.'

Surprisingly, I had. 'Didn't *Money Magazine* rate McKinney as one of the top five places to live in America?'

'It did. After that,' he grumbled, 'and all the publicity from this show, I worry that the population is simply going to *explode*, although I have to admit it'd be good for business.'

'Does Katherine have anyone staying with her during treatment?' I wondered.

His gray eyes caught mine and held. 'Of course. What kind of a person do you think I am? Kat's being treated at MD Anderson in Dallas, so no worries there, and her mother lives close by.'

'I text her, like, every minute,' Melody said, her manicured thumbs flicking rapidly over the keys of her Droid, 'Except the cell phone signal here really sucks.'

'Better get used to it, young lady,' her father warned. 'There'll be no cell phone service at Patriot House at all.'

Melody's head jerked up, her green eyes wide and disbelieving. 'No way. Cell phone signals are everywhere!'

'Not when they're jamming it,' Jack informed her.

Jamming. Great. There went any prayer of clandestine Facetime tête-a-têtes with Paul, assuming I'd even be able to smuggle my iPhone in.

'Is that true, Mrs Ives?' Melody wasn't buying it, seeking a second opinion.

'It's technically possible to jam cell phone signals,' I told her. 'You have to have permission from the FCC, of course, but movie theaters, restaurants, concert halls and churches are issued permits for jamming equipment every day.'

'That sucks,' she said, and I had to agree.

'You'll write to your mother every week,' Jack said. 'The old-fashioned way, with paper and pen.' His eyes darted in Gabe's direction. 'You, too, Gabriel.'

All the while we'd been talking, I could feel Gabe's ice-blue eyes boring into the side of my head. I leaned across the table and lowered my voice. 'Are the children really on board with the experiment, Jack?'

Jack's steely gaze dropped away, back to focusing on his steak. 'You're a Johnny-Come-Lately, so you're probably unaware of the rigorous screening they put us through. *Of course* the children are on board.'

'When Mom was diagnosed, we were all going to quit,' Melody cut in. 'But it was Mom who insisted we stay on. The show was mega important to her.'

'Kat has been home-schooling Melody and Gabriel, but what could be a better educational experience than actually having an opportunity to *live* in the eighteenth century?' Jack added.

From across the table a male voice said, 'May I butt in?'

Back in the parlor, I'd been introduced to the voice's owner, a gangly young man in his mid to late twenties with a fringe of dark hair, but I couldn't remember at the moment whether

he was Alex Mueller, the dancing master, or Michael Rainey,
the children's tutor.

'The children's education will continue,' he said, so I figured
it was Michael. 'They've converted the Paca House gift shop
into a schoolroom. I'll be teaching Gabe and Melody, of course,
plus four other homeschoolers who will be brought in for
classes every weekday.' He snorted softly. 'I almost said
"bussed in." That would have been a neat trick in 1774.'

'That's historically accurate,' Donovan stated airily, just in
case I'd been wondering. 'School teachers were thin on the
ground in colonial times. Only the gentry could afford to hire
them, so children from neighboring estates would be often be
included, and the expense shared.'

I'd done my homework, too, so this wasn't news to me.
Over the weekend, I'd poured over the material in the orientation packet Jud had given me, *The Compleat Housewife,
or Accomplished Gentlewoman's Companion*, for example,
and *The Frugal Housewife, or Complete Woman Cook*, a
cookbook from 1772 where I learned how to dress a turtle
(don't ask!) and prepare such finger-lickin' fare as ragout of
hog's head and ears. Particularly helpful was *The Journal
and Letters of Philip Vickers Fithian*, a charming and extraor-
dinarily detailed account of Fithian's year at Nomini Hall,
the Robert Carter estate in Virginia, as a 'plantation tutor'
to seven of the nine Carter children. Although Fithian wasted
a good bit of time mooning over his girlfriend back in New
Jersey, his impressions of daily life in Virginia are recorded
with insight and the kind of detail one might expect of a
tourist visiting a foreign country which, to a divinity student
from Princeton University in 1774, Virginia almost certainly
was.

Thinking about Fithian being so far away from home
prompted me to ask, 'So, what do you do in real life, Mr
Donovan?'

A corner of his mouth turned up, half smile, half smirk.
'Ah, I see you're getting into your role already, Mrs Ives. The
head of the household is always referred to as "Mister."' He
chased a wayward carrot around his plate, stabbed it with a
fork. 'Or, "sir," depending.'

While Donovan was busy popping the carrot into his mouth, Michael shot me a look: *Asshole.*

I stifled a giggle, narrowly avoiding spewing iced tea out my nose. Playing sister-in-law to such a stuffed shirt and mother to his two sulky children was likely to be a challenge. Didn't Jud tell me that the cast had been carefully vetted? Of course he did, I realized as I mashed my vegetables together with a fork and applied a generous pat of butter. But if every applicant received high marks under the 'Plays Well with Others' column, it wouldn't make for much of a TV show. 'Conflict,' I could almost hear Jud saying. 'That's what makes good television.'

'So, *sir*,' I continued, 'what do you do back in McKinney?'

'JD's Auto Mall,' he said. 'I sell cars. And I'm very, very good at it.'

A used-car salesman as our lord and master. How could we be so lucky?

# SIX

*'Having servants is awesome! I ring a bell and they bring me stuff!'*

Gabriel Donovan, son

On my first day as mistress of Patriot House, I was awakened by a gentle tap on the door.

'Mumppf,' I managed as I opened my eyes, squinted into the semi-darkness and tried to figure out exactly where I was. I struggled into a half-sitting position and patted around on the bedside table looking for my watch before remembering that I didn't have a watch. When the cast arrived at Patriot House the previous afternoon we'd gone through a sign-in procedure more thorough than a security checkpoint at Ben Gurion Airport in Tel Aviv. Watches, jewelry, iPods, iPhones, Droids, even Jack Donovan's hearing aids . . . those technical marvels that make twenty-first century life worth living, all had to be surrendered before we were given a tour of the house and shown to our respective rooms.

Now, as Amy bustled into the room smiling cheerfully and carrying a tea tray, I felt curiously detached from reality. Had it been only two weeks since Jud had showed up on my doorstep like a lost puppy?

'You asked to be awakened at six thirty,' Amy chirped as she set the tea tray down on a small round table between the two front windows. The skirt of her bright blue dress swished as she stood on tiptoe and threw open the curtains, flooding the room with light.

'Ouch,' I said, shielding my eyes.

'The staff is awake, madam,' Amy said. 'Cook said to say that breakfast will be ready to serve by eight. I'll go wake the children, then be back to help you dress.' She lifted a yellow silk dressing gown off a wooden peg near the door and laid it carefully on the foot of the bed, before disappearing into the hall.

My bedroom was located directly over the library at the front of the main house, its two tall windows overlooking Prince George Street. Carefully avoiding the chamber pot, I climbed out of bed, slipped the dressing gown over my shift and crossed to the windows, knotting my sash as I went. It had been a warm evening, so the windows – decorated with the same red and white French toile as the bed hangings – were still open. I stuck my head out, looked down the street to my right, wishing I could catch sight of Paul leaving the house, walking the few short blocks to his office at the Naval Academy, but it was far too early for that.

I settled into an upholstered slipper chair and picked up the teapot, carefully pouring the steaming liquid through the silver strainer Amy had balanced over my cup. I was grateful as I sipped that the two cameramen – Derek and Chad – had been assigned to cover the morning ablutions of The Great Patriot himself, Jack Donovan, who slept alone in the master suite directly across the hall.

Amy returned a short time later, materializing as if by magic through the wall just to the left of my bed. A door-sized portion of the woodwork – wallpaper, wainscoting, chair rail and all – yawned open and I nearly dropped my cup. 'Yikes!' I squeaked. 'You scared the life out of me!'

Amy laughed. 'Sorry.' She carried a tea kettle on a flat, padded pillow, steam drifting lazily out of its spout. 'That door leads to the service staircase. It's a shortcut to the first floor, and to the kitchen. I thought you might want to wash up first,' she added, heading for a washstand I had overlooked the previous evening. Carefully, she poured boiling water into a bowl in the washstand. She added cool water to it from a matching pitcher, tested the water with a fingertip, then draped a flannel cloth over the brim. 'It's ready whenever you are.'

'I'd kill for a cup of coffee,' I told Amy as I dipped the flannel into the warm water, squeezed it out and applied the refreshingly warm cloth to my face. 'A shower, too, but I realize that's out of the question.'

While I washed, Amy set the tea kettle down on the floor near the hidden door, just discernible as a thin crack, now that I knew where it was. She opened a leather trunk at the foot of the bed and pulled out one of my everyday gowns – an apple-green linen that I'd previously seen hanging in the wardrobe trailer with Katherine Donovan's name on it.

'Will this dress be suitable for today, madam?'

When I nodded, she draped the gown carefully over the arm of the chair I'd just vacated. Amy handed me a pair of stockings, a fine white silk, and knelt on the floor in front of me, ready to assist, as if I were an invalid. 'I think I can manage,' I said with a smile. 'Why don't you find my stays?'

While Amy dug the stays out of a dresser drawer, I rolled the stockings up over my knees and secured them there with a fat elastic band. 'Why it took until the nineteen sixties to invent panty hose, I can't imagine. I'm hoping I don't get gangrene below the knee in this get-up.'

Amy watched while I stepped into the under-petticoat. After I'd tied it around my waist, she handed me the stays. I slipped the corset-like device over my head then turned so she could lace me up the back. 'If you don't have a maid, or a husband, you'd never get into this contraption,' I said, regretting my words almost the moment they fell out of my mouth. *Husband.* Shit. Amy's husband was dead.

'I'm so sorry,' I said. 'I wasn't thinking.'

'That's OK,' Amy said, her voice hoarse. She gave my laces a final savage tug before tying them off. 'It's not like I haven't *noticed* that Drew is dead.'

I indicated a chair, the mate to the one I'd been sitting on. 'I've upset you. I'm sorry. Here, sit down for a minute.'

Amy eased her full skirts onto the chair and sat. For a long moment, she simply stared at me. Then she said, 'It hasn't been easy.'

'Do you want to talk about it?'

She sat quietly for a moment, hands folded, as if weighing how much to tell me. 'Do you know what a death notification team is, Hannah?'

'I can guess. Sounds awful.'

'It is. An official car pulls up in front of your house and an officer, a chaplain, a medic and a JAG, all in uniform, step out of it.' She looked up at me through a film of tears. 'Sounds like a bad joke, doesn't it? "An officer, a chaplain, a medic and a JAG walked into a bar . . ."' Her voice trailed off.

'I knew right away, of course. Nobody needed to tell me, but they did anyway, running through their official script, like "Are you Mrs Edward Drew Cornell? Is your husband Lieutenant Commander Edward Drew Cornell? Ma'am, we regret to inform you that your husband . . ."' She swiped a tear from her cheek and sighed deeply. 'According to the Navy, Drew is missing, presumed dead.'

I reached out and touched her sleeve. 'Missing? Is it *possible* he's still alive?'

Amy bit her lower lip and shook her head. 'No.'

'When did this happen, Amy?'

'Ten months ago. Remember that helicopter crash in Swosa?'

My heart did a flip-flop. 'After Madani Sabir Nazari was assassinated? My God! It was all over the news. Two of the casualties were Naval Academy grads, so we paid particular attention to the coverage. Drew was on that mission, too?'

She nodded miserably. 'The Navy's been trying to recover their bodies for months, but the rebel government in Swosa isn't cooperating. But what difference does it make? CNN has videos of the crash. The chopper was incinerated. There can't possibly have been any survivors.'

Outside in the hallway, a patter of bare feet and the putt-putt-putt of a race car screaming by – Gabriel making anach-ronistic noises. Amy looked up. 'Guess I better finish helping you dress. You going to wear hoops?'

I shrugged. 'Might as well go the whole hog.'

Amy helped me tie the figure-eight-shaped hoop Alisha had told me was called a farthingale around my waist, then handed me what looked like an embroidered pouch on a string. 'What's this?' I asked, turning it over in my hands, admiring the handiwork.

'It's a pocket. You tie it on under your skirt. You can put things in it like coins, keys, lipstick . . .' She laughed out loud. 'Just kidding about the lipstick. You reach into the pocket from slits in the side seams of your dress.'

'What made you decide to apply for Patriot House?' I asked
Amy as she helped me adjust the pocket and slip into my
gown.

'Oh, Hannah. It's been awful. After Drew died, everything
seemed to go to hell. I was teaching music in a Catholic
elementary school, but the diocese closed the school in a cost-
cutting measure, then sold the property.'

'Let me guess . . .'

Amy nodded. 'Pedophile priests. Compensating their victims
turned out to be expensive.'

'The price of priestly pederasty spreads far beyond the
original victims. I read about some nuns in Los Angeles who
were evicted from the convent they'd lived in for more than
forty years so that the property could be sold.'

Amy shook her head. 'I'm glad Mother Church is finally
getting around to compensating victims of its pedophile priests,
but the nuns weren't exactly the guilty parties, were they?'

'Where do you live?' I asked as Amy knelt to shake the
wrinkles out of my gown and arrange it more attractively over
the petticoat.

'Virginia Beach. A really nice neighborhood in Lynnhaven,' Amy
continued. 'Or so I thought. Then I started getting harassing
phone calls. I can't prove it, but I think they came from this hate
group out in Topeka, Kansas that calls itself a church. "Thank
God for dead soldiers" the voice would say. They told me that
Drew was killed by an angry God and that whenever God saw
fit to send him home in a body bag, they'd happily picket his
funeral.'

I laid a hand on Amy's shoulder. 'I think I'm going to
be ill.'

'Tell me about it. I reported the calls to the police, of course,
but they had other more pressing cases, so I had my phone
changed to an unlisted number. When the son of a bitch called
that, too, I simply had the landline taken out. Then someone
vandalized my car. Two weeks later, my condo was broken
into. Totally unrelated, I'm sure, but when my mother found
out, she worried – you know mothers – called me three times
a day from Nashua, New Hampshire, left messages on my
cell, insisted I move back in with her, but . . . well, if you

knew my mother, you'd understand why I preferred to run
away to the eighteenth century!' She paused, head cocked
while she concentrated on hooking me into my stomacher.
'There!' She took several steps back, examining her work.
'You look fabulous, but we have to do something about the
hair.'

Over the summer I'd let my usual wash-and-wear, ash-brown
curls grow out. By September they'd reached the length where
I could, with some effort, scrape them into a short ponytail.
Amy sat me at the dressing table, and by some legerdemain,
swept my hair up in wings over my ears, using a hairbrush to
coax the ends into a mass of mini-sausages at the back of my
head. She topped off the do with a soft, lacy mob cap.
Examining myself in the mirror, I had to agree with Amy's
assessment: I looked fabulous – for a grandmother of three
wearing no makeup.

'Where did you learn to do that?' I asked.

Her reflection shrugged. 'I have a little sister. I used to do
it for her. French braids, mostly. Sue married a Mormon and
moved out to St George, Utah.'

'Whew!' I said, patting my curls appreciatively. 'I was afraid
they'd want me to wear a wig.'

'For the ball, yes.'

'You think so?'

She nodded. 'For sure. I overheard Jud talking to Derek
about setting up a shoot at the wigmakers.'

'As long as it's not one of those mile-high creations with
ribbons, feathers and live birds,' I said.

Amy grinned. 'They come with fleas, too. For lice, you pay
extra.'

'Euuuuw!' I rolled my eyes. 'Well, let's hope the producers'
passion for historical accuracy doesn't stretch that far.'

For a house with a dozen (or so) residents, it surprised me
that only five were at breakfast that morning. Alex Mueller,
the dancing master, wouldn't be joining us until later in the
day, I learned, so it was just me at one end of the table and
Jack at the other, with Melody and her brother sitting on the
side facing the windows opposite Michael Rainey, their tutor.

And the cameraman, of course. Derek (or was it Chad?) who was standing as inconspicuously as possible next to the buffet like a black, brooding potted plant, filming us as we ate breakfast.

When I finally managed to arrange my skirts, underskirts and hoops in such a way that I could actually sit down in my chair, Jack offered a quick blessing of the 'Oh, Lord we just . . .' persuasion and I was about to open my mouth to say that we were supposed to be Anglican, thank you very much, saying graces from the *Book of Common Prayer* circa 1662 such as, *Give us grateful hearts, O Father, for all thy mercies, and make us mindful of the needs of others; through Jesus Christ our Lord. Amen*, when French appeared with the scrambled eggs, hominy, fried potatoes and onions – followed by, bless her, cups of rich, dark coffee that brightened my whole day. I hoped Amy and the others were eating just as well down in the kitchen.

I was helping myself to another spoonful of eggs from a covered bowl when someone began knocking at the front door, the sound of the brass knocker echoing sharply through the house. A few minutes later, a man I hadn't met before, dressed in a plain dark suit with gold braid, entered the dining room, carrying a silver tray. 'No reply required, sir,' the man said, holding the tray out in front of Jack. On the tray sat a piece of parchment-colored paper that from my vantage point, looked to be folded in fourths and sealed with a blob of red wax. Jack scooped up the message and said, 'Thank you, Jeffrey. You may go.'

While Jeffrey was busy bowing theatrically and backing out of the room, I said, 'Mr Donovan, may I ask why I've never met that individual?'

'What did you say?'

I'd forgotten about the missing hearing aids, so I repeated the question, only a little louder.

'He's my valet.' Jack picked up his table knife and used it to pry up the seal and unfold the paper.

While Jack was engrossed in reading his correspondence, I leaned in Michael's direction and whispered, 'Why haven't I seen him before?'

'That's Jeff Wiley. From Colorado. He was in Williamsburg early on, but came back to Annapolis before the rest of us to help get the house ready. His room is on the third floor of the main house, next to French's.' Michael pointed at the ceiling.

'Oh,' I whispered back. 'I didn't recognize him. In the photo they gave me, Jeff had a mustache.'

'Shaved it off.' Michael nodded knowingly. 'Tragic. A casualty of learning how to use a straight razor.'

I smothered a laugh with my napkin.

'So, *that's* how it's going to work,' Jack muttered from the opposite end of the table.

Melody looked up from her plate where she'd been rearranging her fried potatoes, constructing little mounds. 'How's *what* going to work, Father?'

'Attention, everyone!' Jack waited until all eyes were turned in his direction, then addressed me directly. 'Mrs Ives, this message is signed by "Founding Father," who informs me that the new styles from France are in at the dressmaker's in Cornhill Street. You and Melody are to be measured for a gown at eleven o'clock this morning. You're to take your maid with you.'

Melody's fork clattered to her plate. 'I'm going to have a gown made? Awesome!'

By 'maid' I presumed he meant Amy. I also presumed this meant the whole expedition would be recorded by Derek and/ or Chad, one of whom had just sidled around to Jack's end of the table, all the better to zoom in on my smiling face as I said, 'I'd be delighted, sir.'

'How about Melody's schooling, sir?' Michael asked. 'She's to be starting Greek at ten.'

Melody frowned. 'Greek? Oh. My. Boring. God!'

Donovan scowled at his daughter, then waved a languid, lace-trimmed sleeve. 'Get her started on her Greek then, Rainey, but missing an hour or so of lessons isn't going to hurt her.'

Melody pressed her pudgy hands together and beamed.

And so, on the instructions of Founding Father, our first outing began. I wore my green, Amy her blue, and Melody turned up wearing a gown of softest gray. We'd tied broad-brimmed straw hats over our mob caps, of course, and pulled gloves over our hands so no neighborhood gossips could titter over their teacups that we were 'no better than they should be.' We strolled down the narrow sidewalk, single-file (how else?) with Chad, the cameraman trotting along behind.

The twenty-first-century people we passed were curious, but didn't seem surprised. Tour guides in colonial garb often wandered the streets of Annapolis; we were three among many. Tourist cameras captured our cheerful little parade up East Street to State Circle – there'd be images of us all over Facebook in half an hour.

Halfway down Cornhill Street, I pulled Amy aside. 'I probably missed this email, Amy, but what are we doing about these people, exactly? Do we pretend like it's 1774 and they haven't been born yet?'

'What people?' Amy quipped.

'I get it,' I said, as we continued on our way. 'Invisible.'

Our destination was a little house near Hyde Alley. A sign hung on an iron bar by the door: *Mrs Hamilton. Dressmaker. By Appointment Only*. We knocked and went inside, setting a bell attached to the door frame jangling.

'Oh!' Melody's gloved hands flew to her mouth.

LynxE had gone to a lot of trouble to turn someone's narrow, colonial-era home into a proper dressmaker's shop. A long table stood to our right, with bolts of cloth stacked up on the end nearest the fireplace. Shelves built along the opposite wall held fabric, too, and hat boxes were stacked in a colorful jumble on top. Bins on a smaller table held buttons and beads, and spools of ribbon – grosgrain and silk – were stored in a corner on upright pegs. In the opposite corner, a beautiful coromandel screen shielded the dressing area from the prying eyes of other customers.

'Welcome, ladies!' A woman I took to be Mrs Hamilton smiled broadly, trying to concentrate on greeting us, but her eyes kept darting nervously toward the camera. 'The moppets are here,' she said. 'Just wait until you see the latest styles from Paris!'

Melody's brow furrowed. 'Muppets? No way. Kermit? Miss Piggy?'

'Moppets, sweetheart. They're fashion dolls, dressed in the most beautiful dresses you've ever seen.' Mrs Hamilton unlocked the door of a glass-fronted cabinet and removed two bisque-faced dolls, one wearing a forest-green gown trimmed in gold braid, the other in a creamy vanilla silk confection with hundreds of miniature rosebuds decorating the bodice, hem and sleeves. Two other dolls, one dressed in red the other in a peach and green stripe, remained standing at attention inside the cabinet.

'I want this one,' Melody said, choosing the doll in the creamy gown, picking it up by the waist and dancing it gently along the tabletop. Her eyes sparkled like a ten-year-old on Christmas morning. 'I collect dolls, Mrs Hamilton. I started out with Barbies and American Girls. I've got a whole lot of Madame Alexanders, too.' She flipped up the doll's skirt, examining its underclothing. 'My specialty is Snow White. I've got her by Madame Alexander, Effanbee, Applause and Disney,' she said, smiling, ticking them off on her fingers.

Mrs Hamilton chuckled. 'Oh, the dolls aren't for sale, sweetheart. They're just models for the dresses. Samples, if you will.' She removed the delicate figure gently from Melody's hands. 'But you can have a gown made exactly like this one if you like.'

Wide-eyed, Melody simply nodded.

'Why don't you measure Melody first,' I suggested. 'Is there someplace my maid and I can sit while I wait for you to finish measuring Melody?'

'Of course,' Mrs Hamilton said, rubbing her hands together briskly, clearly flustered by my request. 'It's a lovely day. Would you like to sit out in the garden?'

'That would be splendid,' I said.

Mrs Hamilton plucked a silver hand bell off the table and gave it a jingle. A young girl appeared from the back of the house – her daughter, I guessed – her head bowed, smiling shyly. 'Amanda, will you show Mrs Ives and her maid to the garden, please? And see if they want some tea.'

'That's very kind, but we've only just eaten breakfast,' I

said, as Amanda led us into the (twenty-first century!) kitchen and out through a back door.

I looked nervously behind me, expecting Chad to be trotting along in our wake, but he'd made an executive decision: viewers would be much more interested in watching a sixteen-year-old strip behind a screen and get measured for a dress than a shop-worn old specimen like me. Besides, LynxE had probably dropped a bundle on decorating the shop, so not one thimble, button or pin could be wasted.

Mrs Hamilton's backyard was enclosed by a high fence. From the back door, a winding path led to a miniature rose garden. Amy and I found a green Chippendale bench between a pink hybrid tea and an orangey floribunda and sat down on it. I removed my hat, closed my eyes and lifted my face to the sun. 'Ah, bliss. Why do I feel as if I've been cooped up for ages?'

Amy laughed. 'Because you have, if you count Williamsburg.'

'But, look on the bright side, Amy. I now know how to milk a cow.'

'French's job, or Karen's, but I guess you'll do in a pinch. Gabe asked for chocolate milk this morning, by the way, but I had to disappoint him.'

I opened one eye and looked at her. 'Don't we have chocolate?'

'Karen didn't think so.'

'Well,' I said. 'I'll put that on the list for when I go to market. Anything else we need?'

'Diet Coke.'

'Ha!' I said. We sat quietly for a while, enjoying the sun. I think I may even have dozed off, when the familiar tri-tone chime of an iPhone brought me out of my coma. 'What was that?'

Next to me, Amy's skirts rustled. She thrust a hand through the slit in her skirt and into her pocket. It came out holding an iPhone. Amy stared at the phone for a few seconds, then, to my astonishment, started to sob. Deep, shuddering, tearless sobs.

'Amy! What is it?' I asked stupidly, forgetting for the moment that we weren't even supposed to have cell phones.

'Oh my God!' she gasped, her eyes still glued to the tiny screen. 'It's not possible! Oh, Hannah, somebody's fucking with my mind!'

'What?'

Amy seemed frozen. I pried the iPhone out of her hand. Written in a green text balloon was this message: Alive. Coming 4 U soon. F U tell anyone, they'll kill me.

I wrapped my arm around the shivering girl. 'Your husband?'

'It can't be. Drew's dead. The Navy said so.'

'Are you sure?'

'Hannah, the helo was brought down by a rocket-propelled grenade. It was incinerated. I haven't seen anything so horrible in my whole life, and CNN ran the footage over and over and over again, interviewed every top military advisor, active duty and retired, as they tried to sort out exactly what happened.' She drew a jittery breath. 'Drew's dead. I'm just waiting for the official paperwork.'

'Screw CNN, Amy. Did the *Navy* tell you what happened?'

She nodded miserably. 'Nazari was supposed to be extracted, but he got shot instead. His people weren't very happy.'

'Oh, God. I remember.' I stared at her screensaver for a few moments, a stock photo of the Earth taken from outer space. Swosa was on the other side of that globe, yet we were still feeling the impact of events that happened there months and months ago.

Amy nudged my arm. 'Maybe it's the same goddamn creeps who were harassing me in Virginia Beach.'

'Look, here's an idea. Why don't you reply to the text?' I slipped the phone back into her hand, but she hardly seemed to notice. 'Ask whoever sent that text message a question that only Drew would know the answer to.'

Amy considered my suggestion for a moment, her lower lip caught between her teeth. 'Like what?'

I thought about the break-in at Amy's condo and wondered if it and the message she'd just received were related. A few seconds later, I said, 'Nicknames, pet names, place of birth, mother's maiden name . . . security questions like that aren't any good because anybody who's really motivated can find out that information by simply walking around your living room.'

As I leaned closer our arms touched and I felt her shiver. 'Ask him this: where was the first place the two of you had sex?'

Amy sniggered. 'OK.' With a nervous glance over my shoulder in the direction of the dress shop, Amy bent her head over her iPhone and swiped it back on. I watched as she typed: OK. F U Drew, where did we first have sex? She tapped Send. Together we watched the status bar creep along the bottom of the screen as the message went on its way.

But it didn't. According to a red exclamation point in a circle on the screen, the send had failed. 'Shit, it didn't go.'

'Try it again.'

Amy tapped the screen, but once again, the send was aborted. This time, a message popped up in a gray balloon: *Error Invalid Number. Please re-send using a valid ten-digit mobile number or a valid short code.*

'See, I told you. Somebody hates me and is doing this to make me crazy.'

'If Drew is alive and on the run,' I suggested, grasping at straws, 'maybe he's using a satellite phone or a throwaway cell.'

'Ten months ago, I might have believed you, Hannah, but now? If Drew were alive, he would have contacted me *long* before this. Trust me, this is just some bastard's idea of a cruel joke.'

'Yoo-hoo! Hannah!' It was Melody, fully dressed, bouncing on her toes, calling to us from the back door. Chad had backed out of the house and down the steps ahead of her and was filming the whole episode. 'Wait till you see what I've picked out!'

Amy hastily slipped her iPhone back into her pocket.

'Why did you keep your phone?' I whispered as we both rose to our feet. I scooped up my hat from the lawn, then linked my arm through hers. 'You know phones aren't allowed.'

'Security?' she said as we hurried to join Melody inside. 'A lifeline to the outside world?'

'You can walk out of Patriot House any time you want, Amy. We're not prisoners.'

I felt her shrug. 'I'm one of those A-type, adult child of an alcoholic who doesn't like to admit failure. I'm a workaholic – when I have a job, that is. When we married, Drew and I agreed I'd be a stay-at-home mom.' She paused, tugged on my arm, holding me back. 'We were planning on starting a family.'

Chad executed an about-face and aimed the camera in our direction. Thinking about Amy's shattered dreams, I wanted to bawl, but I beamed at the camera instead.

'Wanna know how I got the phone past the barbarians at the gate?' Amy kept her voice low.

Since I'd considered trying to hold on to my iPhone myself, I felt a bit guilty giving Amy a hard time about it. 'How?'

'In my shoe.'

'Clever girl.'

She leaned closer, whispered into my ear. 'Made me limp a bit, but nobody noticed. Don't know why I bothered, actually, because of the jamming.

'I wish *I* were having a gown made, madam,' she chirped a few seconds later, purely for the benefit of Chad and his camera.

'When my gown is finished, Amy, you may wear my old one to the ball.'

'Oh!' she gushed. 'That peachy one with the flowers on it?'

'The very one.'

Amy flung out her arms and wrapped me in an impetuous hug. 'Oh, madam, thank you! That will be wonderful!'

Chad zoomed in for a close-up, but I didn't pull away. Even in 1774, hugging one's maid couldn't have been a sin. And if anyone needed a hug at that moment, it was Miss Amy Cornell.

That evening after supper – as was the colonial custom – the women, Amy, Melody and I, prepared to retire to the parlor leaving the men, Jack, Michael and Alex, to linger over their port in the dining room, smoking their pipes and hand-rolled cigars. Gabe had fallen asleep in his chair, clutching a pack of cards, having exhausted himself (and his audience) with fledgling feats of legerdemain.

Using a little silver bell, I summoned French to begin clearing away the dishes. Jeffrey slouched in behind her,

carrying a wooden box which he opened and offered to Jack.
'Cigar, sir?'

'Ah, yes,' Jack replied, leaning forward to peer into the box.
He selected one of several long, cylindrical-shaped objects
that looked more like mummified ape fingers than cigars.
'Rolled 'em myself,' he said, sliding a candlestick across the
tablecloth and using the flame to light the loathsome object.

'French, would you please take young Houdini up to bed?'
I asked.

As French left the dining room with a drowsy Gabe, Alex
made a face at the acrid cloud of burning tobacco smoke
wafting in his direction. 'I didn't think cigars were invented
until sometime in the eighteenth century,' he commented,
reaching for a European-style pipe with orange and brown
geometric designs incised around its belly-shaped bowl.

'Nope.' Jack drew smoke into his mouth, held it there for
a moment, then let it escape in a thin stream from between
pursed lips. 'Cigars arrived here in 1762 with a fellow named
Israel Putnam who'd been serving with the British army in
Cuba when they captured Havana.' He gazed at the glowing
tip of his cigar like a proud father. 'My tobacconist on Maryland
Avenue was able to acquire some for me.'

Michael began stuffing the bowl of a plain white clay pipe
with tobacco, tamping the leaves down with his thumb. 'Thank
God I don't have to inhale,' he said as Jeffrey touched a burning
taper to the bowl and Michael fired it up.

I rose, fanning the smoke away from my face with my hand,
suppressing a cough as I said, 'Well, if you gentlemen will
excuse us.'

A few minutes later, I settled down in the parlor with a
book, leaning as closely as I dared to the candles without
setting my hair on fire, and Melody flounced in and plopped
down on the loveseat to have another go at her embroidery.
After lighting all the candles in the room, Amy began to browse
through the sheet music that was arranged in piles on top of
the harpsichord. Slowly, dreamily, she dusted her fingers lightly
along the whole length of the keyboard and said, 'I think we
should have a little music, don't you? Would you like me to
play something?'

My head jerked around so quickly I was in danger of whip-lash. 'You play?'

'A well-kept secret, but yes, I do. What would you like? Scarlatti? Mozart? Bach? Beethoven?'

'Beethoven wasn't born yet,' I said.

Amy grinned. 'Was too. He would have been four, but I don't think he was composing yet. He wasn't as precocious as Mozart.'

'Mozart would be lovely.'

Amy scooted the bench out, sat down and settled her skirts around her. She rested her fingers lightly on the keys, cocked her head, and began to play from memory. I recognized the tune: Mozart's march from the *Marriage of Figaro*. When she finished the short piece we clapped madly and I said, 'The only thing I miss is the hysterical laugh at the end.'

Melody shot me a what-are-you-crazy kind of look, so I asked her, 'Did you see the movie, *Amadeus*?'

Melody shook her head.

Why was I not surprised? *Amadeus* came out in 1984, years before Melody was born. I felt old as Methuselah. 'When you get home, Melody, rent it from Netflix, and you'll get the joke about the laugh,' I said, before turning back to Amy and urging her to play another piece.

In the middle of Bach's little 'Minuet in G,' the gentlemen joined us, Alex in the lead. He laid a finger against his lips and quietly selected one of the straight-backed chairs that had been lined up in the shadows against the wall and dragged it out into the candlelight. Michael followed suit, while Jack sat down with a grunt on the loveseat next to his daughter.

When the last note died away, Alex Mueller – who was clapping louder than everyone else put together, or so it seemed to me – leapt to his feet and shouted, 'Brava! Brava! Encore! Encore!'

Amy twisted round to face him, bowed her head slightly, smiled and apologized. 'I'm afraid that's all I know by heart. Why don't you play something for us, Alex?'

In three long strides, Alex crossed the oriental rug to the harpsichord and began pawing through the sheet music. 'Here's something,' he announced, waving the music in the air like a victory flag. 'Mozart's sonata for piano and violin in C major. I think we need a duet, don't you?'

Piano and violin? Apparently Alex had hidden talents. I led an encouraging round of applause.

Alex handed the music to Amy, and in the time it took her to spread it open on the music rack in front of her, he'd retrieved his violin from the floor under the harpsichord and removed it from its case. 'An A, please, Miss Cornell?' After a bit of fussing with the tuning pegs and fiddling with the bow, he waved the bow in a dramatic arc and said, 'Ready.'

'Don't you need to see the score?' Amy wondered.

Alex clamped the violin under his chin. 'This one's in my repertoire.' He raised his bow, then lowered it again, turning to address Melody. 'Mozart wrote this piece when he was eight years old. Think about that.' He raised his bow again, nodded to Amy, and they began to play.

Ten minutes of magic ensued.

As the last note of Alex's violin faded away, we sat silently, still mesmerized, until Melody broke the spell by leaping to her feet, applauding like a groupie at a Stones concert.

Alex held out his hand, Amy slipped hers into his and allowed him to guide her out from behind the bench. Standing side by side, hands raised aloft, the two musicians bowed deeply. After a moment, Alex raised Amy's hand to his lips and kissed it. Even in the candlelight, I could see her blush.

Jack, who up to this time had usually sat through family activities like a gargoyle and whose taste in music (I imagined) ran to praise songs like 'Shout to the Lord,' surprised me by clapping and chanting, 'Encore! Encore!' along with the rest of us.

Alex dropped Amy's hand. 'I think it's time for some audience participation, don't you, Amy?'

He returned to the harpsichord, shuffled around through the music, coming up with a handful of booklets composed of folded sheets of parchment, sewn through the center fold with red string. One copy contained the score, which Alex handed to Amy. For us, there was no music, only lyrics to songs popular in the 1770s, collected – according to the handwritten title page – by a soldier named Colonel George Bush from Delaware. Alex made a circuit of the room, passing out the booklets, uttering words of encouragement along the way: 'Come on! Everybody can sing! Yes, even *you*, Mr Donovan,' that charmed the socks off everyone.

'I'll go first,' he said, returning to the harpsichord and indicating to Amy which song he would like her to play. Amy played a short introduction, so we could pick up on the tune, then Alex began leading us in a song of flowers and spring and unrequited love of a swain for a country maid named Katharine Ogie. Like good little do-bees, we joined in, but by the time we reached the end of the song: '*Clouds of despair surround my love, which are both dark and fogie, Pity my case ye powers above, else I die for Katharine Ogie,*' we'd dropped out, one by one, totally mesmerized by the sound of Alex's sweet baritone.

Once again, Melody was on her feet, applauding. 'Your turn now, Amy!'

'What shall I sing?'

Alex leaned over Amy's shoulder and turned to the next page in the booklet, smoothing it down. When it wouldn't behave, he kept a finger on the corner so it'd stay put.

'I'm afraid my voice isn't nearly as fine as yours, Alex,' Amy said, placing her fingers on the keys, gazing up at him sideways through her lashes.

'Sure it is. Go on. We'll sing with you.'

'I'll be sight-reading.' She grinned. 'So don't expect much.'

'Saw you my hero, saw you my hero, saw you my hero, George?' Amy sang, leaning forward, squinting, to better see the words and music as she played. Alex paced behind her back, conducting his motley chorus with his bow.

'*Hark, from the hills, the woodlands, and dales,* (we sang)
*The drums and the trumpet alarms.*
*Ye Gods, I give you charge of gallant hero, George*
*To return him unhurt to my arms.*'

I was just thinking, *ooooh, bad choice*, when Amy's head drooped, and her hands flew from the keyboard to her face.

She rocked forward, then burst into tears and ran from the
room. After a moment of stunned silence, Jack Donovan
blustered, 'What's the matter with *her*?'

Alex bowed, abandoned his violin and rushed out of the
room after her.

# SEVEN

*'I explained to Mr Donovan why I came unglued while I was playing the harpsichord the other day. The advice he gave me came from the heart, but unfortunately it was all about Jesus.'*

Amy Cornell, lady's maid

A week later, I awoke just as fingers of light began to creep around the edges of the curtains. I propped myself up on my pillows and lay in bed with the coverlet tucked under my chin, listening to rain drum against the roof and gurgle along the gutters. I couldn't stop thinking about the abrupt ending to what had been an otherwise delightful musicale, and the text message Amy had received in the dressmaker's garden and wondering who could be so cruel, and why.

A few minutes later, there was a gentle knock on the door hidden in the wall next to my bed, followed almost immediately by Amy, backside and petticoats first, carrying a tea tray. As had become her routine, she set the tray down on the table between the windows, then turned to draw open the curtains. She stood at the window for a few seconds, staring out into the cool, gray day, watching the rain sluice sideways against the antique glass. 'Good day for ducks,' she said.

Amy turned, reached into her pocket and pulled out a letter, sealed with a familiar red blob of wax. 'This came for you a few minutes ago,' she said, propping the letter up against the sugar bowl on the tray.

'I'm beginning to dread these letters,' I confided. 'If it's from our Founding Father, as I suspect, I think I'll need tea first.'

'Allow me.' Amy smiled, set the silver strainer over my cup and poured a cup of tea through it. She set the strainer

containing the damp leaves aside, added a thin slice of lemon
to the cup and brought it over to me where I still lay, like a
slug, in bed.

'Amy, you are a gem,' I told her, lifting the cup and saucer
from her hands and taking a sip. 'Should you ever need a
letter of recommendation as colonial maid of all work, you
need only to turn to me.'

'I'll remember that.' It was good to see her laugh. 'If there's
nothing else you need, I'll go wake up the children, then.' She
curtseyed and let herself out the way she had come.

The secret door to my room opened left off the service
staircase, and a similar door, I had discovered, led off to the
right, directly into Melody's room, the one adjoining mine.
That room had once belonged to William Paca's ten-year-old
niece who had come to live in Annapolis as an orphan, and
had died there, probably of tuberculosis. I hadn't told the story
to Melody, worried that if she knew the truth – that little Henny
Dorsey had literally died in her room – she would have freaked.
I'd been in Melody's room, and I had to admit that being there
gave me a creepy feeling, too.

I could hear Melody moving around next door, singing 'You
Make Me Feel' by Cobra Starship, when Amy returned to help
me dress. 'Did you sleep well?' I asked as she laced me into
my stays.

'Not very,' she replied. 'My windows are tiny, but you know
what I see when I look out? The Naval Academy chapel.'

The cornerstone for the chapel, a Beaux Arts treasure
designed by architect Ernest Flagg, had been laid in 1904.
Amy's room, in the west wing overlooking the garden, would
have an unobstructed view of the chapel's magnificent dome.
'If our Founding Father were here right now,' I teased, 'he'd
tell you that was impossible. The chapel won't be built for
more than a century.'

Amy simply stared at me. Unwittingly, I must have hit a
nerve. I felt like a total shit when she explained, 'It's kinda
ironic, but three years ago, Drew and I were married in that
chapel.'

I laid a hand on each of her thin shoulders and squeezed
reassuringly. 'Oh, Amy, I'm so sorry. Me and my big mouth.'

'It's OK, Hannah. I miss him, sure, but it's over now. Drew's dead. I've sold the condo. The furniture's in storage. It's time to move on.'

Next door, Melody had turned the volume up. 'You make me feel that, la la la la la, you make me feel so, la la la la la . . .'

The moment was so not-according-to-the-script that Amy and I looked at each other and burst out laughing. 'At least somebody's happy,' Amy said.

I picked a hand mirror up from my bedside table and studied my face in the early morning light. 'My eyebrows are pitiful. There's a bit of a uni-brow thing going on here.' Still holding the mirror, I turned to Amy. 'What did they use for tweezers back then?'

'Tweezers? I'm sure they go back to Egyptian times. Do you want me to ask the diary cam?'

I laughed. 'No, I'll do it. I have to do something with these eyebrows if I'm to be seen in polite company.'

With a nervous glance out the window, Amy said, 'I laid out your green silk today, but with the weather . . .'

I hopped out of bed, opened up the trunk at its foot and started pawing through it.

'If they think I'm going to wear a silk gown in this weather, they're crazy. Homespun will do nicely, I think.' I pulled out a dark blue gown. 'What do you think about this?'

'Nice.' She handed me my petticoat. While she waited for me to step into it, she said, 'Drew and I really didn't have all that much time together. First it was the training, then he was deployed.' She shrugged. 'You know what they say after the wedding ceremony, when you walk through the arch of swords on the chapel steps and they whack you on the butt?'

I did, and I said so, but she reminded me of it anyway. '"Welcome to the Navy, Mrs Cornell." I was twenty-five years old, and thought I knew everything, but nothing really prepares you to be a Navy wife, does it? A users' manual would have come in handy.'

Amy helped me into my dress, pinned the stomacher in place, then watched, head cocked to one side, as I arranged a scarf around my neck. Once that was done, I could no longer ignore the letter that sat on the silver tray, its official wax seal staring at me accusingly like a big red eye.

I snatched the letter from the tray, plopped down in the chair, slipped my finger under the seal and opened it up. 'Oh, blast, hell and damnation!'

'What is it?'

'It seems that George Washington is passing through Annapolis on Saturday, a stopover on his way from Mount Vernon to Philadelphia for a meeting of the Continental Congress. He's representing Virginia, no surprise. He'll be staying here overnight. Damn.'

The color drained from Amy's face. '*The* George Washington? As in the first president of the United States?'

'Bingo. But he's only a colonel. He won't be president until . . .' I paused to think. '. . . until 1789. That's fifteen years in the future.'

'But, all our bedrooms are taken! Where will Colonel Washington sleep?'

'Good question.' I thought for a moment, tapping the letter absent-mindedly on my cheek. I certainly wasn't going to move in with Jack Donovan, even if the staff could scrounge up a bundling board somewhere. 'We'll give Washington the best bedroom, no question about that. Jack will have Melody's room. That means that Melody will bunk with me, on the trundle bed.' Just thinking about playing 'musical beds' made me tired. 'I'll have to tell French. We need to make sure we have clean sheets.

'Founding Father also reminds me, in case I'd forgotten, that today's market day. The vendors are expecting us; I'm to pay a visit to the Maryland Table stall. Oh, Amy! Do you think I can get out of it? I *hate* the idea of going out in this rain. Call me cynical, but I think the producers planned it on purpose.'

'Planned what?' Amy wanted to know as she tipped the tea kettle over the wash basin.

'This evil weather. I can just hear them thinking, what could be better than to send Hannah to market on a rainy day? Watch how she ruins her shoes.'

'You should wear your pattens,' Amy suggested.

I'd tried out the pattens, a kind of high-heeled wooden clog that strapped over your shoes and supposedly kept your shoes and the hems of your skirts dry. But after *clack-clack-clacking* around the house in a pair of them, teetering like a drunk, I decided to give them a pass.

'Your water's ready, Hannah,' Amy reminded me. 'Best to use it before it gets cold.'

I dipped the flannel in the water, wrung it out and pressed the warm cloth to my face, being careful not to drip water on my dress. *Note to self. Wash first. Dress second.* After a moment, I said, 'Karen will be accompanying me, of course, but it doesn't say anything in the letter about not taking my maid along.' I draped the damp cloth over the rim of the bowl. 'Would you like to come, too? Get soaked along with me?'

Amy drifted to the window, pressed her forehead against the glass. 'I admit it would be a relief to get out of the house. Melody is driving me crazy with all her mooning over some pimply-faced cowboy named Tim back in Texas. They've only been separated for a couple of weeks, but you'd think it was a year.'

'Don't be too hard on her. I remember being crazy in love at her age. When my father got transferred to San Diego from Norfolk, I thought I was going to die. I'm still crazy in love, believe it or not, and Paul and I have been married for more years than I care to count. If you look to the far right, you can almost see my house from here, but Paul might as well be on the other side of the moon.'

'At least you'll get to see Paul again . . .' Amy's voice broke.

'Amy, I know what you told me earlier, but I can tell you're not over it.'

She flapped a hand in front of her face. 'No, no, I'm all right.'

But I didn't believe her, not for a minute.

After I sat down at the breakfast table, I shared the news about George Washington's visit with Jack. I thought he'd be delighted, or nervous, or apprehensive . . . something, but from behind a facsimile copy of the *Maryland Gazette*, he merely grunted. Melody looked bored, and Gabe was busily sawing

his cinnamon toast into skinny, one-inch rectangles called
soldiers. I wondered what the latest news was on Katherine's
condition, but decided that now wasn't the best time to inquire.

As he'd spent the night on the trundle in Michael's room,
I had expected the dancing master to be joining us for breakfast, but his chair at the table sat empty. 'Where's Alex?' I
asked.

Michael scooped some melon out with his spoon. 'He ate
earlier in the kitchen. He said he had to go over to Brice House
to check out the ballroom. Apparently, there's to be a dance
there next week.'

'A dance? Is that something we'll be invited to attend?'

Michael chewed his melon, looking thoughtful. 'Almost
certainly. I'm sure our friendly neighborhood Founding Father
will be sending out invitations soon enough.'

I spread a bit of butter on my bread and added a dollop of
Karen's homemade strawberry jam. 'What's so fascinating
about the newspaper, Jack? Surely, that's old, old news.'

'You'll find this interesting, Melody,' her father said. 'A
fellow named James Hutchings is announcing a sale at Broad
Creek Ferry on Kent Island. Listen. To be sold, several negroes,
the time of several servant men and women, household furniture, several horses and some black cattle. They will be
disposed of at public sale, for ready cash or tobacco.' He
looked at his daughter over the tops of his reading glasses.
'Imagine. Humans being sold for tobacco.'

'As if . . .' Melody muttered into her porridge.

Jack glared at her over the top of the newspaper. 'What did
you say, young lady?'

'Nothing, Father.'

Jack flicked a crumb off his vest and returned to the paper.
'"The time of several servant men and women,"' he quoted.
'That means indentured servants, Melody, like French.'

Melody grunted.

'I'm going to market today, Mr Donovan,' I informed the
master of the house. 'Is there anything in particular you
require?'

'Oh, can I come, too?' Melody interrupted before her father
had a chance to answer my question.

Her father shot her a withering glance. 'You'll be in school today, young lady.'

'But you let me skip school to go to the dressmaker,' Melody whined.

'That was different. School today and every weekday, and there'll be no arguments.'

'Sir, do you think Gabe's too young to start Cicero?' Michael Rainey inquired. 'As a republican, albeit in Roman times, he undoubtedly inspired our founding fathers. John Adams is quoted as saying of him, "As all the ages of the world have not produced a greater statesman and philosopher united than Cicero, his authority should have great weight." I couldn't agree more.'

Melody rested her head against the back of the chair, crossed her eyes and made a face at the ceiling.

I reached out and grabbed her hand, jerking the little madam back into proper sitting position. 'That's enough! Well-bred young ladies don't behave like that at table.'

Had it been my imagination, or did Jack Donovan's plump lips twitch with approval?

Michael Rainey grinned. 'Perhaps Miss Melody would prefer to study a book I found in the library this morning: *The Ladies Compleat Letter Writer*?'

Wisely, Melody picked up her spoon and resumed eating her porridge.

Gabriel, on the other hand, seemed eager to start his lessons. 'Mr Rainey is teaching me math tricks, Father. Do you want to hear a good one about nines?'

Donovan laid the paper down, picked up his coffee cup and took a sip. 'Yes. Do tell me all about the nines, Gabriel.'

'What's two times nine?' Gabe asked his father.

Donovan furrowed his brow, feigning deep thought. 'Eighteen?'

'Right! And one and eight added together make nine.' Gabe bounced excitedly on the edge of his seat. 'Three times nine is twenty-seven, right? That's a two and a seven, and two plus seven makes nine! Four times nine is . . .'

But as usual when math came into the equation, Hannah Ives, mistress of Patriot House, tuned out.

# EIGHT

*'Hannah showed up in the kitchen with her cookbook
this morning to go over the menu for dinner tomorrow.
I can read the damn cookbook myself, of course, but
that's not the way it works. So I listen to her read and
I measure out the ingredients and I keep my mouth shut.
I'm making an independence cake. I hope George
Washington appreciates the effort.'*

Karen Gibbs, cook

We grew most of our vegetables on the grounds,
either in the greenhouse or in the kitchen garden,
but fresh fruits, other than apples, were just as
scarce at Patriot House as they were in colonial times, so to
obtain them, we'd have to go to market.

No Safeway, alas. No Giant. But, LynxE had made arrangements with several vendors at Market Space on Annapolis'
city dock to carry the meat, cheese, produce and sundry
items that we might need to buy for Patriot House.

One of my jobs was to plan the meals, a challenging task
since – thanks to our Founding Father – I never knew who
was going to be dropping in (or out!) for dinner. This couldn't
be done without consultation with the cook who had her finger
on the pulse of household stores, so after breakfast was over,
I picked up my copy of *American Cookery* and trotted down
to the kitchen.

A fire was burning cheerfully in the large, open fireplace.
Karen's son, Dex, crouched in front of it, using a bamboo
whisk to baste a duck that was roasting on a spit being turned
by a clock-like contraption mounted over the fireplace. When
he saw me, Dex leapt to his feet and bowed deeply. 'Good
mornin', missus.'

'Good morning, Dex. I haven't seen very much of you
lately.'

'I've been chopping wood, mostly. It's gonna get cold soon, and we'll be needing fires in the house.'

On the hearth, the duck began to sizzle alarmingly. 'Hadn't you better get back to the duck?'

'Oh, yes ma'am,' he said, bending again to his task.

'Looks like hard work, Dex.' He looked like such a little man in his white hose, brown breeches and white linen shirt, that I had to smile.

'Oh, not so hard. Much better than emptying the chamber pots, ma'am.'

Chamber pots. I'd been mistress of the house only a little over a week and already I was taking the clean chamber pot that sat under my bed each night for granted. I felt my face redden, not realizing that a lad of ten, who should have been playing Little League baseball or going on a campout with his Boy Scout troop had been taking care of our 'night soil' every morning. History textbooks hid some ugly truths.

'Where's your mother, Dex?'

Dex shrugged and continued to mind the spit.

While I waited, I wandered over to a board near the window where three fresh-baked loaves of bread were cooling. Next to the bread sat two pies. I bent over them, touched a finger to the juice seeping up through a slash in the crust and tasted it – cherry.

On a long table sat the tools of Karen's trade – wooden bowls and spoons, a rolling pin, a mortar and pestle, a cleaver, a salt pig, cones of sugar and packets of spices. On a wooden block nearby lay a dead rabbit, fur and all, and a lifeless chicken. I was just wondering whether I should go look for Karen in the garden when she struggled through the door sideways, carrying two buckets, one of milk and one of water, balanced across her shoulders on a wooden yoke. 'Good morning, ma'am.' She knelt and set the buckets down on the tiles near the door, wiped her face with the hem of her apron.

'The ham was delicious this morning, Karen.' It had been sliced from one of several hams – smoked, wrinkled and green with mold – that hung in the storeroom just off the kitchen, a room I knew had been an office until just a month ago. The space that the desk, computer, printer and fax machine once occupied was now crowded with bins of root vegetables – potatoes, carrots, onions, turnips, beets, cabbages – and various grains, such as wheat, oats, peas, beans and dried corn that we'd need during our time at Patriot House. Sugar, salt and jugs of vinegar, oils and other liquids sat on wooden shelves. Jugs of rum, too, which went into the punch that sat out in a bowl in the front parlor, swimming with sliced fruit, ready refreshment for anyone who came to call. There was also a wine cellar in the room below stairs, but it was kept locked, and Jack Donovan wouldn't trust anyone but himself with the key.

'Thank you, ma'am,' Karen said as she hefted one of the buckets and poured some of the milk into a jug. 'It's all in the soaking. Draws out the salt.'

I pulled up a stool and sat down on it, arranging my skirts around me. 'I've received news that we're having an important guest next Saturday. He'll be spending the night, so we'll need to plan for dinner, supper and for breakfast the following morning.'

Thinking about all the extra work this would entail, I was sure Karen was about as excited by this news as I was, which is to say – not! But, we were both aware of the wall-mounted video camera silently whirring away, capturing for posterity our cozy domestic scene, so she said, 'Who would that be, ma'am?'

'Colonel George Washington. He's actually going to sleep here.'

Karen chuckled. 'If you'll forgive my saying so, ma'am, I think you've just invented a joke.'

I had to laugh, too. 'Since I received the message, I've been thinking about the menu,' I told her. 'We could start with fresh melon slices and some of that wonderful ham, followed by peanut soup, baked oysters, braised beef, roast quail, sweet potatoes – if the market has any – and green peas. Are the peas in the garden ready yet?'

'No, ma'am. The peas are done, but we've got beets, kale and spinach.'

'Spinach, then,' I decided.

When Karen nodded, I continued. 'What do you suggest for dessert?'

'Would a butter cake be satisfactory?'

Even though I'd just eaten breakfast, my stomach rumbled in anticipation. 'Perfect! We'll need a light supper, too. Welsh rarebit? Strawberries and cream?'

'That can certainly be arranged. And there'll be leftover ham and biscuits enough, too.'

I stood up. 'Good. We'll be leaving for market in half an hour. I'm hoping the rain will let up by then.'

'Your mouth to God's ears,' Karen said.

I left her to get started on the chicken we'd be having for supper – its limp feathers and lifeless eyes had been staring at me accusingly from the sideboard all though our conversation – and went in search of Mr Donovan to talk about the wine.

There has been a market house at the city dock in Annapolis since 1788. The most recent iteration, closed since Hurricane Isabel flooded the entire downtown area in 2003, had reopened with great fanfare the previous July after nearly a decade of internecine squabbling and mismanagement. Although glassed in and air-conditioned within an inch of its life, the market felt open and airy, its high roof supported by gold, pole-like pillars, with exposed pipes and ductwork overhead.

After long negotiation, the new market featured local merchants, like Chick and Ruth's Delly Express, and vendors selling Sno-Cones, popcorn, and even Chinese food. Local craftsmen were represented, too, and at the Visitors' Information Center, tourists could get information to go along with their crab cakes. It had been good to see the market thronged with customers again, but I missed the hubbub of fishmongers, butchers, bakers and greengrocers who used to have concessions there. It had been an old-fashioned waterfront market back then, the kind of place where the floors had to be hosed down every night.

The rain had let up, thank goodness. Perhaps foolishly, we'd forgone the pattens, so we had to negotiate our way around the puddles, hiking our skirts up to help keep the hems dry. Chad's Nikes splish-splashed along the sidewalk behind us as he and his Steadicam followed us out of Patriot House heading east along Prince George Street.

'It's creepy,' I commented as we turned into Wayman Alley, a shortcut that led directly from Prince George into Fleet Street. 'I feel like there's somebody following us.'

From behind me, Karen said, 'Duh, Hannah. Chad, one hundred tourists with cameras, a class of fifth graders on a field trip?'

I stifled a laugh with my gioved hand.

As we turned down Fleet Street Amy pointed a gloved finger at a passerby dressed in University of Maryland sweats who had stopped to take our picture. 'Invisible?'

'Invisible,' I repeated, sidestepping a puddle and wishing I'd worn my pattens after all.

Thanks to Founding Father, the vendors were indeed expecting us. The minute we pushed our way through the glass door, we were met by Derek filming from a crouching position, the better to capture our ruined footwear and muddy hems. A clot of tourists surged behind him, most of whom aimed their cell phones in our direction and began clicking away. Like Moses parting the Red Sea, we smiled, nodded, and forged on through the crowd, carrying our baskets and string bags.

'They should have issued me with blinders,' I muttered as we passed Firenzes Gelateria where colorful tubs of gelato (Caramel! Lemon! Passion fruit!) called out to me temptingly, and the aroma of fresh-brewed Italian coffee wafted over, seized me by its tendrils and dragged me totally against my will over to the refrigerated display case, like a scene from a Bugs Bunny cartoon.

'Earth to Hannah?' Karen muttered under her breath.

I snapped out of it. 'Sorry,' I whispered back. 'Lost control there for a moment.'

'There it is,' Amy chirped. 'On the right. Maryland Table.'

Maryland Table, a concessioner who provided organic and sustainable meats, dairy products and vegetables, all locally sourced, was expecting us. In order to make room for an eighteenth-century market stall, they had borrowed a bit of space from Whimsey Cove, an adjoining business selling maps and local art.

Kyle Stewart and his wife, Corey, were decked out in

colonial costume, too. Corey wore a linen dress the color of dark chocolate with a clean, white apron tied around her waist; her light-colored hair was pinned up and covered by a mob cap. When we arrived, she was ringing up two boxes of De Cecco pasta for another customer, so Kyle greeted us. Although his dark hair was too short for a ponytail, he'd slicked it back convincingly and looked sufficiently colonial in his breeches, shirt and vest that Colonial Williamsburg would have hired him in a shot. One of the couple's children – dressed in jeans and a T-shirt – seemed to be rebelling against central casting. He peeked out at us shyly from behind the counter.

While Amy wandered around the market stalls visiting the other vendors and flirting outrageously with the small group of paparazzi in her wake, Karen picked out oranges and blueberries, peppers and mushrooms, then moved on to the meats, some cuts of which I recognized; others could be anyone's guess.

With Karen's help, I selected a beef loin, eight Cornish game hens, a slab of bacon, and a leg of lamb. 'That will be all, Mr Stewart,' I said as Corey began wrapping up our purchases in brown paper.

'You won't want to forget this, Mrs Ives,' Kyle said. He reached under the counter, grunted as he heaved up a package wrapped in burlap and tied with string. He untied the string, peeled away the burlap.

'Oh, gross!' I took a step back. I was staring at a suckling pig – ears, eyes, snout and whiskers, four little trotters and a curly tail. Lying there on the counter, it looked more like a sleeping pet than a future meal. 'There's been some sort of mistake,' I stammered. 'We didn't order that.'

Kyle grinned, clearly enjoying his role. He held up a piece of parchment. 'Begging your pardon, ma'am, but it says here that you did.'

I rolled my eyes. Founding Father, again, damn him. 'How much does it weigh?' I asked.

'Twenty-five pounds, give or take.'

'This must be what we're supposed to serve Mr Washington,' I told Karen. Turning to the shopkeeper again, I said, 'Very well, but we'll have to send someone from the house to pick it up.'

'Do you know how to roast a whole pig?' I asked Karen
as Kyle totaled up our purchases and added it to Jack Donovan's
account.

Karen skewered me with her eyes, but her voice was sweet-
ness itself when she drawled, for benefit of the camera, 'No,
ma'am, can't say as I do.'

In all of the hullabaloo over the pig, I'd lost track of Amy.
I sent Karen next door to Pit Boy Oysters to look over the
seafood while I went in search of my errant lady's maid.
Finally I spotted her in the glass enclosure occupied by the
Annapolis Visitors' Center and, as I feared, she was talking
on her iPhone. Unfortunately, Chad, who was hot on my muddy
satin heels, was about to find Amy, too.

I swayed, touched my left hand to my forehead, flailed
blindly with my right in the direction of the Gelateria counter,
then crumpled gracefully to the floor in a puddle of petticoats.
Almost immediately I heard a woman shout, 'Call 9-1-1!' so
I thought it best to bring a quick end to my charade. I stirred,
opened my eyes, fluttered my eyelashes in a damsel-in-distress
sort of way, and stammered, 'So, so sorry. I don't know what
happened.'

Rather than leap to my assistance, Chad stood to one side,
camera grinding away, as a woman in a pink jogging suit knelt
down and took my hand, rubbing it briskly. 'Are you OK?'

'I think so.'

She helped me into a sitting position just as Amy came
rushing out of the Visitors' Center. 'Hannah! My God, what
happened?' Wild-eyed, she glanced around at the passersby.
'Did she fall?'

I touched Amy's arm. 'No, no. Just a little light-headedness,
is all.' I smiled (weakly) at the gallery of concerned faces that
hovered around me. 'These costumes . . .' I waved vaguely.
'Very hot.'

Befuddlement turned to smiles. Nodding. Tight corset. Of
course.

Several observers went on about their business while Amy
helped me to my feet. Others stayed, cell phones held at the
ready in case I took another spectacular fall that they could
upload immediately to YouTube.

We shuffled back to Pit Boys with me holding on to Amy for support. As we passed Chad, I snapped, 'I could have been having a heart attack, you jerk!' Then I smiled toothily and strolled on.

'What the *hell* were you doing on your cell phone?' I whispered to Amy when Chad was out of earshot.

Amy stopped dead in her tracks. 'You *saw* me?'

I faced her, eye to eye. 'The whole world was about to see you! Why do you think I faked the faint?'

'You were certainly convincing,' she whispered back. 'Georgette Heyer would have been proud.'

'Flattery will get you nowhere, Miss Cornell. I thought we agreed that you'd put the phone away.'

'You're not going to rat me out?'

'No, but you're either going to put that phone away, or turn it in.'

Amy clouded up. I thought she was close to tears. 'I can't, Hannah.'

Chad was closing in, so I rested a hand on Amy's shoulder, inclined my head toward hers. I kept my voice low. 'You *must*. And you didn't answer my question. Why were you talking on that damn phone?'

'When we got here, I pulled it out and saw that I had a message from my Navy contact about Drew. I'm sure it's something to do with the paperwork declaring him officially dead, but I won't know until I call the guy back.'

'So, did you talk to him?'

'No. I left a message, though.'

'Amy, if you want to stay in the cast, you have *got* to get rid of that phone. Change your voicemail message, for heaven's sake. Say you're away and that if they need to reach you in an emergency, call the number that Jud gave us.' I tugged on her arm, and set off in the direction of Pit Boys. 'Frankly, I can't believe you didn't do that already.'

'The battery is about to crap out anyway,' Amy confided. 'I've got the charger, too, but it's no freaking good without electricity.'

Just as we caught up with Karen, I extracted a solemn promise from Amy that she'd deep six the iPhone. Her face looked sincere enough as she spoke, but I worried that she had her fingers crossed behind her back.

With four-dozen fresh Maryland oysters wrapped in paper, not plastic, tucked into my string bag, we headed home. Our last stop was Vivo, an eco-friendly shop at the foot of Fleet Street where everything was strictly off limits except their homemade soaps and candles. I charged six-dozen candles to the Donovan account and asked that they be delivered. Perhaps in his day William Paca had been more frugal, but we had been running through candles at a rapid clip. I had learned how to make candles in colonial Williamsburg out of meat fat and ashes, but like so many things about being a card-carrying member of the gentry, I was happy that our family was rich enough that we could afford to buy them.

# NINE

*'I just got my period and they expect me to deal with it by stuffing rags down my panties. It's totally gross. If you can't bring me some Tampax, I'm out of here.'*

French Fry, housemaid

They say you get used to the cameras; that after a while they become invisible. As if. Derek and Chad followed us around like malevolent shadows. I always seemed to be tripping over one or the other, or knocking into them with my skirts. Not surprising, considering my farthingale gave me the hip-span of a Boeing 747. Moving around the house became an obstacle course. Like an enthusiastic, tail-wagging collie, I could clear a low-lying table of knick-knacks with a single sweep of my skirts.

That day Thing One and Thing Two must have been working on overtime because they filmed us at breakfast, zooming in for a close-up on my fresh strawberries and cream, and tag teamed Amy and me as we kept our appointment at the dressmakers for a second fitting.

At the dressmakers, or in the shops, whenever I made purchases, the shopkeepers simply added the items to our tab, the colonial equivalent of 'charge it.' I had no idea what Jack Donovan made per year – it's not something a wealthy colonial gentleman like Mr Donovan would share with his household minions, but several days later, I learned that thanks to our Founding Father, Jack's pockets were apparently not bottomless.

Jack found me in the parlor where I was squinting in the flickering candlelight, reading aloud from a book I had been delighted to find on the bookshelf in the library, shelved between Middleton's *Life of Cicero* and *Friend on Fevers and Smallpox* – namely, *A History of Tom Jones, Foundling*, the actual 1749 edition. Amy was sitting on a low stool by the

fire, knitting a balaclava out of beige wool for the troops in
Afghanistan. From time to time, I would put the novel down
to help Melody with her sampler, demonstrating, for example,
how to tie the French knots that formed the stamens of the
tulips beds that bordered her work.

Jack loomed over me, fidgeting until I came to the end of
a paragraph. 'Wasteful!' he grumbled when I raised my eyes
from the page to his face, ruddy even in the semi-darkness.
He waved a bit of parchment under my nose. 'Mrs Ives, do
you have any idea how much these candles are costing me?'

'Peasants in India are sewing sequins on T-shirts under
twenty-five-watt bulbs that generate more light than these
candles do.' I paused a beat. 'Sir.'

'Be that as it may, I must ask you to economize, madam.'

'Papa!' I felt, rather than saw, Melody rolling her eyes. Her
skirt rustled as she rose, cupped a palm around one of the
three candles flickering in the candelabra on the table next to
her chair and blew it out. 'There. Happy now?' She plopped
back into her chair, bent her head over her work. 'Besides,'
she added, picking up her sampler, 'it's not like it's *real* money.'

'Of course it's real! Who do you think paid for that frock
you're wearing?'

'Lynx Entertainment?'

Jack scowled. 'The dressmaker sends *me* the bill, young
lady. That frock cost me four pounds, eleven shillings and five
pence.'

'What's that in real money?' Melody wanted to know.

Jack's forehead furrowed as he considered his daughter's
question. 'Allowing for inflation over the past two and a half
centuries, you're gallivanting around in a $700 designer
original.'

Melody, who once confided that her normal taste in clothes
ran to Forever21 and Topshop, gave her father the satisfaction
of emitting a delighted gasp of surprise. 'No way!'

'Best you remember that, young lady.'

I wondered what kind of a dent *my* ball gown had put in
His Majesty's Exchequer, but wisely decided not to ask. Lord
knows I'd tried to get the hang of British money – twenty
shillings to a pound, twelve pence to a shilling had been my

mantra. But, a pound is twenty shillings, except when you add a shilling and it turns into a guinea, and don't get me started on farthings, quids, bobs and groats. And there's no Tylenol here when I need it.

Melody bent over her work, squinted, wrapped the embroidery cotton several times around her needle, took careful aim, and plunged the needle into the linen, drawing the thread slowly down through the cloth and back up again. 'Like this?' she asked, turning the work in my direction for inspection.

'Exactly like that.' Out of the corner of my eye, I saw Jack shift uncomfortably from one silver-buckled shoe to the other. 'Well then, ladies, I'll bid you goodnight.'

'Night, Papa,' Melody muttered without looking up.

'Goodnight, Mr Donovan,' I said, opening my book to the page where I'd left off: '"I saw two farmers' daughters at church the other day, with bare necks. I protest they shocked me. If wenches will hang out lures for fellows, it is no matter what they suffer."'

From the corner by the fire, Amy said, 'It holds up well, doesn't it, *Tom Jones*? Although I have to confess, I much prefer the movie.'

'Bare necks. How shocking!' Melody laid her embroidery down on her lap. 'Well, aren't you going to go on? Read, Hannah, read.'

# TEN

*'This is the end of my third week on the job, and it's back-breaking work. Mopping the hallway floor this afternoon took simply ages, and then along comes Mr Donovan and the little brat with their muddy boots and I had to mop it all over again.'*

French Fry, housemaid

Maybe it was too much work, or lack of sleep, or the late September heat wave that had settled like a hot, wet towel over Annapolis that week, but early in the twenty-four hours leading up to George Washington's visit, I became anxious about the menu. What would the Father of our Country like to eat? Did he have any allergies? What about his dentures? Would the food be soft enough? Out in the garden, helping Karen pick young, tender spinach, I was seized by the irrational thought that I should Google our first president, check out Wikipedia, visit the Mount Vernon website, looking for clues to the great man's dietary preferences.

A visit to the well and a ladle of cool water later, I had come to my senses. He's just an actor, you idiot, I told myself. He probably drives a Porsche, has a full set of cavity-free teeth and enjoys eating blooming onions at Outback.

Fortunately Alex Mueller had taken the children off our hands. For most of the afternoon, Melody and her little brother, Gabriel, as well as the four homeschoolers, had been occupied with dancing lessons at Brice House next door, practicing for Saturday's after-dinner entertainment in honor of Colonel Washington.

Derek and Chad had disappeared, too, accompanying Jack Donovan to Middleton Tavern – directly across from the Market House – where he would be joining a group of socially-prominent Annapolitan men in re-enacting a meeting of the ancient and honorable Hominy Club. The club had actually disbanded in 1773 – possibly due to political differences – but Jud Wilson must have felt it too important a part of the Patriot House story not to be re-enacted, so he'd slipped the date. Since 1750, when Horatio Middleton first opened it as an 'Inn for Seafaring Men,' Middleton's had been a focus of Annapolis social life, and it still was. Jack had been down at Middleton's since noon, and if the punch flowed as freely that day as it had back in 1773, he would be struggling home long after dark on the steadying arm of Jeffrey Wiley, his trusty valet.

In the meantime, French, our housekeeper, was tasked with scrubbing the floors – upstairs and down – while Amy was sent to the dining room to polish the silver. That left Karen and me to manage things in the kitchen. Most of the baking had already been done, except for a butter cake. Karen put another log on the fire, then set a clean bowl on the table, tossed a generous handful of butter into it and began creaming it with a wooden spoon.

'While you do that,' I said from my perch on a kitchen stool, holding a cookbook, 'let me see if I can find a recipe for roast pig.' The book had no index, so I began to leaf through the pages. I found instructions for boiling a calf's head – 'serve the brains mashed or whole, and the tongue slit down the middle' – and fricasseeing lambstones, but it took several minutes of browsing, puzzling over unfamiliar ingredients such as sounds, charr and pluck, before I found it. 'To roast a pig,' I began.

Karen was using her hands to work flour into a pound of butter. 'Uh huh.'

'Spit your pig and lay it to the fire. That seems simple enough. Oh, wait a minute, before you do that, you're supposed to roll some sage, salt and pepper into a piece of butter the size of a walnut and sew it up inside. Actually, that sounds pretty good.

'While the pig's cooking, you keep basting it with flour,' I continued. 'Then, it goes on to say . . . Oh, yuck! You're supposed to keep flouring it until the eyes drop out.'

'Excuse me while I barf.' Karen cracked an egg, used the shells to separate the white from the yolks, then dropped the yolk into the bowl. 'There! That's the last of the eggs.' She picked up a spoon and started stirring the batter vigorously.

I slammed the book shut. 'When this is over, I swear I'm going to become a vegetarian. If you're going to eat meat, it should come cut up and wrapped in plastic and not be so . . .' I paused, searching for the right word, '. . . so recognizable.'

While Karen was stirring the cake batter, Dex came in from the garden, staggering under an armload of firewood. He dropped the logs next to the fireplace, then began to stack them on top of the few logs that still remained after our marathon baking session.

'I hate to see a little guy work so hard,' I said. I lowered my voice so that Dex couldn't hear me. 'He should be in school with the other kids, or taking dancing lessons, not doing chores.'

Dex balanced the last log on top of the pile, then turned to me, wiping his hands clean on his breeches. 'Mama says that my great-great-great-great grandma was a slave.' He counted the 'greats' out on his fingers.

'I think Dex is gaining an appreciation for the sacrifices his ancestors made for him,' Karen said with a smile. 'It's true. Her name was Nellie Moore, and she was a slave on Walnut Creek Plantation in South Carolina.' She stopped beating for a moment, stuck a finger in the batter, tasted it. 'I know that I'm only here today because somebody like Nellie had the will to survive.'

'I wonder what Nellie would have thought seeing you now, Karen. Actually *volunteering* to dress the way she did, work your fingers to the bone like she did.'

Karen laughed. 'She'd probably think I was out of my freaking mind.'

I gathered up the spent eggshells, tossed them in the crock that was designated for compost and sent Dex out into the garden with it. 'I wonder if Nellie endured because somewhere, deep down, she knew that one day, things would be different?'

Karen fixed me with her amber eyes. 'If you'll pardon my saying so, Mrs Ives, that's just a lot of fancy, liberal white lady talk.'

I felt my face grow red.

'No,' Karen continued, 'I think Nellie survived because her will to survive was so strong.

'I've been thinking about her a lot since I came here, Mrs Ives,' she continued after a moment. 'Somewhere between picking peas in the garden, burning myself in the fire, and beating this damn cake – the recipe says I have to do it for an hour! – I feel like I know her, not well, but . . . I wish I could tell her how grateful I am to be her survivor.'

I slid off the stool and returned the cookbook to the shelf. 'I think I know all I need to know about roasting a pig,' I said. 'Here, let me take a turn at that.'

Karen smiled, shook the kinks out of her right hand, and relinquished the bowl and spoon gratefully. While I assumed responsibility for beating the cake, she busied herself stringing the green beans.

Just about the time I thought my arm would drop off, barely five minutes into my shift, Gabriel came barreling into the kitchen. When he saw me, he screeched to a stop. 'Where's Dex?'

'Out in the garden,' I told him. 'Delivering compost to the greenhouse.'

Gabe reached into his waistband and pulled out a leather pouch. 'I've got some marbles, and I need somebody to play with.'

I caught Karen's eye. When she nodded, I said, 'That'll be fine.'

Gabe did a quick about-face, disappearing the way he had come.

'Dancing lessons must be over,' I said, cradling the bowl against my apron and stirring, stirring.

Suddenly, the gardener's dog, Flash – ever true to his name – streaked into the kitchen, followed by Gabe and Dex, in hot pursuit. 'He's got my marbles!' Gabe shouted. Flash darted under the table, and crouched there, Gabe's leather bag dangling from his mouth. I swear the dog was grinning. Gabe got down on all fours and crab-walked toward him, at which point, Flash took off for the door, knocking me off balance.

As the trio of pint-sized ruffians disappeared into the garden,

I was distressed to discover that I'd slopped a good half-cup of Karen's butter cake down the front of my dress. 'Oh, shit! Look what I've done!'

Calmly, Karen handed me a damp cloth and watched while I tried to clean the spill off the linen, but my efforts only seemed to work the batter more thoroughly into the weave. 'Ruined my gown, and your cake, too, I'm afraid.' After all the elbow grease we'd already put into it, I felt like crying.

'Never mind,' Karen said with a grin. 'It'll be just half a slice smaller. Nobody will even notice. Here, let me have the bowl while you go upstairs and change for supper.'

'Thanks. I'll send Amy down to give you a hand.'

But Amy wasn't in the dining room. The candelabra, the tea service, the chafing dishes on the sideboard, all gleamed in the late afternoon light, so I figured she'd moved on to other tasks. 'Amy!' I called, but she didn't answer.

When I reached my own bedchamber, I unhooked my stomacher and slipped out of my gown. I carried the gown over to the window where the late-afternoon sun would illuminate my work, and began to give the stain some serious attention with the damp flannel I usually used on my face. After a few minutes of careful daubing, the biscuit-colored stain had only spread. About the size and shape of a cinnamon bun, it stared up at me, mockingly. I realized that its only hope was a trip to the wash tub on Monday – our usual washing day at Patriot House. I'd turn it over to French. Laundry was her job.

I folded the gown neatly, stain uppermost, then selected a fresh gown from my trunk, a dark wine color that harmonized well with my pale pink petticoat. 'Where's Amy when I need her?' I grumbled as I struggled to fasten the stomacher in place. Eventually, I succeeded, checked my reflection in the looking glass – not bad – then let myself out the hidden door that led to the service staircase.

Somebody was already there, hiding in the alcove to my left.

I stopped short, stifling a yelp of surprise.

But the man was paying no attention. His back was to me and, judging from the pale arms wrapped around his neck, Alex – or so I deduced from the ink-blue suit and the ringletted blond ponytail – was engaged in a serious necking session with some saucy wench he'd backed into the corner. As I watched from the shadow of my doorway in stunned fascination, Alex moaned softly, wrapped his hands around the woman's waist, and lifted her up gently. As her white stocking-clad legs eased around his waist, I caught a glimpse of the pale blue piping I'd seen earlier that day on Amy's petticoat. 'Oh, yes, yes, yes,' she breathed.

Jesus, Mary and Joseph! No wonder Amy was so eager to get Drew declared officially dead, I thought. She'd obviously moved on, rushing past the till-death-do-us-part section of the marriage vows and headlong into her new, post-Drew life. I wondered whether Alex Mueller was to be the destination along that road, or just a comforting stop along the way.

Slowly, I backed into my room and closed the door silently behind me. My face felt hot, flushed with embarrassment. I took a deep breath, and let it out slowly.

What Amy and Alex did on their own time wasn't anybody's business but their own, I thought. But in Patriot House, we had no time of our own; we'd signed contracts that proved it. Amy and Alex should thank whatever god they prayed to that LynxE hadn't installed a camera in that stairwell.

# ELEVEN

*'My legs are all hairy, and before long, I'll be able to
braid the hair sprouting out of my armpits. Oh. My. God.
It's disgusting.'*

Melody Donovan, daughter

I rang the bell for breakfast half an hour early on Saturday.
The children arrived promptly, bursting with excitement
over George Washington's visit. They inhaled their ham
and biscuits and were excused from the table a good five
minutes before the rest of the family managed to straggle
in.

Before long, Melody was back, hovering at her father's
elbow as he buttered his bread. She rolled her eyes, outlined
in black like Cleopatra. 'Daddy, do something about Gabe.
He's out in the garden teasing the rabbits.'

Jack Donovan, whose own eyes bore the unmistakable traces
of an intemperate evening of food, wine and song, smiled
indulgently. 'Boys will be boys. Have some patience, Melody.
He's only nine years old.'

She stamped her foot. 'Well, I'm tired of running after him.
Why don't you get one of the *servants* to do it?'

'You're seven years older than he is, don't forget.'

'How could I? He's a total brat!'

Donovan looked up from his scrambled eggs and noticed
his daughter for the first time. 'What on earth have you done
to your eyes?'

Melody blushed, tucked her chin to her chest. 'It's charcoal.
From the fire.'

'And your lips?'

'Beet juice. Karen gave it to me.' A single tear ran down
her cheek. 'I have to do *something* to make myself pretty for
the party.'

Jack reached out and took his daughter's hand, sandwiching

it between his own beefy paws. 'Melody, you are beautiful just the way you are.'

'No, I'm *not!*' she blubbered. 'Nobody's going to want to dance with me.'

Alex Mueller rested his fork on his plate. 'She's a fine dancer, Mr Donovan. You'll see that for yourself tonight.' To Melody, he said, 'I'd be honored to partner with you, Miss Donovan.'

Melody swiped at her eyes, smearing the charcoal until she looked like a panda. 'You're not just saying that?'

'I am not.' The corners of Alex's eyes crinkled in amusement. 'And I'm sure Colonel Washington will be delighted to dance with you, too.'

I put in my two-cent's worth. 'Melody, back in the eighteenth century, fashionable women would have killed to have skin as white and pale as yours. Do you know how they got it?'

Melody shook her head. 'No, ma'am.'

'They poisoned themselves with lead-based white face powder and rouge.'

'And they looked ridiculous, like clowns,' her father harrumphed.

'They decorated their faces with little black patches shaped like half moons, stars and hearts to cover up smallpox and acne scars,' Michael, the schoolmaster, added. 'And you know what else?'

Melody shook her head.

'Some women even had false eyebrows made out of mouse fur.'

Melody's eyes grew wide. 'Euuuuw!'

'Absolutely true. As Jonathan Swift once wrote, "*Her eyebrows from a mouse's hide, Stuck on with art on either side.*"'

It was my turn to say *euuuuw*. 'After Amy gets you dressed, Melody, come see me. There's a makeup box in my room. LynxE has stocked it with the modern lead-free equivalents of the makeup women used to use back then. I'm not sure we can do much to improve on your natural beauty, but it might be fun to experiment. Are you good with that?'

Melody's ear-to-ear smile told me all I needed to know.

\*     \*     \*

Founding Father had warned us to expect Colonel George Washington, late of the Virginia Regiment, sometime after noon on Saturday. I didn't expect the great man to suddenly materialize on our doorstep with a quiet rap-rap-rap of the knocker, but I was totally unprepared for the eighteenth-century equivalent of the half-time show at the SuperBowl.

Jack Donovan had sent Dex out to the street to keep watch while the rest of us bustled around the house taking care of last-minute chores. I was in the dining room fiddling with an arrangement of chrysanthemums and heliopsis in a cut crystal vase when young Dex came tearing through the front door shouting, 'They're coming! They're coming!'

Within minutes, our entire household converged on the landing where Jack arranged us in two lines, one on each side of the steps, fussing over the alignment as if we were cars on his showroom floor. After switching Amy and French – the pecking order had to be maintained – Jack vacillated between positioning himself at the foot of the steps or at the massive front door, finally deciding that he'd stand near the gate so that he could be the first to shake George Washington's hand.

Spectators lined Prince George Street, too, their cameras on lock-and-load. Someone had provided them with miniature flags – the fifty-star variety – but probably nobody noticed, they were flapping so briskly.

We heard the fife and drum before we saw it – playing 'Yankee Doodle' and 'When Johnny Comes Marching Home,' which I thought was a Civil War song, but never mind. As I strained on tiptoe to see, two drummers and a fifer appeared. Dressed in red uniforms, they led the little parade straight down the street in our direction. Directly behind the musicians, mounted on a white horse, rode George Washington, accompanied by two uniformed aides, also on horseback. Sitting straight-backed and tall in the saddle, Washington looked splendid in a dark blue uniform decorated with gold braid and epaulets, as if he'd stepped right out of a portrait by Charles Wilson Peale. As he drew closer, Washington lifted his cocked hat, and the crowd went wild.

'Who is that?' Amy whispered. 'He looks familiar.'

'He really *looks* like George Washington, doesn't he?' I

squinted, trying to focus on the actor's face. Jutting brow, square chin, a prominent nose, the actor's imperial features fairly screamed authority. No wonder Washington had been unanimously chosen to lead our fledgling nation. 'Wait a minute! I think that's David Morse!'

'Who's David Morse?'

'The actor who played Washington in the *John Adams* series on HBO.'

Amy pressed a hand to her breast. 'No way!'

Washington's entourage halted at our gate and the actor dismounted, handing his reins to Jeffrey Wiley, Jack's valet, who had been standing on the curb.

'Welcome to Patriot House!' Jack's voice rang out.

Again, the crowd cheered.

'Take care of the horses, Jeffrey, and ask Cook to rustle up something to feed Colonel Washington's men.'

Standing on the steps directly across from me, 'Cook' gave Jack the evil eye, but she waited until Colonel Washington had passed into the entrance hall, curtseying along with the rest of us, before motioning for French to follow her down the steps and around to the outside door that led to the kitchen.

'Think Karen'll poison Jack's hot milk tonight?' Amy wondered.

'It wouldn't surprise me,' I said as I led the rest of the household into the entrance hall.

Gabe, being the youngest, was the last to be introduced. He'd been waiting patiently by the punch bowl, hands locked behind his back, but when the moment came, he bowed slightly at the waist and said, as if he'd been practicing, 'Welcome to Patriot House, your majesty.'

Washington snorted. 'I'm but a humble colonel from Virginia, my lad.'

Gabe blushed, flustered. 'Can I touch your sword, sir?' he stammered.

With an indulgent smile, Washington unbuckled his belt and handed it and the sword over to Gabe, who sagged under the weight. 'It's heavy, isn't it, son?'

Gabe nodded.

Jack Donovan snapped his fingers and Jeffrey appeared out

of nowhere to relieve Washington of his hat and Gabe of the
sword. I took the moment to lean closer, look up into the actor's
face and whisper, 'You're David Morse, right?'

George Washington winked a bright blue eye and said, 'It's
been a long, hard ride, madam, and an even rougher crossing
on the ferry. If that bowl contains punch, I could certainly use
a cup.'

By the time dinner was served at three, we were all a bit tiddly.
Jack lurched toward the head of the table while I sat down
(carefully!) at the opposite end, one hand steadying my wig
to keep it from slipping over my eyebrows. After I'd been
seated, Colonel Washington took the chair to my right. His
entourage, I learned after the food had been fulsomely blessed,
had assembled on the campus of St John's College, where
they'd been filmed in front of McDowell Hall, another
Georgian treasure that had been built in 1742 by Thomas
Bladen, the Maryland colonial governor.

Over soup, the discussion moved on, focusing on the business of the Continental Congress at Carpenter's Hall in
Philadelphia. While French bustled about the table removing
the soup plates, the room fell quiet for a moment.

Melody, evidently forgetting that in this century, children
remained silent unless spoken to, took advantage of the pause
in conversation to comment, 'Mr Rainey taught us about the
First Continental Congress in school.'

'It may be the *first* Continental Congress,' George Washington
pointed out with a grin, 'but we don't call it "first" because
the second one hasn't happened yet.'

Below her powdered ringlets, Melody wrinkled her snow-
white brow, as if trying to work that one out. Like me, she wore
a thin veneer of zinc oxide on her face. We'd brightly rouged
our cheeks and lips, but Melody looked surprisingly un-
clown-like, while I could be applying for admission to Ringling
Brothers Clown College. Up in my room that morning, giggling,
Melody'd plastered a tiny half-moon to her cheek where a
dimple ought to be. She'd argued for a half-moon patch over
her left breast, too, but I'd put my silk slipper-clad foot firmly
down. Breast patches are for harlots. Now you know.

'Twelve colonies have sent delegates,' Washington was saying when I tuned back in. 'I, as you know, represent Virginia.'

'Only twelve?' Alex Mueller asked, being the dancer, not the historian among us. He'd clearly skimmed over the history tab in his orientation packet and hadn't exactly been poring over books in the library.

'Georgia is a state full of convicts,' Washington replied, as if that explained everything.

Melody piped up again. 'Like Australia?'

'Exactly like Australia.'

'What are you meeting about, then?' Melody asked.

'We're there to discuss the taxes that have been levied against us of late by the British Parliament. You've heard of the Boston Tea Party?'

Melody and Gabe bobbed their heads.

'That was our first act of protest. Now we're considering a boycott of all trade with Britain if King George III doesn't heed our petition and redress our specific grievances.'

'We have a similar situation here in Annapolis,' Jack chimed in. 'Two days ago, the brig *Peggy Stewart* arrived in Annapolis carrying at least a ton of tea, as well as fifty-three indentured servants. Stewart has paid the tax so that the human cargo can be off-loaded, but in spite of the tax being paid, customs is justly refusing to let the tea come ashore. There's to be another meeting of the committee in two days time, but until then, we have a stalemate.'

As Jack nattered on as if sucked through a time warp into 1774, I fought the almost overwhelming urge to stick the oyster fork underneath my wig and give my itchy scalp a good scratch. Fortunately, Jeffrey arrived – dressed in white gloves and full livery – bearing a platter upon which our roast pig lay in all its splendor.

Jack staggered to his feet, swayed unsteadily, and led a round of applause. Accompanied by a chorus of *ohs* and *ahs,* Jeffrey set the platter down in front of his master who admired the beast for what seemed like a full minute – holding a carving knife in one hand and a fork in the other – before bringing the knife down and whacking off its left front leg.

I averted my eyes from the massacre going on at the head of the table and motioned to Jeffrey. I needed a drink. Jeffrey made another round with the wine, and when my glass was full, I took a sip. Then another.

Jack began slicing meat off the thigh. 'Mrs Ives?'

'Yes, Mr Donovan?'

'I've decided that I need to put my money where my mouth is. Kindly inform Cook that from this day forward until the British government comes to its senses, no tea will be served in this house.'

I was primarily a coffee person, but a mid-afternoon cup of tea was one of my favorite pick-me-ups. 'I'll see to it first thing in the morning, Mr Donovan,' I lied. Then I turned to our guest, lowering my voice to a whisper. 'Ever since *Tales of the City*, I've just *adored* Laura Linney. So, tell me. Is she just as nice in person?'

After the butter cake and the fresh berries, George Washington leaned back in his chair, folded his napkin, sighed with contentment and insisted on giving his compliments personally to the cook. Karen was sent for and when she arrived, she stood in the doorway with her head modestly bowed while Washington offered a toast in her honor.

The ladies adjourned to the parlor for coffee, so the men could get on with their port and tobacco of choice. Around six, Jack appeared at the parlor door, red-cheeked as St Nick and just as jovial. 'Let the dancing begin!' he announced as he tottered in my direction. With each shaky step, my dread increased. I squeezed my eyes shut – *Go away, go away, go away* – to no avail. An eternity later, he paused in front of my chair, bowed, extended his hand and said, 'Mrs Ives, will you do me the honor?'

Amy scooted out of the parlor behind him and before long, I could hear her pounding out an 'A' on the harpsichord so Alex could tune his violin. I was trapped, but I didn't want to embarrass myself in front of Washington/Morse, so I dredged up a smile, pasted it on my face, and allowed Jack to lead me into the central hallway. Behind me, Melody squealed, and a few minutes later she, too, was escorted into the hallway by the Father of our Country himself.

Paca House didn't have a proper ballroom, so the servants had cleared the hallway of furniture for the occasion. At the far end, near the porch on the garden side, Amy sat at the harpsichord. Holding his violin, Alex stood in front, his backside nestled into the natural curve of the harpsichord case. Alex tapped his bow on Amy's music stand, setting the tempo, as Jack led me onto the dance floor. George Washington followed, partnering Melody who must have been blushing furiously under the layer of zinc oxide. From opposite corners we bowed to our partners, and the minuet began.

I curtseyed, Jack bowed, his forehead glistened with sweat. We traced an invisible Z on the dance floor, passing each other diagonally without touching. I sniffed. Jack smelled like a combination of old sweat and Earl Grey tea. We joined hands to the right. 'Sir,' I said, 'what is that cologne you are wearing?'

We joined hands to the left, turned. 'It's called Number Six,' Jack said. 'First introduced in 1752 by an apothecary in Newport, Rhode Island named William Hunter.'

On the next pass, both our hands came together in a chaste little turn, before we ended up in the corners where the dance had begun. As Jack escorted me to the sidelines, he added, 'Number Six is George Washington's favorite. He even sent some to the Marquis de Lafayette as a gift.'

I curtseyed. 'Your attention to detail, sir, is extraordinary.'

'It's astonishing, isn't it?' Jack said with a slight bow. 'Not only can we live, eat and play like colonials did back in 1774, we can smell like them, too.'

'Astonishing,' I deadpanned.

'Caswell-Massey still makes Number Six,' Jack informed me, chest puffed out importantly like a banty rooster. 'Perfumes are like fine wine, Mrs Ives. This one, now, has a delightful undertone of anise, with bergamot and lemon in the top notes. In the middle, there's a faint lavender tone.'

I flipped open the fan attached to my wrist by a silken cord and began flapping it furiously in front of my face. *Locker room in the top notes*, I was thinking, *with a faint undertone of old tennis shoe.*

French, released for the evening from her kitchen duties by papal dispensation, bounced into the hall just then, clean-scrubbed and beautiful, dressed in one of my gowns. She grabbed Michael's hand, and they joined us for the reels and country dances. Everyone danced with everyone else, and at one point, we all hummed the tune aloud so Amy and Alex could join in.

'I don't know how they did it,' I puffed to Colonel Washington as the reel finally ended. 'Dancing is a lot like work!' I pointed in the direction of the punch bowl with the tip of my fan. 'I fancy another glass of punch, sir. How about you?' When Washington nodded, I served us each another ladle. 'We can drink the water these days, sir, I *know* it's safe, but back then?' I took a sip from my glass. 'Our founding fathers must have been staggering around from sunup to sundown. How they got any work done, let alone came up with the Constitution of the United States of America is a complete mystery to me.'

Washington raised his glass. 'We are made of stout stuff, madam.'

I smiled up at the future Father of our Country. 'Indeed.'

Jack sidled up to Washington just then, picking up where he had left off at dinner about the *Peggy Stewart* situation. I seized the opportunity to excuse myself to tell French to help Karen spread out the buffet supper in the dining room, then suggested that everyone join me in the parlor for a game of cards so that Amy and Alex could give their musical fingers a well-deserved rest.

After we'd eaten supper, dancing began again until everyone was drooping with exhaustion. Even Derek and Chad seemed to have fallen asleep on their feet, propped up in their respective corners, the red eyes on their cameras relentlessly winking.

Around ten o'clock, we adjourned to the parlor for a second round of cards. Eventually, French dropped out to help Karen put away the food. That's when I noticed that Gabe had curled up on a loveseat in the parlor and fallen fast asleep.

'Amy?' I gestured at Gabe with the cards in my hand.

With a sideways glance of apology to Alex, Amy laid down her cards and in a rustle of silk, rose from the table. 'It's time the children were in bed. I'll take them. Michael,' she added, 'will you play out my hand?'

Michael assumed Amy's chair and I invited Alex to take mine, leaving the four men to play on while I observed from the loveseat that Gabe – grinding his fist into his eyes – had just vacated. In the meantime, Jeffrey Wiley, our reliable valet cum butler, kept everyone's wine glasses full.

At the end of the next round, George Washington stifled a yawn with his hand, then excused himself, with apologies, from the game. He bowed to Jack. 'I thank you, sir, for your generous hospitality.'

I jumped to my feet when George Washington did, and he made a beeline for me then, took my hand, kissed it and said, 'Thank you, madam, for a most delightful evening.'

I curtseyed and thanked him right back. It's not every evening that you get the inside scoop on what it's like to portray Detective Michael Tritter on television, making life a misery for Doctor Gregory House.

'I'm for bed, too,' Jack announced, and headed upstairs to Melody's room, while Michael set off for the west wing with Alex, who would be sharing a trundle in his room.

A colonial housewife never trusted the fine crystal to the care of her servants, so I collected the dirty glasses that were scattered about the house and carried them downstairs to the sink where French and I would wash them in the morning. Then, I headed for bed myself. The long case clock in the upstairs hall was striking eleven thirty as I crept past, the candle in my hand casting flickering shadows against the wall. Not wanting to disturb Melody, I pushed the door to my bedroom open slowly, then slipped inside.

A candle still burned on the bedside table, but the bed was already occupied. Amy had removed her shoes and stockings and was fast asleep, propped against my pillows with Gabe's head cradled in the crook of her arm. She'd been reading them a bedtime story – the book lay open, face down, on her chest. On the trundle next to the wall, Melody was snoring gently.

I tiptoed to the dressing table, removed my wig with a quiet sigh of relief and arranged the instrument of torture on its stand. Using my fingers, I fluffed up my hair, digging vigorously into my scalp. I doubted that I'd picked up any fleas, but it sure as hell felt like it.

I turned to consider my options. My bed scarcely had room for two, let alone three, so I smiled a motherly smile, blew out the bedside candle – waste not, want not, as Jack Donovan, the Patriot, had been known to say – picked up my own candle, still flickering on the dressing table, and quietly left the room.

I stood in the hallway for a moment, staring at the LynxE camera mounted on the back wall. *Time to make an executive decision, Hannah.* Shielding my candle with one hand, I tiptoed across the floorboards and descended the Chippendale staircase.

# TWELVE

*'I cornered Amy on the back staircase the other day and gave her a kiss. Unfortunately, I think Hannah caught us at it. I hooked up with Amy later in the garden and we took up where we left off. As long as Amy's here, I think I'll be able to hack it.'*

Alex Mueller, dancing master

Less than five minutes later, I stood on the second-floor landing of the west wing listening to Michael (or was it Alex?) snore. It had been a long night for everyone. With every muscle in my body aching, screaming out for rest, I slipped into Amy's room just across the hall from Michael's and silently closed the door.

I positioned my candle on the narrow walnut table next to Amy's bed, sat down and kicked off my shoes. I couldn't wait to get out of my gown and the underlying stays that had not seemed quite so tight that morning – before losing the battle against Karen's excellent food and Jack's fine wine. I unhooked my stomacher, slipped out of my gown and let it fall to the floor. Twisting and squirming like Houdini escaping from a straight jacket, I managed to reach the ties on my stays and release myself from their tyranny, too. Last came the stockings. Almost before they had time to reach the floorboards, I had crawled under Amy's coverlet.

I lay flat on my back, staring at shadows dancing on the ceiling. Damn, the bed was uncomfortable. I wasn't as sensitive as *The Princess and the Pea*, but something was digging into my back.

I hopped out of bed and knelt on the floorboards, lifted the mattress off the rope webbing that supported it. Nothing was underneath. I untucked the sheet, moved the candlestick closer so I could examine the mattress ticking. Horsehair was poking out through a four-inch slit in the seam.

*Eureka!*

I eased my hand through the slit, feeling around gingerly in the stuffing until my hand encountered the object that had disturbed my royal slumber – Amy's iPhone.

I extracted it from the stuffing, pushed the 'on' button. When the screen lit up, I could see that the battery indicator was a thin line of red – almost exhausted – and the signal strength indicator read NO SERVICE. 'Bummer,' I muttered, and returned the useless lump of metal, silicon chips and microprocessors to the mattress, tucking it well to one side where it wouldn't bother me.

That done, I crawled back into bed and pulled Amy's coverlet up to my chin. Using my thumb and forefinger, I reached over and pinched out the candle.

Immediately, the room was plunged into a darkness so absolute that I felt as if a black velvet bag had been drawn over my head. It was a moonless night, and no streetlamps – ancient or modern – shone into the room from the garden side of the house. The Naval Academy had even been persuaded to turn off the floodlights that usually illuminated the Chapel dome. After straining for a moment to distinguish something, anything – the bulk of a dresser, the outline of a chair – in the profound darkness of the room, I closed my eyes and fell instantly asleep.

*Paul is wearing a midshipman's uniform. We're having a race, and I struggle to keep up. As Paul runs he glances over his shoulder, signals with his arm – C'mon Hannah! – laughing like a boy. He's leading me . . . where? Suddenly, he flings up his arms and disappears. I follow, panting. Wait for me! Wait! Then I'm falling, falling into darkness, suffocating darkness.*

I couldn't breathe.

A hand was clamped over my mouth, pressing hard against my nose. I flailed against it. *Oh my God, I'm being raped!* Desperately, I tried to remember what I'd learned in self-defense class: *Scream. Scream bloody murder.* But I can't scream, I can't even breathe with his hand pressing down like that, hard then harder.

*Relax, don't fight. Not now. You need air.*

'Shhhh, shhhh,' his breath, rancid with coffee, hot in my ear. 'It's me, Amy, it's me. Please don't scream.'

Beneath his hand, I nodded. *Mumpf.*

I gulped air as his hand slipped away, traced my arm and found my waist, circling it, drawing me closer.

I breathed into the dark, eyes straining to see. 'Alex?'

He stiffened, his cheek, rough with bristles, pressed against mine, his erection hard against my back. 'Who's Alex?'

'I . . .' I began.

But he didn't wait to hear. 'Shhhh, shhhh.' His mouth wet against my neck, his lips seeking mine. 'Oh, God, Amy, God.'

'I'm not Amy!'

He froze, then catapulted out of the bed as if I had morphed into a bolt of lightning. 'Christ!' Stumbling in the dark, feeling along the walls for the door.

'Drew?' I stammered, heart still thrashing. 'It's Drew, isn't it?'

He paused, breathing hard.

I had no way to relight my candle, but what kind of SEAL doesn't come prepared? 'Do you have a flashlight?'

A barely audible rustle of cloth, a click, and a thin beam of light wavered across the floorboards, touched the foot of the bed, moved along the coverlet and found my face. I put up a hand to shield my eyes.

'You're the woman in the front bedroom.' A fact, not a question. 'Married to that flaming asshole.'

For a moment I was puzzled, then I realized he meant Jack Donovan, not Paul. 'No, he's supposed to be my brother-in-law.' I wondered how long Drew had been watching me, and fought down the creepy feeling that crawled over me.

'Where's Amy?' Where his wife was concerned, Drew had a one-track mind.

'She's asleep in my bedroom with the two children.'

'I need to see her.' The beam snaked across the floor, searching for the door.

'Wait!' I whispered. 'If you show up suddenly like this, you'll give her a heart attack. Amy believes that you're dead.'

'I sent her . . .' Drew began, then clammed up.

'She had an iPhone, but it was, uh, confiscated,' I lied. I had promised not to rat Amy out, and even though Drew was her husband, I didn't plan to make an exception. 'No electricity in Paca House anyway,' I said, pointing out the obvious.

Drew's face, lit from beneath by the flashlight, stared back at me ghoulishly, like a creature out of *Friday the Thirteenth*. 'Look, I'm sorry about what just happened here,' he said contritely. 'I didn't know . . .' He paused, as if considering how much to tell me. 'I've been watching the house for days. I thought this was Amy's room. Obviously I made a mistake.'

While he talked, I scooted into the corner at the head of the bed and drew my knees up to my chin, the coverlet along with them. If Drew was begging for forgiveness, he was standing on the wrong street corner.

'Fuck. Why am I telling you this? I need to see Amy. Your room, then?'

The light flicked off.

I heard the door creak. 'Drew! You can't! Not if you don't want to be seen by a couple of million people when *Patriot House* goes on the air.'

Another creak. 'What the hell are you talking about?'

'You picked a hell of a night to break in, Drew. George Washington is sleeping in Jack's bedroom and they've got extra cameras set up everywhere. How did you get in, anyway?' I asked, knowing as the words left my mouth how dumb it was to warn Drew about the cameras and to ask him such a question. SEALs knew one hundred ways to get in and a hundred-and-one ways to get out of any dangerous situation, without being seen.

'Never mind,' I said. 'Don't answer that. But, you should understand that Amy is here because she really wants to be. She's signed a contract. If she breaks the rules, she'll forfeit fifteen thousand dollars as well as opening herself up to the possibility of a million-dollar lawsuit.'

'She doesn't need fifteen thousand dollars.'

'I didn't get that impression.'

'Well, that's crap. Amy's getting my pay and benefits now, but soon she'll receive a tax-free death gratuity of one hundred thousand, and there's a four-hundred thousand dollar life insurance policy, too. I'm married to a wealthy woman.'

A light bulb flicked on in my brain. 'As long as you stay dead.'

Drew was quiet for so long that I was afraid he'd used his super stealth skills to slip silently out of the room. 'Drew?'

'I'm here.' The straight-back chair next to Amy's dresser groaned in protest as Drew sat down in it. 'It's better to be dead. Better for me, less embarrassing for the Navy.'

'Why on earth would you say that?'

'I screwed the pooch.'

*Screwed the pooch.* A term from the Mercury days of the U.S. space program. Like Gus Grissom, Drew must have screwed up, big time. 'I understand, honestly. If it's important that the Navy doesn't find out Drew Cornell's not a pile of ashes in Swosa, then I'm sure we can figure out a way for you to talk to your wife about it, if she wants to.'

'What do you mean, "if she wants to?"'

I thought about Amy and Alex, but wisely kept my mouth shut. 'Ten months is a long time, Drew. If you didn't die on that helicopter in Swosa, where the hell have you been?'

'Getting myself out of a sticky situation.'

'Can you tell me about it?'

'Why should I trust you?'

'Because my Dad is retired Navy? Because my husband teaches at the Naval Academy? I *know* what it means to be a SEAL, Drew. Just to be selected for SEAL training is a major accomplishment, but to successfully complete the training, be sent on dangerous missions . . .' I paused, choosing my words carefully. I needed Drew to trust me. 'You're DEVGRU,' I said. 'Elite among the elite, but the stress has to be enormous.'

Drew caught his breath. 'DEVGRU,' he repeated, then he laughed.

'DEVGRU's less of a mouthful than the Naval Special Warfare Development Group,' I said, 'but you gotta admit that the old name, Seal Team Six, sounds a hell of a lot sexier.' I thought about Drew's key role in the mission to extract a high-value target like Nazari from Swosa, and it hit me like a thunderbolt. 'You're Gold Squadron, right? It doesn't get any more select than that.'

When Drew didn't respond, I said, 'Amy and I have become

close over the past several weeks. She's very proud of you, you know.'

Drew snorted. 'In the early days, maybe. When I was everyone's hero, quietly picking off Somali pirates in the Arabian Sea. Now? I'm shit under their shoes.'

'Just a moment ago you said that it would be less embarrassing for the Navy if you stayed dead. I'm trying to work that one out. The mission to capture Nazari was fully-sanctioned by the U.S. government, right? That's what they kept saying on CNN.'

'Capture, not kill. They wanted Nazari trussed up and delivered to the ICC for crimes against humanity.'

'ICC?'

'The International Criminal Court in the Hague. In March of 2009 Nazari was indicted by the ICC on eighteen counts of genocide, torture and rape. He'd been a fugitive ever since.'

'A monster,' I said. 'Not fit to breathe the same air as the rest of us.'

'Yeah, but the brass thinks that I stepped over the line. We broke into the compound, cornered Nazari in an upstairs bedroom. The bastard was unarmed. We could'a taken him alive, easy. Just one sorry excuse for a human being hiding behind a curtain with his wife and children. He massacred millions of his own people, sure, I could deal with that, but when he grabbed one of his daughters and tried to use her as a human shield I looked the son of a bitch straight in the eye and said to myself, screw it, you're a waste of space. You've forfeited your right to live. I double tapped him. End of story.'

'But it wasn't, was it? The end of the story, I mean.'

'Fuck, no. All hell broke loose. Women crying, children screaming, guards popping up out of nowhere. We killed a bunch of guards on our way out, and I covered for my team as they ran to the chopper, but I missed the guy with the rocket launcher.'

'We saw the explosion on CNN. Everyone assumed you were aboard, too.'

'Sometimes I wish I had been.'

'But it's better to be alive, Drew, surely. What's the worst thing that can happen to you if the Navy finds out you're not dead?'

'After being AWOL for almost a year? Let's just say that I'm not planning on doing any time in Leavenworth.'

'So, what happened next?'

'After the explosion, I took out the guard, borrowed his clothing and got the hell out. It took me a while, but I'm here.'

'How did you get out of Swosa with no passport, no money?'

'It helps to be fluent in the language, and . . .' He paused and we both heard the door across the hall creak open. There was a light tap on the door.

'Amy? I heard voices. You OK in there?'

Alex.

I wasn't sure I could imitate Amy's Yankee twang, so I mumbled sleepily, 'Fine. Just a nightmare. Sorry I woke you. G'night.' I held my breath, fearful that Alex might decide to comfort Amy in person, but after a few seconds, the light pad of stocking feet confirmed that he'd returned to the room he shared with Michael.

As much as I wanted to hear the rest of Drew's story, I knew it could be dangerous for everyone if he stuck around much longer. 'We're going to church at nine o'clock tomorrow,' I whispered. 'Amy and I will figure out a way for the two of you to talk.'

'St Anne's, you mean? On Church Circle?'

'Yes,' I said, thinking fast. 'The restrooms are through the door to the right as you enter the narthex. Nobody should be using them during the service, so you can wait for Amy there.'

A slight creak of the chair, a whispered, 'Thanks.'

For several minutes I remained huddled in my corner, arms wrapped around my knees, imagining I could still hear him breathing. 'Drew?'

But Amy's husband was gone. And I'd never even seen his face.

# THIRTEEN

*'I've never been a morning person, so waking up at 5:30 a.m. to start cooking breakfast for a whole houseful of people is a real chore. It's getting so I don't mind eating porridge, but the next time one of the cameramen sashays into my kitchen with an Egg McMuffin, I'm going to kill him.'*

Karen Gibbs, cook

After Drew left, I couldn't get back to sleep. I lay in bed with my heart pounding, trying to calm it. *Breathe in, breathe out. Repeat.* But my heart still pulsed hot in my ears like a piston.

I lay shivering in bed until dawn's pale light began to filter in, giving shape to the room's spare furnishings. I got up, pulled Amy's robe off the hook on the back of the door, wrapped it around my shift. Leaving my ball gown lying in a heap on the floor, I crept from Amy's room, tiptoed into the hall and down the stairs, through the hyphen into the main house where the occasional wine glass abandoned on a window sill or on the steps of the Chippendale staircase were reminders of the excesses of the previous evening.

On the second floor I paused, smiled demurely at the camera. So what if future viewers thought Hannah'd been bed-hopping? It might even juice up their ratings.

When I let myself into my room a few seconds later, everyone was still asleep, but sometime during the night, Amy had awakened and pulled the bedcovers over Gabe and tucked him in.

I approached the bed and shook Amy gently by the shoulder. 'Amy,' I whispered. 'Wake up.'

There was no response, so I shook her again until she stirred.

One eye opened. 'What?' As if suddenly realizing who she was and who she was supposed to be, she propped herself up on one elbow and said, 'Oh, Hannah, I'm sorry. I must have fallen asleep. What time is it?'

'Dawn. Sunday,' I said. I needed Amy wide awake before I told her about Drew. 'We need to talk, but not here.' As Amy climbed out of bed and began tugging at her corset, smoothing her rumbled clothing, I slipped out of her robe and began rummaging in the half-light through the chest at the foot of my bed, coming up with one of my everyday gowns, a simple linen frock – could have been blue, could have been black – that laced up the front.

'In the kitchen?' Amy asked, sounding worried.

'No. Meet me inside the summer house. There are no cameras there. And go quietly. I'll join you in a few minutes.'

In the garden, dew glistened like cobwebs on the grass. To save my shoes, I kept to the terraced walkway that bisected the garden and led straight down to the two-story summer house that had been William Paca's pride and joy. A statue of the god Mercury balanced on tiptoe at the peak of its octagonal roof.

I crossed the Chippendale bridge that spanned the fish pond and found Amy sitting on a bench inside the folly. I sat down next to her and took her hand.

'It's bad news, isn't it?' she said.

I squeezed her hand. 'Honestly, Amy, I don't know. You'll have to be the judge of that.' I'm not one of those break-it-to-'em-gently kind of people. Best to dive right in, get it over with. 'Drew's alive.'

Amy covered her mouth with both hands and screamed into them. She turned to face me, eyes wide and dry. 'No, no.'

'It's true. Last night I slept in your room, and sometime in the middle of the night, Drew broke in. He expected to find *you* there, of course.'

'Why didn't he . . .' Amy fumbled for the words.

I finished the sentence for her. 'Why didn't he simply knock on the front door, say, hey, it's me, the rumors of my death have been greatly exaggerated?'

She nodded.

'Drew believes it's important that he stay dead for a while, but he wants to see you very much.'

'I don't understand. The helicopter . . .'

'I'm not sure I understand either, Amy, not entirely. Drew will have to explain. He knows that we're going to church this morning, and is going to wait in the restroom. During the service, we'll have to figure out a way to get the two of you together for a talk.'

Amy didn't look happy at the prospect of seeing her husband again, which puzzled me until she said, 'But, I don't want to leave the show.'

'Why would you have to?'

'You don't know Drew.'

That was true. I didn't even know what her husband looked like, since carrying wallet-sized photographs of loved ones in our handbags had been forbidden, too. And nobody had any Hans Holbein miniatures, either. But I figured if Drew had been trained to extract a foreign dictator from his armed compound in a foreign country, surely he could extract his wife from a historic home in Annapolis, Maryland. There must be something holding him back. 'You'll need to talk to him, Amy. Then you can decide what you need to do.'

Jack Donovan was out of sorts at breakfast Sunday morning. Not long before dawn, George Washington (Founding Father informed us) had been whisked away. Not the way he had come – on horseback – but in a black limo, in order to make an early morning flight from BWI to New Orleans, where he would be shooting an episode of *Treme*.

Jack took Washington's desertion as a personal insult. 'Inconsiderate,' he sputtered as he stood at the buffet heaping smoked bluefish on his plate. 'Especially when we went to all the trouble preparing this spread.'

*We? What do you mean, we?* Jack's sole contribution to the breakfast feast spread out before him had been the bluefish itself, a ten-pound beauty given to him by one of his Middleton Tavern cronies at their last meeting. Karen – who had smoked the fish, scrambled the eggs, pickled the herring, sliced the ham and balled the melon that Jack was busily tucking into – Karen was the only individual with any claim to being put out, in my opinion. Or possibly French Fry, who stood behind

Jack's chair at that particular moment, crossing her eyes and sticking out her tongue.

I had to smile. At least we would be attending St Anne's that morning, a *real* church, rather than experiencing the torture of sitting through one of Jack Donovan's bowdlerized versions of Morning Prayer. As I slathered butter and a glop of Karen's strawberry jam over my bread, I remembered a previous Sunday when gusts of wind had hurled sheets of rain furiously against the windowpanes. Jack had pronounced the day too unspeakably foul to consider going out in it, and ordered Amy to pass the word that our presence was required in the parlor, where we found Jack, balancing the *Book of Common Prayer* on his open hands. When all had assembled, even little Dex, Jack – heeding the admonition to 'read with a loud voice' – had stumbled over the *hasts* and *doeths* all the way to the end of the Apostle's Creed where, good Baptist that he was, he skipped over the troublesome bit about the 'holy Catholick Church.' I had been amused rather than annoyed when Jack refused to pray for 'the King's majesty' or to 'bless the royal family,' but fully half his captive congregation seethed in silent anger and for all I knew were seething still when – for some reason known only to Jack – the New Testament scripture lesson was taken from Luke 17, verses 7–10, the Parable of the Dutiful Servants. *Would he thank the servant because he did what he was told to do? So you also, when you have done everything you were told to do, should say, 'We are unworthy servants; we have only done our duty.'*

'A beautiful day,' I commented to the table at large. 'Nice and sunny. I shall enjoy the walk to church.'

Melody shot me an *as if* glance. Judging from the cockeyed arrangement of curls on her head I gathered that Amy had been too preoccupied with worries over Drew to help Melody with her toilette. Thank goodness for mob caps and bonnets, I thought, fingering my own hack-handed do. They covered a multitude of sins.

At a quarter to nine, wrapped in our cloaks against the cooler weather, Jack Donovan and his little family, including several of his Dutiful Servants, began the Royal Progress toward St Anne's where our (very) late benefactor, William Paca, had served as a vestryman from 1771 to 1773.

I attended St Katherine's Episcopal Church in West Annapolis where my friend Eva Haberman served as rector, so I didn't know whether the black-robed rector who greeted us when we passed through the door was a regular at St Anne's or some 'talent' that LynxE had brought in for the day. Would we get to sit through an hour-long sermon delivered by a firebrand like Peter Muhlenberg from Woodstock, Virginia who, in 1776, threw off his clerical robes and stood before his startled parishioners wearing the full uniform of a Virginia militia officer declaring, 'It is a time for war!' Or would the service be more or less business as usual for the nineteenth Sunday after Pentecost?

Little had changed with the actual language of the Anglican service since the 1662 Book of Common Prayer was first published. Even Thomas Cranmer (who began working on the first version more than a century earlier) would have been right at home that day in Annapolis, Maryland. Priestly vestments hadn't changed much since then, either, but gratefully, the Reverend Thomas Dyer kept them on as he delivered a long, rambling monologue based on the parable of the Good Samaritan.

Next to me, his arm often brushing mine, sat Jack, listening intently, nodding in agreement whenever Reverend Dyer made a point with which he agreed. Amy sat in the pew directly behind me, between the two Donovan children who had to be separated. They'd been squabbling over an origami frog that Gabe had folded out of a scrap of his father's fine vellum writing paper.

'Some among you may not appreciate the do-gooder inter-pretation of this parable,' Dyer was saying when Amy tapped me lightly on the shoulder with her gloved hand, as we had arranged.

'I don't feel well, Mrs Ives,' she whispered feebly. 'I need to visit the necessary.'

'Perhaps, then, it could better be characterized as the parable of a man who is saved by an enemy.' Dyer droned on.

I patted Amy's hand and whispered back, 'Go ahead.' I turned slightly, observing with an obvious show of motherly concern as Amy gathered her skirts close about her and eased past Gabe, out of the pew and into the aisle. She dipped her head in reverence to the cross, then spun around and drifted toward the rear of the church.

A sudden movement in front of an elaborately carved screen in the north transept drew my attention. Chad, Steadicam attached to his chest like a phantom twin, was making a move to follow.

I caught his eye, glared ferociously and mouthed 'bathroom,' which seemed to settle him down.

The service wore on, and Amy had yet to return. The final hymn – 'O For a Closer Walk with God' – was appropriate to our century, having been written by William Cowper in the 1700s and set to Caithness, a seventeenth-century tune. I noted this arcane fact as I paged nervously through the hymnal, trying to distract myself and not worry about Amy.

She had still not returned when, from the chancel steps, the Reverend Thomas Dyer raised a hand in blessing. 'The grace of our Lord Jesus Christ, and the love of God, and the fellowship of the Holy Ghost, be with us all evermore. Amen.'

'Amen,' I repeated softly, desperate to leave, but the singing of the final hymn intervened.

As the last note of the organ died away, I tensed, ready to bolt for the door, but Jack looped my arm through his and escorted me down the aisle, greeting the congregation, nodding and smiling, paternally patting my hand where it lay in the crook of his arm, acting oh so lord of the manor.

In the narthex, I reclaimed my hand. 'I need to check on Amy,' I told him.

He looked puzzled. 'Amy?'

'In the necessary,' I said, bobbing my head in the direction of the restroom. Jack hadn't even noticed that my lady's maid had gone.

'Very well,' he said. 'We'll wait outside.'

But Amy wasn't in the restroom, and there was no sign that she had ever been there. I checked all the stalls. No discarded clothing, no telltale twists of toilet paper, no messages scrawled on the mirror with a bar of soap.

Amy Cornell, my lady's maid, had disappeared.

# FOURTEEN

*'I have no idea where Gabriel has gotten to this morning. It's hard to keep track of him in a house this large. I worry that he's spending too much time hanging out with Dex, the cook's boy, and wonder if it's appropriate for him to fraternize so much with the servants, and then I remember, this isn't for real, Jack. When it's over, we go back to Texas.'*

Jack Donovan, Patriot

Founding Father was not going to be happy.

Neither was Jack Donovan.

I needed to think. I scrunched up my petticoats and backed into one of the stalls, sitting myself down on the toilet-seat lid and leaning back against the tank.

One of two things had happened. Either Amy had decided to leave the show voluntarily, or she hadn't. In which case, Drew – or someone he'd hired – had kidnapped his wife. Unless Amy had done a one-eighty turn since our talk the previous morning, I figured her departure had not been by choice. But before I blew the whistle, I needed to be sure.

When I rejoined my family on the lawn in front of the church, they'd already attracted a crowd. Jack had gone all *pater familias,* gathering his sullen offspring around him, grinning broadly for the cameras. When he spotted me standing on the church steps, he waved me over. 'Mrs Ives! Join us. I have good news.'

I dredged up a smile from somewhere and pasted it on for the benefit of our audience, then sashayed in their direction with my skirts sweeping the brick sidewalk. 'Indeed, Mr Donovan. Pray tell, what news is that?'

Jack withdrew a familiar buff envelope from his waistcoat pocket. A message from Founding Father, dammit. He waved it in the air. 'We're to have tea at Reynolds Tavern,' he announced. 'Come along, or we'll be late.'

If I hadn't been preoccupied with worries about Amy, I might have guessed as much. Derek had already positioned himself on the corner where Church Circle meets Franklin, preparing to film our grand entrance into the historic tavern, another authentic colonial treasure, built in 1749 by Annapolis hatmaker, William Reynolds, who dubbed it the Beaver and Lac'd Hat. Except for stints as Farmers National Bank and later, the Annapolis Library, it'd been a tavern and B&B ever since.

Jack answered my next question before I could ask it. 'I've sent Jeffrey home to tell Cook that we'll have dinner somewhat later,' he said in a rare display of sensitivity to the rhythms of the household. 'But, where's Amy?'

'She's ill,' I lied gracefully as he guided me across the street. 'I've sent her home, too.'

'I hope it's nothing serious,' Jack said. 'It'll be hard to manage without her.'

'It's that green ham, I'll bet,' Melody chimed in. 'Gross.'

'Nonsense, Melody,' said her father. 'That ham is cured, and it's perfectly safe.'

'"Do you like green eggs and ham; I do not like them, Sam-i-am. Would you like them here or there? I would not like them anywhere."' Gabe channeled Dr Seuss as he trailed into the tavern behind us.

'Behave, Gabriel,' cautioned his father. 'You're being watched,' he added unnecessarily, as if none of us had noticed Derek's camera.

Tavern staff attired in colonial garb seated us in the elegant front dining room, next to the fireplace. Over the mantel hung a portrait of our recent dinner guest, Colonel George Washington as painted by Rembrandt Peale. Although servers laid a grand 'Savory Tea' out on tiered trays in front of us – scones, tarts, and an assortment of finger sandwiches – I could barely taste my food. As I sipped tea out of a flowered Wedgewood cup, I kept staring out the window at St Anne's Church, praying that Amy would reappear on the steps at any minute.

But she didn't.

When we returned home from the tavern, I made straight for Amy's room. I opened the door to her wardrobe and looked quickly through it. Nothing appeared to be missing. If Amy had run off, it was in the clothes she was standing up in.

On my instructions, French had already made up the bed and tidied the room, removing the gown I had cast off so hastily the previous evening and returning it, freshly pressed, to my room. I stared at Amy's bed for a few moments, reliving the terror of waking up to an intruder in my bed.

I shuddered, shook off the recurring panic, and approached the bed. Kneeling alongside, I lifted the quilt, untucked the sheet, stuck my hand inside the slit in the mattress and began rooting around. Amy's iPhone was still there. That settled it, at least in my mind. If Amy had *planned* to leave with Drew, there's no way she would have left her iPhone behind.

I turned the phone on, and was rewarded with a thin line of red on the battery indicator – the iPhone still had some juice – but the message, NO SIGNAL still taunted me. I turned the phone off to conserve what little power remained, then tucked it into my pocket.

I needed to tell Jack about Amy's disappearance – I couldn't cover up her absence for very much longer – but decided that could wait until dinner. In the meantime, I opted for a stroll, leaving the house by the back door.

At one time, William Paca's garden would have overlooked the Severn River, but now it overlooked the Naval Academy. Damn. Would everything remind me of Drew, and of Amy?

I wandered down to the middle terrace where I hoped that the geometric preciseness of the heirloom rose garden would help order my mind.

It didn't. It only reminded me of Amy Lowell's heart-wrenching anti-war poem, 'Patterns,' a poem I'd memorized in high school, snatches of which began to float about my head, bringing tears to my eyes. *I walk down the garden paths, in my stiff brocaded gown. With my powdered hair and jeweled fan. I shall go up and down, in my gown. Gorgeously arrayed, boned and stayed. For the man who should loose me is dead. In a pattern called war.*

Eventually, I found myself drifting down to the lower terrace, skirting the fish pond, and meandering along serpentine paths, each turn bringing into view a fresh bed of native plants. At one point, the path paralleled the wall that separated the garden from a three-story apartment building so far from the Paca House that I wondered if it might be out of range of the LynxE cell phone jamming equipment. All the time I'd been walking, Amy's iPhone had weighed heavily in my pocket. I brought it out then, and switched it on: NO SIGNAL.

I was about to switch it off, when I noticed that the fan-shaped wireless signal strength indicator was displaying a single bar. I walked a little distance along the wall and the indicator jumped to two bars. I tapped the Settings icon and discovered that Amy's phone was picking up an unprotected wireless signal – hellcat3 – that was apparently leaking from an adjacent apartment. My heart fluttered. I couldn't telephone Paul, but maybe I could email him.

Holding the iPhone in front of me, blessing hellcat3, whoever he (or she) was, and praying that the iPhone's battery wouldn't die, I began wandering along the garden wall like a prospector with a metal detector, searching for a stronger signal. Just outside the privy, I got three bars, so I ducked inside and hooked the door shut behind me.

It was dark inside the one-holer, muggy and slightly fetid. I opened up the email app and with my thumbs literally flying over the virtual keyboard, composed a message to Paul – subject URGENT from Hannah – hoping that the unfamiliar address won't get caught up in his nitpicky spam filter. 'Need to talk. Critical. Look for message in bottle on back wall.'

I pressed SEND, held my breath until I heard the comforting *swoosh* of the email going merrily on its way, then leaned against the wall of the privy, weak with relief.

I was about to send a second message as an insurance policy, when the screen faded to black.

I pressed the ON button. Dead as a doornail.

As oppressive as it was inside the privy, I remained there for a few minutes more, holding the dead phone, contemplating the bucket of dried corn husks that served as our toilet paper, and wishing I were back in the land of quilted Charmin. Even the privy seemed preferable to facing Jack Donovan – and Founding Father – with the truth about Amy.

*    *    *

I sensed Karen before I saw her, standing behind me, hands on hips, watching in mild amusement as I rummaged among the items on the pantry shelves in search of a bottle the appropriate size and shape to hold a rolled up message. I was holding an empty gin bottle – square, and with a pig snout top – but it was too big and the mouth too small for my purposes.

'Can I help you find something, ma'am?'

'Guilt' might as well have been written in letters two inches high across my forehead. 'An empty bottle,' I said, 'for some experiment that Gabe is working on.'

'He's not going to be blowing things up, is he?'

I laughed. 'I don't think so. It's something to do with, uh, sympathetic inks.'

'Lord, what's that?'

'You write with something like lemon juice or vinegar and it's invisible until you hold it up to the heat. Most of these bottles are too big.'

Karen chuckled at the foolish amusements of the idle rich, ambled over, lifted the gin bottle out of my hands and set it down. She reached behind a crock and came out holding a brown bottle about the size of an old-fashioned Coca-Cola bottle, only square. The mouth was a little small, but if I rolled the message up tightly, like the size of a pencil, it might just fit.

'This isn't an original, is it?' I asked, worried that if Paul had to break the bottle to get the message out he'd be destroying a priceless antique.

'Heavens, no. Look on the bottom where it says 'Made in China.''

'Ah, well, that's a relief.' When I sniffed the bottle, it smelled like my grandmother's Christmas cookies. 'What was in it originally?'

'Vanilla. We use a lot of that around here.'

I tucked the bottle into my pocket and followed Karen back into the kitchen where a roast duck rested on a platter, wreathed with perfectly round potatoes the size of golf balls. 'I'm sorry if Founding Father's tea party upset your schedule, Karen.'

'I'd be lying if I said it wasn't an inconvenience, but that's what slaves are there for, right? To be inconvenienced.'

'Is dinner ruined?'

'Oh, Lawsy, no!' She beamed. 'Youse dealin' wif a pro, Miz Hannah.'

I laughed out loud. 'How on *earth* do you manage to keep a sense of humor with all the thankless, back-breaking work we ask you to do?'

Karen shrugged her broad shoulders. 'It is what it is.'

'When this gig is over, Karen, have your girl call my girl. We'll do lunch.'

I trotted up to the library and sat down at the desk, grateful that everyone else seemed to be occupied, so I had the room to myself, except for the watchful eye of the SelectoZoomMini, of course. I made an elaborate show of extracting a fresh sheet of paper from a drawer and smoothing it out on the blotter. A small glass vase held three goose quill pens. I took my time selecting one of them, then uncapped the ink bottle. I dipped the pen in, and began to write, carefully at first, keeping my pressure light so the ink wouldn't squirt out all over the page on the first 'D' of Dear Paul. One line, then two, using round letters, drawing rather than writing them.

After thirty minutes, I was done.

I waited for the ink to fully dry, then folded the letter once and tucked it into my pocket. Aiming a self-satisfied smile at the camera, I left the room.

Outside, in the privacy of the privy, I started at the narrow end, rolling the paper up carefully. I inserted it into the bottle where it uncurled, filling the bottle. A tear-jerker by Nicholas Sparks; a song by The Police; instructions to my husband. They were all messages in a bottle.

A few minutes later I stood in the wilderness area of the garden, past the bee hives, behind the spring house, nestling the bottle in one of the vertical slits in William Paca's brick wall. If Paul found the note as planned – rather than some curious tourist – he'd know exactly what I planned to do.

# FIFTEEN

*'Life without my laptop totally sucks!'*
                                    Michael Rainey, tutor

It was four o'clock before we sat down to dinner. I'd intended to tell the family about Amy right away, but Jack had received another message from Founding Father that sent him off on a dissertation that lasted until the soup bowls were cleared away. There was to be a meeting of his compatriots at Middleton Tavern in the morning. Things weren't looking good for the owner of the *Peggy Stewart* and its cargo.

When Jack wound down, Michael Rainey seized the opportunity to discuss the children's progress with their lessons. 'While Gabe excels in mathematics, Melody fairly dazzles us with her Greek. These abilities are natural, sir, but need to be nurtured once this . . .' He waved a fork. '. . . this experiment is over.'

'*Ánthrōpos métron*,' Melody said, as if to prove Rainey's point.

Her proud father beamed. 'What does that mean, Melody?'

'Roughly translated, "Man is the measure of all things."'

Jack's head bobbed. 'So very true.'

Just then, Jeffrey appeared at my elbow proffering the sauce-boat. I waggled my fingers over my plate to let him know that I'd like some gravy on my duck, please, and a bit on the roasted potatoes, too, then took a deep breath and said, 'Mr Donovan, there's something I need to tell you.'

Jack paused, a forkful of meat half way to his mouth. 'Yes?'

'My lady's maid, Amy Cornell. She's gone.'

For a long moment, Jack considered me over the top of the gleaming candelabra that stood on the table between us, partially blocking our view of one another. A flash of movement in the corner by the buffet let me know that Derek had taken notice, too. Jack rested his fork on his plate, crossed it with his knife, giving me his full attention. 'Gone, madam? What do you mean, gone?'

I decided to skip the part where I was in collusion with Amy at St Anne's, but I didn't want to lie, so I said, 'When we got back to the house after church, I went to Amy's room to see how she was feeling, but she wasn't there. I've looked everywhere, Mr Donovan – throughout the house, in the garden, in the summer house, even in the necessary. I don't know where she is.'

Jack leaned back in his chair, tented his fingers on his chest and flexed them, like a spider doing push-ups on a mirror. 'Well,' he said. 'Well, well, well.'

Melody made a little *peep*; Gabe said, 'Can I have some more meat, please?' but the rest of us sat there in stunned silence.

Jack's gaze swept around the table. 'Do any of you know anything about this?'

A chorus of noes, uh-uhs, and no-sirs.

Jack turned to Derek. 'You?'

Derek shook his head, red light on his camera relentlessly winking.

While Jack was interrogating everyone with his eyes, I turned to Alex Mueller. His deer-in-the-headlights expression said it all – he had no idea where Amy was, either.

Michael Rainey was the first to speak up. 'If you'd like my observations, sir, Amy seemed to have a lot on her mind recently. The one-year anniversary of her husband's death in Swosa is coming up, and I think it's fair to say she's been a bit melancholy of late.'

Melancholy. I hadn't heard anyone use that word in years, but it was a perfect fit. *Gloomy, sad, down in the dumps, depressed.* Amy had been all those, true, but not for the reasons everyone thought.

Jack nodded sagely. 'Yes, yes. I remember how affected she was by that love song several weeks ago. I thought it was merely, you know, her time of the month.'

'Daddy!' Melody snapped.

Her father raised a conciliatory hand. 'Sorry. I was out of line.'

Melody scowled, not the least mollified.

'I'm quite sure Amy will be back,' Alex cut in; desperation tinged his voice. 'Do we have to report it?'

'I believe we already have.' Jack pointed to Derek, who had moved from the corner of the buffet to a spot over by the door, presumably to better zoom in on our reactions.

'I believe she'll be back, too,' I stated with more confidence than I felt. 'But it will be up to Founding Father to decide what to do with her when she does.'

'She's in breach of contract,' Michael added. 'It might not be pretty.'

Jack's mouth formed a grim line. 'Do we need to request another lady's maid, madam, or can you manage as we are?'

I folded my hands in my lap, squeezing hard, thinking. I risked a furtive sideways glance at Melody, who had sucked in her lips and was shaking her head almost imperceptibly from side to side. If we asked for another maid, there'd be no spot for Amy when – and if – she returned. 'No, sir,' I replied. 'Melody and I can assist one another with our toilette, and French can assume some of Amy's other duties.' I paused, then added to emphasize the point, and to keep my options open, 'For the time being.'

'Very well. So be it.' Jack tucked his napkin back into his collar, leaned forward and picked up his knife and fork. He skewered a potato and popped it into his mouth, whole. 'I'll miss our little musicales.'

'I can still play, sir,' Alex threw in half-heartedly.

'Yes, yes, of course, Mueller. But you know what I mean.'

'We can put an ad in the paper!' Gabe suddenly exclaimed, his eyes bright as crystal buttons.

His father glanced up. 'What are you talking about, son?'

'You know, in the old newspapers you're always reading! "Ran away from the subscriber in Annapolis, an indentured serving woman named Amy Cornell, about twenty-eight years of age, about five and a half feet high . . ."'

Jack threw back his head; his whole body shook with laughter. 'What clever little ears you have, Gabriel Donovan. I had no idea you were even listening when I read the *Maryland Gazette* out loud.'

Melody swiveled in her chair the better to glare at her

brother. 'That is so dumb. Amy isn't an indentured servant, French is. Amy's a free woman. Besides, the *Maryland Gazette* is like three hundred years old. Duh!'

I smiled. At least one of the Donovans wasn't mired in a time warp. Like his son, Jack Donovan was sometimes so into 1774 that I amused myself by picturing him, months after the television show had aired, throwing boxes of Lipton tea off the shelves at his local Safeway.

Dinner proceeded somberly after that, momentarily brightened when French appeared – to *ohs* and *ahs* – carrying a crystal trifle bowl brimming with wine-soaked biscuits, fresh fruit and whipped cream. As I served up dessert, I remembered something that nearly caused me to drop the spoon. In the market house, Amy had said: 'I've got the charger, too, but it's no freaking good without electricity.'

I resisted the urge to manufacture a reason to leave the table and check it out immediately, but my eagerness seemed to make dinner drag on interminably. Everyone required seconds on the trifle – myself included. And then there was the coffee, of course.

Released at last from my duties as hostess, I left the men at table to drown their considerable sorrows in fine port and Cuban cigars. I shooed Gabe to the kitchen with orders to play with Dex, thereby relieving the little boy of his clean-up duties in the scullery. Melody settled in the parlor with *Tom Jones*. 'The necessary,' I said simply. 'I'll be right back.'

A few minutes later, kneeling on the floor by the bed in Amy's room with my arm stuck up to the armpit inside her mattress, I found it. Nestled near the foot of the bed – a plastic Ziploc containing her iPhone charger.

I twirled the bag over my head in silent celebration.

Then quickly sobered up. I had a charger, true, but as Amy said, where the hell was I going to find any freaking electricity?

That night I lay in bed staring at the bed curtains as they swayed gently in the autumn breeze that wafted through my open windows. Coals still glowed hotly in the grate. I listened, ears straining, as the house grew quiet around me. No whisper of an overhead fan, no heating system kicking off then on, no icemaker churning out cubes, *ka-chunk*, into the freezer bin. Only the occasional *thrum* of a passing car kept me anchored – tenuously – to the present.

I had told myself that I'd sleep on it, and sleep on it I was: Amy's iPhone and charger were tucked under my pillow.

The solution was simple: find an electrical outlet. But the only working outlets in the house were behind a locked door, the forbidden door that led to the conference room where LynxE stored their equipment. I decided to check it out.

I slipped out of bed and into my robe. I found my candlestick and lit it from the coals in the fireplace with a twist of paper. Carrying the candlestick, and with the Ziploc bag containing Amy's iPhone and charger tucked under my arm, I let myself out the door that led to the service staircase and tiptoed downstairs, pausing at every creak of the boards beneath my bare feet.

When my feet hit the cold bricks I froze, looking right and left. I turned my back to the kitchen, thereby avoiding its ever-present camera, and scurried along to the conference room area.

I stood before the locked door, contemplating both the lock and the fatal results of feminine curiosity in song and fable. Lot's wife, Pandora . . . I was one of Bluebeard's ill-fated wives attempting to enter The Forbidden Room. Except Bluebeard's wife had a big brass key, and the lock glistening back at me in the candlelight was made of cold, hard steel, with an array of push buttons like a cell phone on steroids.

I'd learned to pick locks in college – don't ask! – but paperclips weren't going to work on this baby. I squinted – a King Cobra by Schlage. The day Jud brought me to the room to hand me the contract I'd watch him open it, but I hadn't been paying particular attention. I squeezed my eyes shut, trying to recall what buttons he pushed. There were four, I remembered, all in the same column, and he'd punched them up quickly with his thumb.

I could eliminate 1-4-7-* and 3-6-9-# because * and # are not numbers, so that left 2-5-8-0, but I didn't know the correct sequence. If Paul had been standing next to me, shivering in his nightgown, too, he would have been quick to inform me that 'a four-digit number with no repeating digit has twenty-four possible permutations,' but I didn't find that out until much later, so I just set my candle down on the floor and started methodically punching. 2-5-8-0, push the handle, no. 2-5-0-8, push the handle, no.

I got lucky on the eighth try – 2-0-8-5 – when the lock clicked open.

Giving myself a mental high-five, I picked up my candle and Ziploc bag and let myself into the conference room.

In the candlelight I noticed a wall switch to the right of the door, but I didn't dare turn it on. Shielding the flame with my hand as best I could, I circumnavigated the conference table, searching for outlets in the walls, but they seemed to be made out of solid brick or stone. There had to be electrical outlets somewhere, I reasoned. Where else could Historic Annapolis plug in laptops for PowerPoint presentations, or recharge their equipment?

On my second lap around the room, I stepped on something even colder than the bricks. I bent down, held the candle close and discovered a circular brass outlet cover, buried flush with the floor. *Eureka!* Praying that the outlet was hot, I flipped up the cover, plugged Amy's charger in, hooked up her iPhone and held my breath. When the white Apple logo appeared, I sat down on the floor, blew out my candle, and prepared for a long wait.

How long does it take to completely recharge a dead iPhone 4? I'll never know. The next thing I remember is a hand on my shoulder, a firm shake, and a gravelly voice saying, 'Mrs Ives, wake up.'

I opened an eye. Derek was looming over me, like a friendly vulture.

'Oh, God!' I scrambled to my feet. 'This is so embarrassing,' I stammered, as I hopped around on one foot trying to get the circulation going while simultaneously attempting to straighten my robe and tug the sash a bit tighter around me.

'Are you all right?' Derek asked in a voice that was so deep, rich and full that it surprised me. If Derek ever decided to hang up his Steadicam, he could do voiceovers for Darth Vader.

'Yes, I'm fine,' I told him, fighting back a wave of nausea.

I forced myself to smile. 'A little stiff, but that'll pass.' Surreptitiously, I felt around with my foot, trying to make contact with Amy's iPhone so I could shove it under the table and out of sight, but Derek had already spotted the forbidden object.

'Yours?' he asked.

'No. It's Amy's.' I reached for the back of a chair, grabbed on. Why was I so dizzy? 'I thought maybe I could . . .' I let my voice trail off.

Derek's eyes darted from mine to the iPhone. He squatted, unplugged the device, wrapped the charger cord around it and held it out. 'Fully charged, I see. Here.'

I took it from him and slipped it into the pocket of my robe, then heard Amy's words coming out of my mouth. 'You're not going to rat me out?'

'You're worried about her, aren't you?'

I nodded silently. 'But there's no cell phone signal, so what's the point?'

'You can always use it to play Bejeweled Blitz or Solitaire under the covers at night. Wouldn't be any skin off my nose.'

*Dodged that bullet.* Clearly, Derek hadn't considered the possibility that there'd be rogue Internet signals wandering like wraiths about the premises.

'Thanks, Derek. I'm just keeping it for Amy. I'm hoping that she, you know, comes back.'

'Yeah, I know. They're out looking for her now.'

My stomach lurched. 'Who's "they?" The police?'

Derek snorted. 'Police? Shit, no. Jud's put somebody on it.'

'"Somebody?" Somebody who?'

'His security team. Some private outfit out of Washington D.C. Former cops and soldiers, mostly. You know the type. Dark blue suits, shoulder holsters, sunglasses.' He circled a finger next to his head. 'Curly wires snaking out of their ears. They'll find her and bring her back, don't you worry.'

I shuffled toward the door on leaden feet. 'Amy's broken her contract, though, hasn't she? Won't they just let her go?'

'Unlikely. They've got a lot of time and money invested in Amy. The camera loves her, what we call "mediagenic."'

Derek held the door open for me. 'She's here, she's gone, she's back again. No matter what her reasons, it's going to make good television. Besides, she plays a really mean harpsichord.'

'What if Jud's people can't find Amy?'

'They'll find her. Trust me.'

I stepped into the hallway, staggered, grabbed the doorframe.

'You sure you're OK? You look really pale.'

I touched my cheek. It felt hot, even to me. 'It's just the makeup,' I told him. 'Colonial ladies are supposed to look pale. Only mad dogs and Englishmen go out in the noonday sun.'

'Well, if you're sure . . .' He didn't look convinced.

'Derek, I really appreciate your not saying anything about Amy's iPhone.'

Derek switched off the overhead light, pulled the door shut behind him, gave it a tug. 'No problem. If you don't tell anyone that I left the door unlocked.'

I smiled, marveling at my luck. 'It's a deal.'

When I got back to my bedroom, it was still dark. I leaned against the bed, pulled the iPhone out and checked the time: 4:25 a.m. I wandered over to the window, tapped Settings, and looked for a wireless signal, but there was none, rogue or otherwise, leaking into my bedroom. No way, then, to check for any emails from Paul. I'd have to do that in the morning from the privacy of the privy.

Following Amy's example, I looked around for a good place to hide the iPhone, finally deciding on one of the blue and white Chinese vases that decorated my dresser. I slid the charger in first, followed by the iPhone.

The effort seemed to exhaust me.

I stumbled to the bed and fell against it, desperate to climb in and burrow under the covers, but inexplicably unable to lift myself up. Nausea continued to sweep over me, wave after wave. I sank to the carpet, grabbed the chamber pot and clutched it to my breast only seconds before vomiting into it all that remained of the supper I had eaten the night before.

'That's what you get for sleeping on a cold, hard floor,' I heard my late mother say, and then everything went dark.

# SIXTEEN

*'It's nine o'clock on a Monday night, and ordinarily I'd be watching* Dancing with the Stars. *Last night, Hannah was sitting in the parlor in front of the fire reading* Tom Jones *out loud. As soon as I finish washing up the glassware, I'll be going upstairs so I can hear the next chapter.'*

French Fry, housemaid

As I lay under the covers in a sweltering fog, the noises of the house went on around me. The clatter of dishes being carried down to the kitchen for washing, the drumming of Gabe's feet as he ran along the hallway, Melody's voice – yelling – 'Quiet, or you'll wake up Mrs Ives. She's sick, you dope.' At one point, I thought I heard Amy playing the harpsichord, but I must have been dreaming, because Amy is gone.

When I opened my eyes again, the sun was just setting, casting long shadows across the floorboards of my room. A man stood at the foot of my bed. He was tall, fair, sturdily built, wearing a suit of dark blue wool, trimmed with gold braid. He peered at me curiously through a pair of wire-rimmed eyeglasses. 'I'm Doctor Kenneth Glass, Mrs Ives. We've been worried about you.'

If I hadn't been so out of it, I'd have been worried about myself, too. I opened my mouth to reply, but the only thing that came out was a croak. My tongue had grown fur, and was several sizes too big for my mouth.

I didn't realize French stood at my bedside until she said, 'Would you like a drink of water, Mrs Ives?'

I started to nod, but it hurt too much to move. I heard water trickling, followed by a cool, wet cloth being laid across my forehead. 'Thank you,' I whispered.

'You can put it over there, Samuel,' French said after a moment. She was speaking to a black man who had entered the room carrying a wooden box by a pair of rope handles. Samuel set the box down on my dressing table, then turned to Dr Glass and held out his arms expectantly. The doctor handed over his gold-handled cane and his tri-corned hat. Samuel set them down on the table next to the fireplace, then returned to help the doctor remove his elegant coat.

Dr Glass pulled up a chair and sat down next to the bed. 'Tell me how you feel,' he said.

'Headache,' I mumbled. 'Fever. Upset stomach. Probably the flu.'

In the shadows by the window, a red light winked. Oh, hell. Derek lurked there filming, or maybe it was Chad.

I considered the doctor's well-groomed wig, his expensive wardrobe, the finely-wrought gold chain that ended at the watch peeking out of the pocket of his weskit. I began to panic. 'Are you a *real* doctor, doctor, or do you just play one on television?'

Dr Glass smiled, his blue eyes twinkling. 'I'm a real doctor, Mrs Ives, both in the eighteenth century and in the twenty-first.' He lifted my wrist and took my pulse. 'Hmmm,' he muttered enigmatically, thereby confirming his credentials.

'How come you don't carry a stethoscope, then?'

Dr Glass was checking the lymph nodes in my neck, under my arms. 'Remember when you signed the contract to be on *Patriot House*?'

I grunted in reply.

'There's a clause in that contract where you agree to be treated for minor medical problems using eighteenth-century medicines and techniques. Do you recall that, Mrs Ives?'

'That contract was longer than *Atlas Shrugged*,' I moaned. 'I think I missed that chapter.'

'Well, they didn't have stethoscopes in colonial Annapolis. Didn't have them anywhere until 1816, in fact. Looked like ear trumpets.'

Dr Glass asked French to hold up the sheet to shield me from the camera while he checked the lymph nodes in my groin. Then, he cautiously pressed his fingertips into my stomach.

I screamed in pain.

'Sorry. This will be over in a minute. Take a deep breath now.'

I tried to comply, but it hurt too much. I felt tears rolling sideways down my cheeks.

'Your stomach is distended, as you've undoubtedly noticed. But I see you've had your appendix removed, so appendicitis can be eliminated. What have you eaten lately?'

I tried to remember. 'Nothing that the rest of the house hasn't eaten.'

'You could be suffering from verdigris, which is usually caused by eating tainted meat. Have you eaten any meat that's turned green?'

Before I could answer, French sputtered, 'We'd *never* serve meat that had turned green in Patriot House!'

Dr Glass held up a hand. 'Fine, then, fine. Are you having diarrhea, Mrs Ives?'

Just thinking about having diarrhea in a house with no bathrooms made my stomach roil. I curled over. 'I'm going to vomit!'

French held a basin while I retched, but there was nothing left in my stomach to hurl except nasty yellow bile. I fell back on my pillows, exhausted, as my brain bounced painfully back and forth against the inside of my skull. Even the roots of my hair ached.

'How about melons? There's been an outbreak of lysteria linked to cantaloupes grown out in Colorado.'

'We grow cantaloupes in our greenhouse right here, Dr Glass,' French informed him. 'And before you ask, no night soil is involved.'

I closed my eyes for a moment, and my lids scratched hotly against my eyeballs.

'What kind of treatment would an eighteenth-century doctor usually give in a case like this?' French asked as she straightened the sheet and tucked it in around me like a cocoon.

Dr Glass had crossed to the washstand where Samuel stood at attention holding the pitcher. As he scrubbed his hands vigorously with soap, the doctor said, 'Pretty much as I'm doing now, except for the hand washing part.' He grinned back at French over his shoulder. 'I must be a visionary. The connection between germs and disease isn't going to be discovered for another half century or so.' Samuel rinsed the doctor's hands with water, pouring it over them into the wash basin, then held out a towel.

Dr Glass dried his hands, then returned to my bedside. 'There could be something more serious going on, of course, such as a partial obstruction or blockage of the bowel. We'll have to watch for that.' He patted my hand where it lay on the sheet, limp and boneless. 'The odds are, though, that it's something viral and self-limiting.'

I grabbed the doctor's wrist, using what little strength I had to pull him down until his ear was close to my lips. 'Could I have been deliberately poisoned?' I croaked.

His pale eyebrows shot up under his wig. He straightened, but I kept my vise-like grip on his wrist. Dr Glass laid his hand over my clenched fingers. 'I very much doubt that, Mrs Ives.'

'Who would want to poison you?' French clucked. She gave the doctor a knowing glance. I read the message in her eyes: poor woman must be delusional.

How about a disgruntled Navy SEAL, I thought, who wanted to make sure that I kept his secret?

'What's in the box?' I wondered miserably, as I watched Samuel lift up the lid.

'Ah, those are my medicinals, my mortar and pestle. I've bleeding instruments in there, too. Lancets and such. Sometimes I carry leeches. But don't worry. We don't generally bleed post-menopausal women.' He paused, nodded to Samuel, then bent again to whisper in my ear. 'I am going to take a blood sample, however, and send it out for testing. Just to be sure.

'Everyone out now!' He made shooing motions with his hand, the lace at his wrist flouncing gaily. 'Miss Fry, please fetch some more hot water.' He paused, glared into the shadows where Derek was trying his best to blend into the curtains. 'That means you, too, young man; you *and* your camera.'

When everyone had gone, Dr Glass rolled up the sleeve of my shift, swabbed the inside of my forearm with cotton soaked in alcohol, and took a blood sample in the twenty-first-century way, using a rubber tourniquet and a syringe.

'They didn't know how to do that back then, did they?' I asked stupidly as he transferred my blood from the syringe to a sealed test tube, gave it a shake. He handed the tube off to

Samuel, who wrote something on the label with an anachronistic ballpoint pen.

'Of course not, Mrs Ives, but I refuse to take chances with a patient's health, no matter what century she fancies she wants to live in.' He handed the used syringe to his assistant who disposed of it in a red plastic bag and sealed it shut. 'As I said, I'm having your blood tested, and if it turns up anything serious, I'll be back with proper medication.'

'Can you give me anything now? I feel like shit.'

'We'll brew up some tea out of white willow bark. It's what the American Indians used for pain. It contains salicin which was one of the components used in the development of aspirin.'

'Popcorn, peanuts, chocolate, tobacco . . . and aspirin. God bless the Native Americans, doctor.'

Dr Glass smiled and patted my hand like a favorite uncle.

When French came back with the tea kettle, Dr Glass began issuing orders. He had her fill up a pottery hot water bottle, wrap it in cloth and tuck it under the covers next to my feet. 'Build up the fire,' he instructed. 'Make sure you keep the windows open to let the putrid air out. And if you've got any fir boughs, you can spread them out on the floor. I'm not exactly sure what that's supposed to do, but it was common practice back then. Probably served as an air freshener.'

While Samuel packed up his case, Dr Glass sat at the table and wrote something out on a piece of paper. He handed it to French. 'The tea should take care of the pain, but if you take that to the apothecary, he'll give you something for her fever.

'In the meantime, white willow bark tea. There'll be some in the kitchen. Don't be alarmed when you see it. In spite of the name, when it's brewed up, it's ruby red in color. You can add a stick of cinnamon if she doesn't like the barky taste. In the morning, you can start her on a broth, chicken or beef. Cool, not hot.'

Samuel helped his master back into his coat; handed him his hat and cane. At the door, the doctor turned, adjusting the lace where it protruded from his sleeves as he spoke. 'Send for me if you feel worse, or there's any change. I know you're reluctant to leave the project, Mrs Ives, but if *I* think you need modern medical attention, I'll sling you over my shoulder and carry you off to the hospital myself.'

'In a horse-drawn carriage?' I murmured.

'If I have to,' he chuckled. 'I'll come back tomorrow, same time,' the doctor said, and he was gone, with Samuel and the box of medicinals in his wake.

French placed another cool compress on my forehead, then scurried off to the kitchen to brew up the tea. Half an hour later, she returned and helped me sit up. Propped against several pillows, I cradled a cup in my hands and sipped the brew slowly, knowing that if it didn't stay down, it couldn't work its magic. It tasted like tree bark with cinnamon in it, but felt deliciously warm and soothing as it trickled down my throat.

Soon, I felt myself nodding. French relieved me of the cup, tucked the comforter in around me, then settled into the upholstered chair next to the fire with her feet curled up under her.

'You don't have to stay,' I whispered as sleep began to overtake me at last.

'I don't mind,' she said. 'Would you like me to read to you?'

'Yes, thank you.'

She opened the book and began, 'Eight months after the celebration of the nuptials between Captain Blifil and Miss Bridget Allworthy – a young lady of great beauty, merit, and fortune – was Miss Bridget, by reason of a fright, delivered of a fine boy. The child was indeed to all appearances perfect; but the midwife discovered it was born a month before its full time.'

'They don't write 'em like they used to,' I thought, as I drifted off.

I'm not sure what woke me. It could have been the cool October wind that was making the bed curtains dance around me as it whistled through the open windows. It might have been my bladder, in eminent danger of bursting from all the liquid I'd been force-fed over the past several hours. I needed to use the chamber pot in the worst way, but the thought of leaving the warmth of my bed effectively paralyzed me.

A fire still flickered in the grate – somebody must be tending it – but the chair that French had occupied was deserted. Our novel – *Tom Jones* – lay open on the table next to the chair, a strap of fringed-leather marking the place where she'd left off.

The book could wait, but my bladder couldn't. Gritting my teeth and thanking my lucky stars that I didn't have to rush outside to use the privy, I slid out of bed and found the chamber pot, wincing as I pulled up my shift and sat down on the ice cold porcelain.

As relief washed over me, I heard the long case clock in the downstairs hall strike the quarter hour. But the quarter of *what* hour? I'd lost complete track of time.

When I finished, I stood up, wobbly. My head swam. My legs felt like cooked spaghetti and I grabbed for a bed post.

I looked to the windows for a clue to the hour, but it was still dark outside. Then I remembered Amy's iPhone.

It was probably less than eight feet from my bed to the dresser, but the distance seemed to stretch out forever before me. I released the curtain and shuffled to the straight-backed chair, clung there for a moment, head pounding, then moved on. At the dresser, I rested, breathing hard, as exhausted as if I'd just run a marathon. Even the Chinese vase felt like lead, but I managed to scoot it toward me across the dresser top, tilt it toward me and stick my hand inside.

But the vase was empty.

Amy's iPhone had gone.

# SEVENTEEN

*'Amy's been sight-reading from a collection of songs some-body put together in 1779. I guess they got tired of ye olde songs like "The Twins of Latona" because they're up there right now singing songs from Stephen Foster. I'm OK with "I dream of Jeannie with the light brown hair," but when they get to "All de darkeys am a-weeping, Massa's in de cold, cold ground . . ." Well, I'm here to tell you that not everyone feels the same way about Ole Massa.'*

Karen Gibbs, cook

'You shouldn't have tried to get out of bed, you know.' Someone was swabbing my hands and arms with warm water. A cool compress lay over my eyes. 'There's a bell on the table. Next time, madam, you use it.'

'I'm sorry, French, but I had to pee.'

'It's not French, it's Amy.'

I whipped off the compress, instantly alert. 'Amy! My God, I've been so worried!'

Amy dipped the flannel in water, calmly wrung it out. 'I can see that. But you needn't have made yourself *sick* over it.'

'Where . . . ? How . . . ?'

'All in good time. You need to rest now.' She concentrated on my hands, working the cloth between each of my fingers. 'I'm sorry I wasn't here when you needed me, Hannah.'

'How long have I been out of it? I've lost all track of time.'

'Just two days.'

'*Two?*'

'Uh huh. French told me they sent for the doctor. You're such a troublemaker.'

'I'm sorry.'

'You should be. If you hadn't been such a damn fool, your fever might have broken earlier.'

'I had to pee,' I explained again. I didn't mention her missing iPhone.

'The doctor came to see you again last night,' Amy said. 'Your blood sample was normal, he said. Best guess, you've got a bad case of flu. Wait a minute, I wrote it down.' She reached into her pocket for a slip of paper, squinted as if trying to decipher the handwriting. 'CDC H3N3,' she read. 'Ah, the Center for Disease Control says you had the H3N2 virus that's making the rounds.'

'The doctor came again?' I had no recollection of that. I remembered dreams, weird and disjointed. Amy. Alex. Paul and the Phantom of the Opera duking it out.

'You don't remember?'

'I had a long discussion with René Descartes about the existence of God and the immortality of the soul.' I raised the arm she had just washed and pointed. 'He sat right there at the foot of the bed and explained it all to me. What's more amazing, is that I understood every word.'

'Ah, that explains the French.' Amy said, dropping the flannel back into the basin. '*Je pense donc je suis*. How's your head?'

'Better.' Amy looked skeptical, so I said, 'Really.'

'I'm going to fetch you some broth. Are you up for that?'

'Only if you promise to sit down next to the bed and tell me what's been going on.'

'First you eat.'

When Amy returned a few minutes later holding a tray, I asked, worried, 'Is Derek in the room? Chad?'

'No,' Amy said. 'Everyone's off to see a production of *The Beggar's Opera* in the Annapolis Summer Garden Theatre building down by the docks.' She fluffed up my pillows and propped me up against them. She handed me a cup of yellow liquid with specks of green floating on top.

I took a cautious sip, 'Bleah! It's cold!'

'It's *supposed* to be cold. Pretend it's vichyssoise.'

'That's a stretch.' I took another sip and swallowed. 'But I think it's going to stay down.'

'Good.' Amy scooted the straight back chair closer to my bed and sat down on it. 'So, where to start?'

'At the beginning,' I said. 'At St Anne's. In the restroom.'

'I never even *got* to the restroom,' Amy told me. 'When I entered the vestibule, Drew was already there, waiting, thumbing through the brochures on the tract rack. He saw me, literally scooped me up, and the next thing I know, we're in the back seat of a cab speeding out of town on Rowe Boulevard, heading straight for the airport.'

'Where was he taking you?'

'To the Four Points Sheraton at first, and then South America. Argentina, to be exact, in Flores, which is a yuppy-fied barrio in the heart of Buenos Aires, or so I gather. You can get lost among thirteen million people, he says. Drew had it all laid on. False passports. A private plane. A suitcase of clothes for me, all bought for cash at Macy's.' She blushed. 'He even remembered my size.'

'So how come you aren't in Argentina?'

Amy gave me a look.

Oh, I got it. First things first. The hotel. *Sex.*

'But thank God for that,' Amy continued, 'because it gave me time to negotiate.'

'Successfully, apparently.'

She nodded. 'But it wasn't easy.'

'So, what future is there in it for you, Amy? Some sort of Do-it-Yourself Witness Protection Program?'

'You could say that. In a few months, the Navy will declare Drew officially dead. I'm to collect the $100,000 survivor benefit and cash in his $450,000 life insurance policy. Then I join him. He's arranged passports, as I said. New identities. He had training as an accountant, so he even got somebody to dummy up a convincing work history for him. Low-level jobs at large corporations where nobody will ever bother to check.' She smiled grimly. 'I was once a teacher. Ditto on my new résumé.

'Drew is fluent in five languages, but I don't even speak Spanish, so what kind of work can *I* do in Argentina? "You can learn," he said. Ha! Honestly, Hannah, I married the man for better or for worse, and this is definitely for worse. He probably wants to keep me at home, barefoot and pregnant.

'He looked different,' she rattled on. 'Sunburned, bleached, brittle, so . . . hard.'

'It was pitch dark the night he visited me in your room. I never saw him, Amy.'

'His hair is long now, tied back in a ponytail. It was always kind of dirty blond, but it's been bleached almost white by the sun. And he's no longer Drew, by the way. His name is Donald. I *hate* the name Donald.'

I had to agree. 'I had an evil boss once named Donald. We amused ourselves by inventing devious ways to kill him. And there's always Donald Duck.'

Amy laughed mirthlessly.

'Drew knew how much staying on the show meant to you because I told him. Why did he risk getting you kicked off the show by taking you away?'

'In a way, it's the show that saved me, Hannah. He was going on about living in luxury for the rest of our lives. I let him think I was on board with it, too, but dammit, I don't want to live life on the run. I'm not particularly close to my mother, but I have a sister, and a niece and a nephew, and I don't want never to see them again. Besides, it's been ten months. I have new friends now.'

'New friends,' I repeated. 'Like Alex.'

Amy fell back against the chair. 'You noticed?'

'I stumbled across the two of you in the service staircase one day.'

'Shit.'

'He's been worried sick about you, Amy.'

'Oh, Hannah, what am I going to do about Alex? I'm sweet on him, sure, but now that Drew's back in the picture . . .' She leaned forward, grabbed my hand. 'Alex doesn't know about Drew, and if Drew finds out about Alex, I hate to think what might happen!'

'Maybe you need to let Alex down gently,' I suggested.

'Alex is such a sweet, gentle spirit,' Amy said, 'while Drew . . .'

'Doesn't Drew have family?' I asked. 'Other than you, I mean.'

'His father was killed in Vietnam, in the final days during the fall of Saigon. His mother died of cancer when Drew was only twelve. Drew's grandmother raised him, but when she died . . .' Amy shrugged. 'I'm the only family he has. Everything Drew loves goes away.'

'If he wanted you to stay with him so badly, Amy, how on earth did you escape?'

Amy shrugged. 'I gave him some of the best sex he's ever had, and in the afterglow, I put him off. I pointed out something that should have occurred to him in the first place if he hadn't been thinking with his . . . you know. It would only attract attention if I disappeared from the show in midstream. *60 Minutes* and *48 Hours* would be all over it.' Amy held an imaginary microphone to her mouth, stared at me intently and said, 'Why would the young widow of a Navy SEAL run away from the set of a major television show? Where is she hiding? And why? Stay tuned. We'll be right back.

'If I wait until the show is over, I pointed out to him, then I could leave without comment, not have to worry about a million-dollar lawsuit, collect his insurance money, shave my eyebrows, dye my hair black or whatever, join him in Argentina, and I'd even be $15,000 to the better.'

'But, if you don't intend to run away with Drew, what *are* you planning to do?'

Amy's face clouded up. 'I don't know, Hannah. I'm just trying to buy a little time while I work it all out.'

'I hate to sound like an old mother hen, but I'd give it some careful thought because it doesn't sound like Drew is willing to leave without you.'

'Oh, Hannah, I used to be so in love with that guy! But, now? I *can't* go away with him, Hannah. Drew is not the same man I married. He's changed. He's hard, cynical. I don't know whether it's PTSD or what, but if I met him today, we'd never get past the first date.'

Drew had told me a little bit about the incident in Swosa, but I wanted to get details from Amy. 'Did he ever fully explain to you why he's on the run? I figure it has to be more than wanting the insurance money.'

'If the Navy found out he was alive after all this time, he'd be subject to courts martial. In Swosa? Drew was the triggerman. The Swosians had closed-circuit TV in the bedroom at the palace, so they got it all on tape. If the Swosa loyalists knew Drew had escaped, they would be all over him, too. Alive, everyone would be out to get him. Dead.' She shrugged. 'Dead is better.'

'There were tapes?' Drew hadn't mentioned that. Possibly he didn't know.

'You bet. When the Navy were shown the tapes, they were embarrassed, but at least they don't have to parade Drew out before a congressional subcommittee to explain why he murdered a foreign national when he wasn't authorized to do so. And the Swosians believe that the triggerman died with all the others when one of their brave boys shot down the helicopter after being fatally wounded himself. With Drew dead, no loose ends. On either side.'

'As long as he stays dead.' I set my empty broth cup back down on the tray.

'Right.' Amy took the tray from where it rested on my knees and set it on the floor outside the service entrance to my room. 'Dex!' she yelled down the service stairway. 'Come fetch the tray!'

While she waited for Dex to appear, Amy said, 'I don't need the money, not desperately, but Drew does, and since he's dead, he needs me to get it for him.' She held the door open, occasionally checking for Dex over her shoulder. '*He* can move to Argentina as far as I'm concerned. Once the money comes to me, I'll send it all to some bank account in Buenos Aires.' She flashed a smile. 'But don't tell Drew that. He still thinks I'm coming with him.'

'Amy, if the authorities find out you've done that, *you* could go to jail for fraud.'

'Nobody will find Drew unless he wants them to. I'm convinced of that. Losing his parents at an early age made him tough.'

'He's AWOL, big time. Isn't he worried that he'll be caught?'

'Not Drew. Remember that line in *The Right Stuff* where Dennis Quaid is driving a convertible and asks his wife who's the best pilot she's ever seen, and that she's looking at him? Well, that's Drew. He pumps up his abs and says, "I'm a U.S. Navy SEAL. I'm trained not to be caught."'

'I can believe that,' I said. 'He made it out of Swosa alive, and not many men would be able to accomplish that. Did he

tell you the story? It's been more than ten months. Why did
it take him so long?'

'Naturally, he had no money, no passport. He was on foot.
It took him weeks to make his way out of Swosa and over
the border into Tanzania. Eventually, he ended up in Dar es
Salaam, where he hung out on the beach with all the other
ex-pats until he hooked up with an American sailboat captain
looking for crew. The guy was circumnavigating, and in no
hurry, so Drew simply signed on. I gather the lack of a passport
wasn't a problem.' She grinned. 'Drew can be pretty convincing.
When the boat finally made it to the U.S., Drew jumped ship
and disappeared into a crowd of tourists in Charleston. That
was a month ago. He's been hiding out in that hotel by the
airport ever since, keeping an eye on me, making plans.'

There'll be a *New York Times* bestseller out of this, I thought,
by Drew Cornell as told to whom? Tom Clancy? Or maybe
it'd be the other way around: BY TOM CLANCY and DREW
CORNELL. A movie later, I'll bet, produced by, directed by and
starring Tom Cruise. An EA computer game. The possibilities
were endless.

Watching Amy bustle about my bedroom, tending to my
wrinkled gowns, straightening up, rather than being holed up
in a hotel room with a sex-starved fugitive made me enormously happy. 'I'm so glad you're back,' I said, as she helped
me change into a clean, white shift that smelled like fresh
soap and sunshine.

Since Amy had broken more clauses in her contract than a
shady real-estate developer, I wondered why Jud Wilson had
agreed to let her come back. Was Derek right? Was Amy too
mediagenic a 'product' to let slip through their fingers?

'What happened after you left Drew?'

'He gave me some cash, put me in a cab, and the cab brought
me here. I simply walked in through the kitchen door.'

'Brazen hussy.'

'Damn right! Karen gave me a big hug, but I must have set
off an alarm somewhere because Jud Wilson appeared after
about fifteen minutes and marched me into the conference
room. You should see it, Hannah! Long walnut table, upholstered chairs. Very deluxe.'

'I can imagine. So, what did you tell him?'

'When he asked why I'd run away, I lied. Karen told me that Jack had once cornered her in the kitchen, so I said he'd made a pass at me, too. Said I freaked. I told Jud I didn't think I could hack it, being recently widowed and all, so I took a few days off to think.'

I wasn't exactly in love with Jack, but still, pinning a sexual harassment charge on the jerk seemed a little harsh. 'Amy, you didn't!'

Amy puffed air. 'You know what Jud told me? They knew all about the incident between Jack and Karen, too. Seems Jack snuck down to the kitchen one night where Karen caught him red-handed eating a piece of pie with his fingers, right out of the pie plate. He was a little tipsy, and he backed Karen into the corner. Smeared cherry pie juice all over her breast before she clocked him with a rolling pin.'

I laughed out loud at the picture.

'They caught it all on tape, Hannah. Jud said the viewers were going to *love* the way Karen told him off. If she'd been a real slave, he told me, she'd have been whipped after that. Probably ended up on the auction block, too.'

I cringed, thinking how glad I was to be living in the twenty-first century. 'I can't wait to see how the show comes out when it finally goes on the air.'

'At least I won't be watching it from Buenos Aires.'

'Tell me something,' I said later as Amy was brushing my hair. 'You mentioned that Drew's new name is Donald. What's the name on your fake passport?'

'Angela,' she said. 'Angela Clark. Do I look like an Angela to you?'

'Probably to Drew you did.'

'In his dreams.'

# EIGHTEEN

*'I want some toothpaste! Can you hear me, Founding Father? A fringed stick dipped in lemon juice and salt is simply not going to cut it.'*

Hannah Ives

Wednesday dawned sunny and unseasonably warm. For the first time in three days, I was able to get out of bed, get dressed – with Amy's help, to my great relief – and join the family for breakfast.

Melody leapt to her feet when I entered the dining room, fairly bounced across the carpet and smothered me with a hug. 'Mrs Ives! You're all well!'

My stomach muscles were still sore from two days of vomiting, and I tried not to wince as I untangled myself from her embrace. I smiled, looked into her emerald eyes and tapped her on the chin with my index finger. 'Thank you. I'm glad to be back, too, Melody.'

Melody grabbed my hand and led me around the table to my customary chair. She dragged it out from the table and helped scoot it back in after I sat down.

Gabe glanced up from his porridge. 'We're going to see the burning of the *Peggy Stewart* today, Mrs Ives. It's a big ship with a lot of tea on it.'

I helped myself to a soft boiled egg. 'Are you, now?'

'Are you coming, too?' Melody asked as she reclaimed her own seat.

Jack looked up from his paper, another facsimile of the *Maryland Gazette*. 'Now, Melody, don't you overtax Mrs Ives. Remember, she's been ill.'

'I feel very well, thank you, Mr Donovan. And I'm very much looking forward to the burning of the *Peggy Stewart*. The last time I saw a boat go up in flames, it was in Cambridge, Maryland.' I winked at Melody. 'It wasn't exactly planned.'

I had captured Gabe's attention, too. 'What happened to it?'

'Gas fumes had built up in the engine compartment. When the captain turned the key to start the engine, there was a spark. *Kaboom!* Fortunately, he was able to jump overboard.'

Gabe turned to his father, eyes wide. 'Are they going to burn a real boat?'

'I don't know, son. Do you, Mrs Ives?'

I whacked the top off my egg with the edge of my knife. 'I have absolutely no idea, having been out of the loop for a couple of days, but LynxE isn't particularly tight-fisted with their dollars – can you imagine how much they had to pay to get David Morse to play George Washington? So it'll probably be quite a production.'

'What shall I wear, Mrs Ives?' Melody wanted to know.

'The dress you wore to church on Sunday would suit, I should think. The pink one with all the bows?'

'And you should wear your blue, Mrs Ives. The one with the ruffles running down the front and the tiny seed pearls. I think that's *so* beautiful!'

'Why, thank you.' I leaned closer and whispered, 'Shall we leave our wigs at home, then?'

'Oh, yes, please, Mrs Ives. It itches like crazy.'

'We'll save them for the ball.' I salted my egg and dug in, not realizing how hungry I was until I was scraping the inside of the shell and looking around for another one. Jack passed me the biscuits with ham when I asked for them, and I was happily munching away when Alex said, 'Women often think that men aren't particularly interested in fashion, Miss Donovan, but may I suggest that I'm the exception? For the outing today, I'll be wearing a pale blue suit with silver braid and I'll have a matching blue cockade on my hat.' While Melody stared at him, mouth slightly ajar, he continued. 'And I'm honored to say, that Miss Amy Cornell has agreed to accompany me.'

'Cool!' Melody cooed.

My mouth was half ajar, too, thinking, too much, too soon, Amy. You're treading on dangerous ground. What if Drew . . . ? I pushed the thought away. 'Are you coming, too, Michael?' I asked instead.

'Indeed I am. I imagine the whole household will be there.' He waved a fork. 'Founding Father says.'

Jack took a sip of coffee. 'Mrs Ives,' he said. 'Normally I would have consulted you first, but since you were, uh, indisposed, I told the servants they could have the day off.'

'Perfectly appropriate, Mr Donovan,' I said. 'From noon on?'

'Exactly.'

'I'll speak to Karen, then, about laying out a cold buffet this evening.'

'I already took the liberty.' He stood, laid his napkin on the table. 'Now, if you will excuse me, I have some accounts to take care of.'

One by one, they left the table, leaving me to savor my coffee alone. I can't say that I minded.

Later, following a trip to the privy, I finally had a chance to check the wall where I'd left the message in the bottle for Paul all those days ago.

To my delight, the bottle was gone.

It seemed like the entire state of Maryland had turned up for the burning of the *Peggy Stewart*, which had taken place exactly two-hundred-thirty-eight years before. For the Patriot House residents, on the other hand, yesterday was today: October 19, 1774.

We gathered in the hallway – chatting and giggling in anticipation – and left the house together just as the long case clock was striking two. Jack Donovan, Patriot, in the lead, looked resplendent (I admitted reluctantly) in his black wool suit, wearing a tricorn hat over his powdered wig and carrying a cane. I scooted along behind, followed by Melody who did her best to mind her little brother while at the same time curtseying and waving to the crowds like a royal bride.

Alex strolled alongside Amy, Michael (I was pleased to see) escorted French, Jeffrey strutted on bravely alone, poor thing, followed by Karen and her son, Dex, who kept running ahead, wild with excitement, so she had to keep herding him back.

We proceeded en masse toward the harbor, along streets thronged with people, both residents and tourists, many of whom had turned up wearing colonial costumes. By now, it was no secret what was going on at Patriot House. Gawkers often gathered on the street outside the house, cameras at the ready. We were used to it.

Cameras were out in force – Derek and Chad had been supplemented by two additional cameramen from LynxE – and the boys in black had competition from the networks, too. As we pushed through the crowds in V-formation, Jack still in the lead, I caught sight of television crews from WBAL in Baltimore as well as WRC and WJLA in Washington, D.C. Maryland Public TV caught up with us at the corner of Dock Street and Randall, and no matter where we were, cell phone cameras recorded our every move.

The area around the Market House and City Dock had been cordoned off using the same portable chain link fencing used for the two annual boat shows – sailing and power – that had concluded the previous two weekends respectively. Only appropriately-costumed spectators were allowed inside.

As we marched down City Dock, costumed vendors dressed especially for the occasion popped up everywhere, roaming the streets and handing out stick candy to the crowds. I watched as a pair of pint-sized Davy Crocketts grabbed more than their share of the sweet, then offered pieces to Gabe and Dex as we paraded by. (An offer they couldn't refuse!)

'Where are we going to stand?' Gabe asked me as he ripped the waxed paper off his candy and stuck the end in his mouth.

'On the dock, I think, over there,' I said, pointing in the direction of the Harbor Queen tour boat where a white canopy at water's edge was decked with bunting decorated with the familiar LynxE logo.

'Oh, goody. Maybe I can sit down. My feet are killing me,' Melody complained.

But there were no chairs, only shade. Being under the canopy afforded a bit of relief from the crowds pressing in around us, however, while at the same time putting us on display.

Once we were under the canopy, Amy, wearing the peach dress I had given her, sidled up to me. 'Just checking to see how you're feeling, Mrs Ives. You OK?'

'I'm fine, Amy, honestly. A little tired maybe, but I'm not going to upchuck all over the mayor.' I pointed with my gloved hand to a young man dressed in white breeches and a black, gold-buttoned frock coat who was making a beeline for Jack Donovan from across the quay.

'*That's* the mayor? How old is he? Fifteen?'

I giggled. 'I think he's thirty-eight.' I poked her in the stays with my elbow. 'Shhh. We're about to be introduced.'

The mayor extended his hand. 'On behalf of the citizens of Annapolis, let me welcome you to our city. I'm Josh Cohen.'

The arrival of the mayor must have been the signal to start the show. Almost immediately, a large wooden rowboat set off from the dock, manned by two oarsmen. The vessel's passengers included three men in full patriot regalia, carrying torches.

'Those actors are representing Anthony Stewart, the owner of the vessel, and the brothers Joseph and James Williams, the merchants who ordered the tea,' I heard Michael tell the children.

Melody tugged on my sleeve. 'Mr Rainey says that Anthony Stewart named the boat after his daughter. It must have sucked to have to burn it down.' A few minutes later, I heard her say, 'Father, if you had a boat, would you name it after me?'

Jack laid a hand on her shoulder. 'I think Melody would be a lovely name for a boat.'

The city couldn't burn an actual two-masted sailing ship, of course, especially not an antique one, so they'd duded up a barge with poles and second-hand sails, decked it with flags and banners, and moored it in the middle of Annapolis harbor just off the Naval Academy sea wall.

As the rowboat neared the *Peggy Stewart*, the crowd on shore began waving and shouting. My preparations for a sunny day out had included a fringed parasol, so I held it aloft and shouted 'Huzzah,' along with everyone else.

When the rowboat pulled alongside, 'Stewart' and the 'Williams brothers' tossed their torches into the replica. There was a flare-up as the accelerant ignited. The crowd went wild. Higher and higher rose the flames, licking at the ropes, gobbling up the sails. You'd have thought it was Army-Navy game day in Annapolis the way the crowd roared.

The rowboat returned to the dock and the trio of arsonists climbed out. Jack Donovan sauntered over to greet them, shaking their hands, clapping them on the back in a job-well-done sort of way. Then the four men wandered off together, presumably to lift a pint at Middleton's, pursued by one of the auxiliary LynxE cameramen.

As the flames consuming the *Peggy Stewart* replica began to die down, the crowd gradually lost interest and began to wander. I'd thought I'd lost track of Amy and Alex, and then I spotted Amy, standing with French next to a fellow in a makeshift colonial costume who was trying to chat her up, but Amy appeared to be staring at the burning ship, pretending not to listen. I decided to bail her out, so I gathered up Melody and Gabe, ducked out from under the canopy and traipsed over to join them. By the time I got there, however, the pesky individual had moved on.

For our day out, Founding Father had issued us vouchers, redeemable for treats at the Market House and other local business. I reached into my pocket and pulled out three of mine, facsimiles of Maryland colonial currency in two-dollar denominations. I handed them to French. 'Why don't you take Melody and Gabe over to Storm Brothers and buy them some ice cream?'

'Where's Alex?' I asked Amy after they had gone.

'He's off with Michael, buying a beer. They're supposed to be fetching me the eighteenth-century version of a Sprite, but it's been a while, so I think they must have meant beers, plural.'

'Alex certainly looked handsome today,' I commented as we watched one of the charred masts snap and topple into the water.

'Hubba hubba,' Amy said. 'Don't you think it's totally unfair how *guys* are born with the gorgeous fringed eyelashes?'

'Totally.'

'*There* you are!' said a familiar voice behind us. Michael, carrying a can of Sprite in one hand and a bottle of Sam Adams lager in the other. 'Sorry, Hannah,' he said, handing the Sprite to Amy. 'I should have asked if you wanted anything. Sip of my beer?' He tipped the bottle my way.

I screwed up my face. 'No, thank you. Stomach still delicate.'

Amy popped the top on her soda after fumbling a bit because of her gloves. She took a grateful sip, then said, 'Where's Alex got to?'

Michael shrugged. 'He got waylaid by a guy who wanted to talk about *Patriot House*. I think he was angling for an introduction to you.' He nudged Amy's arm.

Amy tossed her head and made an elaborate show of rolling her eyes. 'Sure he wasn't a reporter?' she asked.

'Gosh,' Michael said. 'I bet you're right. Alex better mind his Ps and Qs.'

Watching rivulets of condensation drip down Michael's beer bottle made me desperately thirsty. 'Take care of Amy, will you? I'm going to get something to drink. Non-alcoholic,' I added.

I flipped open my parasol, held it over my head and began weaving through the crowd in the direction of Starbucks. As I passed Aromi d'Italia, I thought I caught sight of Alex's distinctive blue suit over by the harbor master's office. As Michael had said, Alex appeared to be talking to someone. I made a left turn and headed in their direction, but just as I got within hailing distance, his companion wandered away. 'Alex!' I called, waving my parasol to attract his attention.

'Hannah?' Alex glanced quickly over his shoulder, then back at me.

'Who were you talking to?' I asked.

'Some tourist from Raleigh, up for the day.'

'Ah. Michael was worried that he might be a reporter.'

Alex flushed. 'Shit, Hannah. I know better than that. I'm not itching to get canned. Besides, I need the money.'

'Amy's been wondering where you got to.' I smiled, looped my arm through his. 'Shall we?'

Alex covered my hand where it rested on his arm. 'I'm very fond of Amy,' he confided. 'As you are no doubt aware.'

'A person would have to be blind not to notice,' I teased. 'No wife or girlfriend at home, I suppose?'

'Do I seem like a rogue to you, Mrs Ives?'

'Not at all, Mr Mueller.'

We'd reached the boardwalk when Alex said, 'I had a fiancé

until six months ago. She dumped me for a motivational speaker from Des Moines. Seems there's more money in the touchy-feely biz than in music.'

'Motivation, schmotivation.' I squeezed his arm. 'I'd rather listen to you play the violin any day.' I looked up, smiled. 'How long have you been studying?'

'Since I was five. Mom bought me one of those teeny-tiny violins and took me to a woman who taught the Suzuki method.' He laughed at the memory. 'Suzuki believed that children who hear fine music from the day of their birth and learn to play it, develop discipline, endurance, and sensitivity, as well as a beautiful heart.'

That certainly described Alex, I thought, tears pricking at the corners of my eyes.

'And the dancing?'

He shrugged. 'Just a hobby.'

As we neared the place where I'd last seen Michael and Amy, I was suddenly distracted by a handsome chap wearing a dark green suit with gold buttons. His khaki breeches fit his slender frame to perfection. He'd topped off his ensemble with a powdered wig and a tricorn hat, and as we approached him along the boardwalk, he removed his hat and bowed deeply.

'Paul!' I grinned up at Alex. 'Sorry, Mr Mueller, but I know this gentleman.'

Alex released my arm, doffed his hat and bowed deeply. 'Later, alligator.'

My heart raced as I closed the distance between me and my husband. Paul gathered me in, crushing me and hundreds of yards of fine silk fabric to his own equally well-costumed chest. I flipped the parasol so it shielded us from Chad's Steadicam and planted a kiss on my husband's lips. He returned it hungrily.

'Watch it, bub, or I'll roger you right here,' I whispered, my lips close to his ear.

'Is that a promise?' he murmured into my hair. 'I've been worried about you, Hannah. Jud told me you'd been ill.'

'He shouldn't have worried you, Paul. I'm fine. Really. A touch of the flu. No big deal.'

'Thank God.' He kissed me again, then said, 'I got your message.'

'Both of them?' I knew about the bottle-mail, but wasn't sure about the email.

'Both. You should take up calligraphy. That note was a work of art.'

'For a beginner,' I said, leaning back so I could look him in the eyes. 'Amy's back now, thank goodness. Problem solved.'

He raised an eyebrow. 'So she's no longer in any danger?'

'She and her husband talked it out. I think she's safe, at least until Drew figures out that she's not going to go along with his plan. But that won't happen, if it happens at all, until Amy leaves Patriot House. Till then?' I shrugged. 'What could be safer than a house full of people where cameras are rolling practically twenty-four seven?' I looped my arm through his, and urged him along the sidewalk back toward the water: Mr and Mrs Colonial Annapolis on an afternoon stroll.

'What about the fugitive, Drew Whats-his-name?'

'Cornell. Outside of Amy and Drew, nobody knows that Drew is alive except you and me, and Amy doesn't know about you.'

'Don't you think you should turn him in?'

'I've never laid eyes on him, Paul. He's like a phantom. But then, that's what SEALs are trained to be. Shadows. Besides, who would believe me? I have no proof. The only proof would be the man himself, or his body, and Drew Cornell is making himself scarce.'

'Amy?'

'Maybe, although I think she figures Drew is entitled to the money after the hell he's been through.'

The sun beat down hotly on my bonnet. I shifted the parasol to better shade my face, then reached for my fan. 'Is it hot, or is it just me?'

A look of concern crossed his face. 'Is it too soon for you to be out? We don't need any relapses here.'

I smiled up at him. 'I was on my way to Starbucks when I was – how shall I say? – interrupted.'

'How about some water?' Paul reached inside his coat and came out holding a bottle of Deer Park spring water. He twisted off the cap and handed the bottle to me.

I took an unladylike swig. 'Ooooh, that tastes good,' I said, dabbing at my lips with the back of my gloved hand. With the parasol and the fan, the bottle would require three hands, so I gave it back to him. 'Where did you get that fabulous costume, Paul?'

'I borrowed it from the Masqueraders' costume room,' he said. '*School for Scandal* opens in a couple of weeks. I think this outfit properly belongs to Sir Benjamin Backbite, but it fit, and the director is a colleague of mine, so there you have it.'

'Is some midshipman running around the stage in his skivvies?'

Paul laughed. 'Don't worry, I'll get it back in plenty of time for the dress rehearsal.'

As the flames of the burning vessel died down, the wind fanned the embers, sending sparks spiraling up into the sky. Spectators began to drift away, to the bars, to the restaurants and to the souvenir vendors that were waiting to separate them from their money.

'Walk me home, will you, Paul?' I suddenly felt drained, weary. Maybe I *had* ventured out a little too soon.

'Do we need to get permission from Founding Father first?' he asked, taking my arm.

I shook my head. 'We've been surprisingly free to wander today, although they have beefed up their film crew.' I pointed my parasol at Chad. 'Exhibit A, or maybe B. Maybe he'll get tired of following us. Find other fish to fry.'

A few minutes later we did, in fact, lose Chad. I had steered Paul purposefully toward the canopy where I'd last seen Karen and Dex. There, in the space the VIPs had vacated, we found Gabe and Dex kneeling on the ground, playing a game of marbles. Irresistibly cute and quintessentially mediagenic. One look at the kids and Chad was a goner.

Paul escorted me up Prince George Street where we stopped at the Paca House gate. A security guard dressed in the red and white uniform of the Maryland Militia was guarding the door. 'Your house, I believe, madam. Mine is just up the street.' He bent down and kissed me on the forehead. 'Are you sure you're all right?'

'Of course I am, Paul. It was only the flu. I just need a little rest. Probably tried to overdo it.' I touched his cheek.

'Will you email me again?'

I whipped off my hat and shook out my curls. 'Can't. Amy's iPhone went AWOL.'

'Ah, that explains why you didn't answer. But I did leave you a message in the bottle.'

'You did? When?'

'Just before climbing into this get-up and going downtown to meet you.'

'What did it say?'

'Aside from arranging to communicate with you through the proprietors of Maryland Table at the Market House, not much. Just a little something of my own. I call it "Heart Foam." I shall not publish it,' he said, quoting from a favorite Gilbert and Sullivan operetta, *Patience*.

'I set everything up with Maryland Table just like you asked in your note,' Paul continued. 'Kyle was happy to cooperate.' He reached into his waistcoat pocket and pulled out a tiny blue notebook decorated with white stars. Strapped to it with a rubber band was a ballpoint pen about three inches long. He pressed them into my hand. 'Here, make it easy on yourself.'

'Thank you,' I said, tucking the notebook into my pocket. 'And you can do another something for me in the not-so-according-to-my-contract department.'

'What would that be?'

'Go to CVS or Walgreens and buy some lipstick, eyeliner and blush. As small as they come. Then go to the travel section where they've got those sample-sized bottles of shampoo? Get a couple of those. Oh, and deodorant. And toothpaste . . .'

Paul held up a hand, palm out. 'Whoa. I'm going to have to take notes.'

I grinned. 'It doesn't really matter. Wrap them up in brown paper and string, and leave them with Kyle at the market.'

'Got it, but what for?'

'If I need to get a message to you, and I can't get to the market, I'll send Melody. It's just a little incentive for the wee lassie. Am I brilliant, or what?'

He stroked my cheek with the back of his index finger. 'I miss you, Hannah Ives.'

'And I miss you, too.'

'Aside from the flu, are you having fun yet?'

'I think so. But I'll be glad when it's over, and I can sit on the sofa with you and watch the whole thing from the *other* side of the camera.'

He kissed me sweetly on the mouth, then said, 'It's a date.'

With one eye on the guard, I asked, 'Do you want to come in for a minute?'

'Tempting, but I've got a department head meeting in thirty minutes. I could attend in all my sartorial splendor, but I think I'd better shower and change.'

'Shower? Hot water, too? My God, you do know how to torture a gal.' I planted a kiss on his cheek, then turned and scampered up the stairs. When I reached the front door, I wheeled about and waved.

Paul swooped off his hat, placed it against his chest and bowed deeply. I laughed out loud. It was all too Georgette Heyer for words.

# NINETEEN

*'I don't have a problem with having servants. If they weren't serving us, they wouldn't have a job.'*
                                        Jack Donovan, Patriot

The servants had been given the day off, so except for the security guard there appeared to be nobody in the house but me.

In full view of the SelectoZoomMini mounted on the back wall, I made a leisurely show of dropping my hat, kicking off my shoes, and peeling off my stockings, leaving them in an untidy heap on the floor. Then I wandered into the garden in my bare feet.

The stones were hot, so I took to the lawn, descending the terraces one by one until I reached the pond. Extending my arms like a tightrope walker, I teetered playfully along the bricks that lined the canal that carried water from a natural spring into the pond, one foot ahead of the other, gripping the stones with my toes.

The bee hives were buzzing in the late afternoon sun, so I gave the industrious insects wide berth, skirting behind the spring house until I reached the wall. As Paul had promised, the bottle was wedged into the same vertical slit where I'd left it for him several days earlier. I eased it out, then leaned against the bricks, enjoying their warmth against my back as I tried to determine the best way to get at my husband's message.

The cork came out easily, but extracting the note was quite another matter. I stuck my index finger into the neck, but only succeeded in spinning the note around. I'd need a tool, I decided, and if that failed, I could always break the bottle. I slipped the bottle into my pocket where it could make friends with the notebook Paul had given me, and headed back to the house.

As I passed the spring house again, I pulled up short.

Something (or someone) had disturbed the grassy plot just in front of the door. Fed by the same natural spring used by the bathhouse and the pond, the spring house, set about four feet into the ground and lined with brick, remained cool throughout the year. It was where we kept our milk and butter. Had someone been pilfering?

And then I saw the hat. A black tricorn with a blue cockade.

I took a deep breath, wrenched open the door and peered inside.

Lying in a puddle of milk on the bricks below, wearing the same suit I had seen him wearing at the burning of the *Peggy Stewart*, was Alex Mueller. Nearby lay a crock of milk, a fist-sized chunk broken out of its side. 'Alex!' I scrambled down and knelt beside him. I touched his cheek, hoping for a sign of warmth, but it was cool, clammy. Then I felt his neck for a pulse.

Nothing moved under my fingers.

Alex's beautiful eyes stared blindly at the wall, the lashes hanging over them like awnings. There was a nasty gash on his temple. 'Oh, Alex, what the hell were you doing out here? Did you fall?'

I remembered the muddy grass, the torn up bits of sod and thought: Drew Cornell. He'd been watching the house. He'd been *inside* the house. He knew what room everyone slept in. Had he discovered the relationship between Amy and Alex the same way I had? Had he killed Alex in a jealous rage? Struck him on the head with a blunt object and pushed him into the spring house, leaving him to die, cold and alone?

Fueled by rage, I hoisted myself out of the spring house and sprinted through the boxwood. I raced up the long walk, taking the stairs as I came to them two at a time. When I reached the porch, I paused to catch my breath. I needed to dial 9-1-1, but to do that, I'd need a telephone.

'Help! Help!' I screamed as I ran into the house.

Where was everyone? Where was the security guard, for that matter? Using both hands, I pulled the front door open, looked right and left, but the guard had inexplicably disappeared.

I closed the door, fell back against it and tried to think.

To one side of the entrance was a red fire alarm box, and at that moment it seemed to be shouting, 'Hey! Look at me! Look at me!' I reached out, took firm hold of the handle and pulled down.

Covering my ears against the wail of the claxon, I retreated to the front steps where I nearly ran into the security guard, rushing into the house, in the act of zipping his fly.

'Where *were* you?' I shrieked, although the evidence of the fly probably told the whole story.

'I had to take a piss,' he said. 'There aren't any bathrooms in this freaking house so I had to use the freaking privy. What the hell is going on? Where's the fire?'

'I needed to call 9-1-1,' I babbled, 'but I didn't have a phone and I couldn't find you, so I pulled the fire alarm. Alex Mueller, our dancing master, fell into the spring house. I think he's dead!'

'Jesus.' He reached into his pocket and pulled out a cell phone. 'I'll call it in.'

'You wait here.' I jabbed a finger at the sidewalk: X marks the spot. 'I'm going back to stay with Alex until they get here. Do you know where the spring house is?'

'Yes, ma'am,' he said, sounding professional at last. 'I'll show them how to get there.'

I've seen dead bodies before, more than my share. When the spirit's gone, it's gone, abandoning the body it no longer needs, leaving nothing behind but a hollow shell. I knew there wasn't anything I could do for Alex Mueller. One minute, two minutes, three minutes, four. It wouldn't matter to Alex how quickly I got back to the spring house where he lay, but I couldn't stand the thought of leaving him alone. As I looked down at his body again from the doorway, at his open eyes and slim, beautiful fingers, fingers that had coaxed magnificent music out of an otherwise un-pedigreed violin, I grieved for his talent, silenced forever.

It was cold in the spring house, damp. I resisted the urge to return to the house for a blanket to cover him with, or a shawl, because I knew better than to add or subtract anything from the scene before the police got there.

So I sat down near a rhododendron in a patch of sun, hugged

my knees to my chin and wept. Barefooted and bare-legged, my torn gown and stained petticoats pooled around me, I must have looked like Cinderella, sulking in front of the fireplace long before her fairy godmother turned up to wave her magic wand.

In the time it took for the first emergency vehicle to arrive, I kept turning a single thought over and over in my mind. Back in Amy's bedroom, when I didn't know who had climbed into bed with me, I'd said his name: 'Alex?'

Had I signed Alex Mueller's death warrant that night?

# TWENTY

*'I knew I'd miss safety razors and toilet paper, but you
know what I really miss? RC Cola and Moon Pies.'*
Michael Rainey, tutor

Historic Waterwitch Hook and Ladder #1 was, quite
literally, just around the corner on East Street, but had
been sold to the Chesapeake Bay Foundation in the
1980s and converted into offices. I wasn't sure how long it
would take the Annapolis Fire Department to reach us from
their firehouse in West Annapolis, considering that they had
to navigate a labyrinth of circles and radiating one-way streets
that had been all the rage in urban planning back in 1696. Ten
minutes after I pulled the lever, however, with sirens screaming,
they arrived. Seconds after that, a team of paramedics hustled
down the promenade carrying stretchers, bags and boxes of
equipment that I knew wouldn't be needed.

After pointing out the spring house, I rocked back and did
my best to fade into the shrubbery while the paramedics did
what they were trained to do. After a few minutes, I heard a
Nextel crackle to life, a sputtered reply. They were calling it
in to the police.

'Ma'am? Ma'am?' Somebody had noticed me at last. I tried
to focus on the paramedic's face through a veil of tears. He
was young, not more than twenty, and his face was open and
sympathetic. 'Do you know what happened here?'

I heaved a shuddering sigh. 'No. I came out to the garden
to . . . to . . .' What *had* I come out to do? The vision of Alex
lying dead in the spring house was driving everything else out
of my mind. 'I went for a walk,' I managed at last. 'I noticed
a torn up patch of grass outside the spring house, a hat. I was
curious, I looked inside. I tried to help him, but it was too
late.

The young man extended his hand, I grasped it and he pulled

me to my feet. 'You've had a shock. Let's get you into the house. Is there somebody here . . . ?'

'No,' I said, 'I mean, yes. There are at least a dozen of us living here. We've been out today watching the burning of the *Peggy Stewart*.'

'Ah, I know about that,' he said as he escorted me to the promenade, made sure I was steady on my pins, not about to take a nose dive into the boxwood. 'We had our fire boat out there to make sure it didn't get out of control.'

While his colleagues were busy packing up, the young man walked alongside me as we mounted each of the three sets of stairs, catching my elbow once when I stumbled and steadying me, then accompanying me up the long flight that led up to the back porch. Once I was delivered safely inside the house, he seemed to relax. 'Where would you like to sit, Mrs . . . ?'

'Ives. In the parlor, thanks.'

I'd just passed the main staircase when French and Michael rushed through the front door, grave-faced and out of breath. 'My God! What's with all the fire trucks?'

'Parlor,' I said, nodding my head in that direction.

Before I sat down on the loveseat, I pulled aside the parlor drapes and peered out the window. Fire trucks, indeed. In addition to the trucks from West Annapolis, the distinctive red units of the Eastport Volunteers had also responded to my call. I wondered if Paul had noticed all the hullabaloo, too, before remembering that he would be locked up in a meeting at the Academy.

The paramedic's eyes ping-ponged between Michael and French, made an executive decision and took French aside. 'She's had a shock,' he told her in a whisper that could have been heard round the world. 'I think she could use something to drink.'

'Brandy,' I said. Then added quickly, 'Please.'

After French left to fetch the brandy, Michael knelt at my feet like an ardent suitor, rested a hand on my knee. 'Hannah, what's happened?'

I told him.

I watched his face go white. 'How . . .' he began.

I flapped a hand, fresh tears coursing down my cheeks. 'Give me a minute.'

Once French returned with the brandy and he saw that the snifter had been placed in my hand, the paramedic waited until I took a sip, then said, 'I'll be going now, but a detective will be here shortly. He'll want to talk to you – all of you – so I wouldn't go anywhere.'

I nodded dumbly, then took a second more generous sip of brandy, coughed, slapped my chest with the palm of my hand. 'Smooooth,' I croaked.

Michael filled French in, whereupon she burst into tears, which set me off on another crying jag. Michael blinked rapidly, trying to maintain control over his own emotions.

'Where's Amy?' I asked, the brandy burning its way down my esophagus.

Michael answered. 'Last time I saw her, she was with Melody and Gabe, watching a Punch and Judy show on the dock near the Alex Hailey memorial.'

'Jack?'

Michael shrugged. 'Middleton's, I think.'

French wiped her nose on her sleeve. 'Karen took Dex to the memorial, too.' She sniffed so hard that her nostrils slammed shut. 'She was telling him the story of Alex Hailey and how he traced his ancestor, Kunta Kinte, to a slave ship that docked right here in Annapolis. I think Dex was more impressed with the statues, though. He kept posing next to the two little bronze kids as if Hailey was reading to him, too. The tourists were going bonkers.'

'Michael,' I said. 'I'll stay here with French. Will you go outside and wait for the others? Tell them what happened? I don't think I can bear to do it again. When Karen returns, please ask her to make some tea and some sandwiches and bring them up here to the parlor. I have a feeling we'll be needing them. Oh, as they come in, tell everyone else to join us here.'

When the detectives finally appeared, everyone had returned to Patriot House except Amy and the children. Jack Donovan was beside himself with worry and sent Jeffrey out to look for them.

The detective who introduced himself as Lt Pickett was string-bean tall and wore a dark blue business suit. A uniformed officer accompanied him whose sole purpose seemed to be to nod and take notes.

For the third time, I explained how I had happened to find Alex, and it didn't get easier with the telling. 'I tried to help him, Lieutenant, but it was too late.'

Lt Pickett eyed my soiled and torn gown. 'Was there a scuffle?' he asked.

'What?'

'An argument.'

'With me? No. Absolutely not. He was already dead when I got there.'

'And what time would that have been?'

I stared at Lt Pickett's well-tanned face, his bright blue eyes accented by minuscule wrinkles, like tiny cat's whiskers. 'I don't know. I don't have a watch.'

'Will someone please explain what the *hell* is going on here?' It was Jud Wilson, red-faced and wild, barging into the room like his hair was on fire. 'The fire trucks. The goddamn police.' Catching sight of the police officer, he screeched to a halt. 'Uh, sorry, Officer.'

Lt Pickett seemed unflappable. 'One of your, uh, actors, or do you call them cast members . . . ?'

'We prefer cast, actually.'

'One of your cast, a Mr Alex Mueller, was found dead in the spring house this afternoon.'

'Christ on a crutch!'

'If you say so, sir.'

Jud swiped a hand through his hair, paced in the doorway. 'Oh, God. This is terrible.' His eyes swept the room, focused on one of the four chairs set around the card table. He crossed the room and lowered himself into it, wearily, as if he were a hundred years old. In the last minute, his face seemed to age by a decade, too.

'Mrs Ives here found the body. We were just asking her about what time that was.'

I squeezed my eyes shut, trying to hold it together. 'As I *said*, Lieutenant, it was not long after the *Peggy Stewart* celebration was over.' A sudden thought made my eyes fly open. 'Wait a minute! There's a videocam in the entrance hall. You

should be able to tell what time I came in by looking at that.'
I swiveled in my chair to face Jud, looking for confirmation.
'The tapes are time stamped, aren't they?'

Jud stopped chewing on the knuckle of his index finger and
said, 'We'll see to it that you get copies of all the videotapes,
Detective.'

'*All* of them? How many are there?'

'Eight? Nine? We're taping a reality show here, Detective,
so we have pretty broad coverage. You'll see when you get
them.'

'Are there any in the back garden?'

Jud shook his head. 'None outside the house, I'm afraid.
We use handhelds for the outside shots.'

Standing next to the door, the junior officer was scribbling
away when Amy rushed in, Melody and Gabe in her considerable wake. 'Jeffrey came to get us. What's going on?'

I patted the cushion on the loveseat next to me. 'Here. Sit.'

Jack sprang to his feet. 'Let me take the children out of
here.'

Melody clouded up and stamped her foot. 'I am *not* a child!'

Her father glanced at me uncertainly. He was leaving the
decision to me.

'French,' I said, 'would you take Gabe down to the kitchen,
please? He can play with Dex. And for heaven's sake, tell
Karen not to let the boys out into the garden.'

'Yes, ma'am,' French said, actually looking relieved to be
leaving the room.

'Melody, you may sit next to your father.' I gestured with
my head in the direction of the sofa.

When everyone had settled in again, I picked up Amy's left
hand in both of mine and just said it right out. 'Amy, Alex is
dead.'

Amy's eyes grew wide as saucers. 'Dead? How can he be
dead? I just saw him!'

'We don't know, sweetheart. It looks like he fell into the
spring house. Hit his head . . .' I shrugged helplessly.

'Fell?' Amy's face was dangerously red. '*Fell?* No. Nobody'd
fall into the spring house. That's just bullshit.'

Privately, I had to agree.

Across the room from us, Jack stirred. 'What would he be doing out there at this time of day anyway?'

'A reasonable question,' said Lt Pickett. 'Who was the last to see him?' His eyes scanned the room.

Michael raised his hand, waved it like a schoolboy. 'It may have been me. We bought a couple of beers at McGarvey's during the *Peggy Stewart* celebrations. Alex was supposed to be bringing Amy a Sprite, but he got involved in a conversation with some reporter, so I said I'd take the soda to Amy. And I did.'

'Can you describe this reporter you saw talking to Mr Mueller?'

Michael shrugged. 'Black frock coat, three-cornered hat, powdered wig. Impressed me that he was kinda getting into the story, you know? Wait a minute, his ponytail had a little black bag tied to the end of it.'

'A tag?' asked the junior officer.

'B-A-G, bag,' Pickett corrected.

'Ponytail with a bag on it,' muttered the junior officer, his ballpoint pen scratching away. 'I can't believe I'm writing this.'

'Do you know what the two were talking about?'

With a nervous glance at Jud, Michael said, 'Not really. Because of our contracts, we're not supposed to be giving interviews, so I split.'

I raised a hand. 'I saw Alex, too, Detective. But whoever he was talking to had just left.' I swiveled on the loveseat to face Michael. 'Michael, how do you know it was a reporter? Alex told *me* the guy was a tourist from Raleigh.'

Michael scowled. 'If he was a tourist, then I'm a prima ballerina.'

So, Alex had lied to me. That stung. I stole a quick glance at Amy, but Detective Pickett drew me back to the matter at hand. 'What happened next, Mrs Ives?'

'We walked for a bit, then we ran into my husband. I didn't see where Alex went after that.'

'What happens now, Detective?' Jud wanted to know.

'As soon as we finish processing the scene, we'll be transporting the body up to the medical examiner in Baltimore for autopsy.'

Next to me, Amy gasped.

Lt Pickett addressed her directly, his voice gentle. 'It will help us find out what killed him, Miss. Whether it was an accident, or . . . or, something else.'

'Accident, had to have been an accident,' Michael said. 'Who would want to hurt Alex? He was one of the nice guys, you know?'

Jud frowned. 'What impact will this have on the continuation of our show?'

'Until we get the autopsy results, which, barring complications, should be in a couple of days, I must ask that nobody leaves town.'

Amy's giggle had a manic edge. 'That's a laugh! We're stuck here for the duration anyway, right?'

'From a policeman's point of view, it's awfully convenient having all of you together in the same house,' Pickett admitted. 'Like one of those Agatha Christie novels where everyone's snowbound at Chipping Monktip for the weekend.'

Melody, who had been staring at a spot on the wall, sitting bolt upright with her hands folded demurely in her lap, suddenly roused herself. 'All of the suspects are right here in this room,' she intoned.

Jack gave me a look – see, I told you the children shouldn't be here – and I gave him one right back. Chill out, Jack.

'That's what always happens on *Masterpiece Mystery*,' Melody forged on, unchallenged. 'Hercule Poirot comes into the room *et voilà!*' She pursed her lips, furrowed her brow. 'Eet iz zee brain, zee liddle gray cells, on which one must rely.' What *we* need, is Hercule Poirot.' She favored us with an elaborate sigh. 'But he's a fictional character.'

Amy and I exchanged glances.

Both she and I knew that one of the suspects was *not* in the room, and he was far from fictional.

# TWENTY-ONE

*'What's two-penny worth of yeast, anyway? A teaspoon?*
*A cup? Then it says to beat for three-quarters of an hour.*
*No wonder they needed slaves.'*

French Fry, housemaid

Two nights later, with the table set, candles lit and the food laid out for dinner, Jack summoned the family and all the staff to the dining room.

With a face like Mount Rushmore, he cleared his throat several times, then said, 'I have an announcement to make. Founding Father has just notified me that according to the medical examiner, our dear friend, Alex Mueller, died of a broken neck as the result of a fall. His death has been ruled accidental. Let us pray.'

Almost without taking a breath, Jack launched into a rambling grace that touched on food, death, the souls of men (and women) and the downtrodden people of the third world. While the food on the platters cooled, and Jack showed no sign of winding down, I dared to raise my head and look at Amy. She stood by the buffet, hands folded in front of her – even in the candlelight I could see that her knuckles were white. Her mouth was a thin line, and she was shaking her head and mouthing, 'No, no, no, no.'

Late that night, Amy came to me in my chamber. 'Would you like me to brush your hair?'

'Oh, yes.' I threw back the covers, slid out of bed and sat in the chair in front of the vanity table. 'I'd give anything for some Pantene,' I mused as she came up behind me and started brushing the tangles out of my hair. 'One of those itty-bitty bottles of shampoo you get in hotels. Is that too much to ask?'

'You and me both. From the Waldorf-Astoria or Holiday Inn, wouldn't matter. My hair is so stiff from that bar soap we made that it looks like I'm wearing a helmet. Karen says I should try rinsing it with vinegar.'

'Phew!' I said.

Amy brushed in silence for a while. 'Your husband works at the Naval Academy, right?'

'Uh huh.' I was enjoying the gentle massage of the bristles against my scalp.

'Drew murdered Alex, I *know* he did.'

'The medical examiner determined that it was an accident, Amy.'

'I don't believe that any more than you do, Hannah.'

'You're right, I don't. I think it's *possible* that Alex broke his neck in a fall, but not very probable.' I twisted around in my chair. 'What is Drew's motive, Amy?' When I saw the expression on Amy's face, I froze. 'Did he know about you and Alex?'

Amy blushed. 'Alex has been visiting my room at night. If Drew has been watching the house . . .' Her voice trailed off.

'That sounds like motive to me.'

'So, how can we *prove* it?'

'That's the hard part,' I said. 'Drew is a phantom. And, according to the government, which we all know is infallible, Drew Cornell doesn't even exist.'

The brush stopped. 'Do you think *I'm* in danger?'

'No, I don't. Drew needs you to collect the insurance money for him. He believes you'll join him after that happens, no matter what. You are essential to his plan.' I waved a hand. 'Brush!'

'One thing I wonder about,' I said after a bit. 'Why didn't Drew contact you sooner? Even third world countries have cell phones and Internet cafes.'

'I had my cell number changed after the break-in. My email account was hacked, and my Facebook page was hijacked so badly that I couldn't even log on. I had to set up new ones.' The brush stopped. 'Then I came here, so it took Drew a while to track me down. Otherwise?' In the mirror, I saw her shrug. 'Maybe he was afraid my phone would be tapped. Maybe he thought I was being watched and I wouldn't act like a proper widow if I knew he was actually alive?'

'You asked me about Paul. How can he help?'

'He has friends in high places?'

I laughed. 'High military places? I suppose he does. Midshipmen who Paul used to teach are now captains, and I think there's even one vice admiral among his former students.' My eyes locked on to hers in the reflection in the mirror. 'I could tell Paul that Drew is alive, sure, and he could pass that information on to the Navy brass, but that wouldn't *prove* anything.'

'I don't care. We can't let him get away with it. I know he murdered Alex just as sure as I'm standing here brushing your hair.'

'But you *aren't* brushing,' I reminded her gently.

'Right.' She began again, slowly, rhythmically. 'I wasn't in love with Alex,' she reflected, 'but he was in love with me. I told him how I felt, and he was OK with it, really. I think he thought I'd come around eventually, and he may have been right. But it was just too soon after Drew to get into another serious relationship, you know?'

'I know. If something happened to Paul . . . Gosh, breaking in one husband is hard enough. I don't understand how women like Elizabeth Taylor and Zsa-Zsa Gabor managed it. After they talk me off the railing of the high span of the Chesapeake Bay Bridge, I'd probably just sell up and move to a cottage in the south of France.'

'No you wouldn't, Hannah.'

'No?'

'Your daughter? The grandchildren? How about them?'

'You have a point.' I laughed. 'Look, I have an idea. What we need is to snatch off his cloak of invisibility, draw Drew out. What would make him show himself?'

'Jealousy. If Drew killed Alex, it was because he was jealous.'

'We have to assume that Drew is still watching us,' I said.

'That gives me the heebie jeebies, Hannah.'

'I'm not comfortable with it either. So, under that assumption, let's make him jealous. Get somebody to come on to you.'

'But that could be dangerous, especially for the object of my so-called affection.'

'That's where the people Paul knows might come in handy.'

I thought for a moment while Amy brushed. 'If Drew *is* watching you, I'll bet he'll turn up at the State House Ball. It's the next time that we'll all be outside Patriot House and it'll be a mob scene. He could easily sneak in, just like he did at the burning of the *Peggy Stewart*, if we assume, like I do, that the so-called reporter Alex was talking to was actually Drew.'

'We'll need help, Hannah. I'm certainly not going to flirt with *you*!' She laughed, genuinely amused. 'That would push Drew over the edge for sure! SEAL's wife throws him over for another woman.'

'It probably wouldn't be the first time,' I observed ruefully. 'OK, it's decided. In the meantime, then, it's business as usual. Let me get a note out to Paul. I'll try to talk to him. See what he can do.'

'A note to Paul? How will you arrange that?'

I put a finger to my lips. 'Need to know, Amy. Need to know.'

# TWENTY-TWO

*'I had to help the cook pluck a chicken today. When this is all over, I think I'm going to become a vegetarian.'*
French Fry, housemaid

'**M**elody,' I said as we strolled through the rose garden one morning after breakfast, cutting flowers we planned to arrange in the vase on the entrance hall table. 'I need you to run an errand for me.'

Melody snipped off a white damask rose and laid it gently in her basket. 'As long as it doesn't involve Gabe, I'll consider it.'

'I'm sending you to the market with Karen today. You'll be purchasing a roast for Sunday dinner, and anything else that Karen thinks we might need.'

Melody's face lit up. 'I'd adore that. But, how come you aren't going?'

'Founding Father sent me an invitation to tea at Hammond-Harwood House this afternoon. No way I can get out of it.' I reached into my pocket and pulled out the note I had written to Paul using a leaf I'd torn out of the little blue notebook he'd given me. I pressed the note into her hand. 'This is for my husband. Please leave it with Kyle or with Corey at the Maryland Table concession. They may have a packet for you, too.'

'But isn't that, like, cheating?' Melody asked. With a furtive glance over her shoulder at the hulk of Paca House looming behind us, she accepted the note and tucked it quickly into her own pocket, a willing accomplice.

'Technically, it is. But I'm hoping that this will be our little secret.' I touched her arm. 'Thank you, Melody. And whatever is in the packet they give you? It's yours to keep.'

Her eyes widened, she beamed. 'Awesome.'

I cleaned up for the tea party as best I could, scrubbing my face and neck with soap and warm water, and paying particular attention to my underarms. My Savannah-born grandmother had often said, 'Hannah, honey, horses sweat, men perspire, but women glow.' After the fever, the exertion and the tension of the previous weeks, I had done more than glow; I sweated buckets. One of my gowns was so ripe, in fact, that I was certain it could walk out of the room and down to the laundry tub quite of its own accord.

For the occasion, I chose one of the few remaining everyday gowns in my wardrobe, a yellow silk with green lace trim that had probably looked smashing on Katherine Donovan but only made my skin look sallow, more tired and drained than I already was. I was a winter; yellow didn't appear anywhere on my color palate.

Through my fund-raising work for breast cancer research, I was already acquainted with the hostess, Mrs Sandra Bordley-Bowen, a local realtor who could trace her ancestry directly back to Stephen Bordley, the eighteenth-century Maryland attorney general, and rarely missed an opportunity to interject that historical fact into any conversation.

When I arrived at the Hammond-Harwood House, an Anglo-Palladian villa built in 1774 by renowned architect William Buckland, Chad the Cameraman took some time to capture the impeccable front door, then ducked in ahead of me the better to record my grand entrance for posterity. A liveried servant took my cloak, and I was shown to the upstairs ball-room where two pianists, a man and a woman, sat at the pianoforte, and were just beginning to play the second move-ment of a Mozart sonata for four hands.

Mrs Bordley-Bowen's lips drew away from her laser-white, predatory teeth in what passed for a smile in the over-botoxed set and gushed, 'Mrs Ives. Delighted you could join us today. May I introduce you to the others?'

'Of course.' I scanned the audience and realized that I already knew most of the others, a half-dozen women from Mrs Bordley-Brown's book club, dressed, like her, in colonial costumes, mob caps perched precariously (and ridiculously) atop their freeze-dried hairdos. Shallow women, these, whose conversations ran the gamut from A to B, as Dorothy Parker famously said, and read Oprah books almost exclusively, depressing novels where life sucks, things get worse, and everybody dies. I didn't like these women any better now than I would have nearly two and a half centuries ago. Nevertheless I gathered my skirts around me, sat, folded my hands demurely in my lap and prepared to enjoy the music.

The event turned out to be more of a soiree than a tea. There were sandwiches and sweets, of course, and the inevitable ceremonial pouring of the tea. At the end of the Rondo, one of the pianists retired to a Chippendale armchair, and a soprano took her place, treating us to some delightful solos from the ballad operas of Thomas Arne and William Boyce. Following the musicale, when the pianists were finally allowed some refreshment, Mrs B Hyphen B divided us up into two groups with a cheery, 'It's time for whist!'

After the card games began, I could no longer avoid their questions about the terrible accident at Patriot House, and how I felt about it.

We had no access to modern-day newspapers at Patriot House, of course, but I quickly learned from the ladies that Alex's death had been in all the papers. Fortunately, neither *The Capital* nor *The Baltimore Sun* had mentioned exactly who had found Alex Mueller's body, so I could smile wanly, claim shock, and suggest that with time, I might possibly get over it, which was the honest truth.

The sun was low in the sky before I could politely excuse myself, send for my cloak, and hurry home to Patriot House, just two blocks away, with Chad hot on my heels. If Melody had done her part, I would have an appointment with Paul at the back wall, and I didn't want to miss it. But first, I'd have to ditch Chad.

I paused at the Paca House gate. 'Don't you have a place to go home to?' I inquired sweetly.

'Yes, ma'am,' he drawled, 'and as soon as I lock this camera up, I'm going there.'

At that time of year, the sun set around seven o'clock, but it wasn't well and truly dark until seven thirty. I waited in my room until the long case clock chimed the half hour, then threw my dark cloak over my neon-yellow dress. I entered the garden through the kitchen, skirted the flower and holly parterres by way of the green houses, scampered as quickly over the footbridge as possible before melding into the darkness of the wilderness plantings along the back wall.

Paul was waiting for me. Through the vertical slit in the wall, we touched hands. 'I feel like I'm in the visiting room at the Maryland state penitentiary,' he said as his fingers met mine.

'It feels that way to me, too.'

'I got your message,' Paul said, cutting to the chase. 'What's going on?'

'I have a job for you, and I think it might be dangerous.'

'Yes?'

'At the State House Ball? I want you to seduce Amy . . .'

'What?' he sputtered before I even had time to finish the sentence. 'Are you completely out of your mind?'

I squeezed his hand. 'Sorry, let me rephrase that. I want it to *appear* as if you've got a thing going with Amy.'

'And that's different, how?'

'She will know you don't mean it, for one thing. What's even more important, so will I.'

'Hannah, I've gone along with some of your hare-brained schemes before, but this one really takes the cake. No. My answer is No. N, O. No.

'Amy and I have talked it over, Paul, and it's the only way we can think of to draw Drew out of hiding, make him show himself. He'll be at the ball, we feel certain of that.'

'And suppose I agree?'

'I'm going to pretend to be outraged, of course. I'm an old hag, tired and worn out. You're the elder statesman, virile, devastatingly attractive.'

'What bullshit. Never mind. What does this Drew person look like?'

'Longish hair, bleached white. Otherwise, I don't know. Amy had pictures of him on her iPhone, but they disappeared along with the phone. Her Facebook account was hijacked, so the photos on her wall are inaccessible, too. There may be photographs on the Internet, but I doubt it. Drew was, *is* a

SEAL, after all. People in covert ops don't generally post their mug shots all over cyberspace. Do you have any buddies who can pull something out of the official records?'

'I'm not sure I have any buddies who are *that* good, but I'll try.'

I rested my forehead against the bricks, still radiating heat from the sun. In spite of their warmth, a sudden chill crept over me. I shivered. 'I feel like someone's watching us.' I kept my voice low. 'Look over my shoulder, Paul. Do you see anything?'

'Where?'

'Anywhere!' I said impatiently. Cautiously, I turned, straining my ears, listening for the rustle of a bush, the snap of a twig, looking for the sudden flick of a curtain in the window of one of the condos in the building next door.

Paul squeezed my fingers. 'You're letting your imagination run away with you, sweetheart.'

Again, I shivered. 'I know that Drew's out there somewhere, watching, always watching. It gives me the creeps.'

'Do you think he's going to rise up out of the fish pond wearing a ghillie suit?' In the gathering dark, I couldn't see my husband's face, but I could tell from his voice that he was smiling.

'Did you get my note?' he asked, steering the conversation away from disgruntled SEALs who may or may not be hiding among the bulrushes, dressed like Sasquatch.

'What note?'

'The one I left in the bottle.'

I pressed a hand to my mouth. 'Oh my gosh! I totally forgot. I'd just picked it up and was heading back to the house when I found Alex . . .' I took a deep breath. 'It's been sitting in my pocket all this time. I'm so sorry, Paul.'

'Never mind. It wasn't all that special anyway.'

'I'm sure I'll treasure it,' I said. 'Once I have enough light to read it by.' I leaned closer to the opening in the wall. 'Guess I better be going in.'

His fingers found mine. 'I guess. See you at the ball?'

'At the ball, then.'

'And Hannah?'

'What?'

'I'm bringing back-up.'

I smiled. 'That's what I hoped you'd say.'

Back in my bedroom, I lit the candle on my bedside table, then fished the little bottle out of my pocket. Using the tweezers that Amy had managed to scrounge up for me, I teased Paul's note out of the narrow mouth, dropped the note onto the table, then smoothed it out and read, not the silly poem I expected but this:

*Can't wait to see you at the ball, Mrs Ives. Something tells me you'll be needing a date.*

It wasn't Paul's handwriting.

That night, I crept out to the summer house, let myself in, and gave the diary cam a piece of my mind.

*Jud! Listen up. This is important. Amy's husband isn't dead. You hear me? Drew Cornell is alive, he wants Amy all to himself, and he's not going to let anything stand in his way. I'm convinced he murdered Alex Mueller. Did you get that? He murdered Alex! Now he's sent me a note saying he's planning to crash the ball. It's a long story, but I'm worried that he's going to harm my husband. You've got to get your security team on Drew right away. If anything happens to my husband, I swear to God, money or no money, I'm going to walk. Got it?*

# TWENTY-THREE

*'I've got this recipe for battalia pie, and it calls for . . .*
*hold on a minute while I find the page . . . sheep's tongues*
*and shivered palates, two pair of lamb's stones, twenty*
*to thirty cockscombs, with savory balls and oysters. Lay*
*on butter, it says, and close the pie with a lear. Jesus,*
*where's Wikipedia when I need it?'*

Karen Gibbs, cook

D ressing for the ball would have been exciting in any case, but in anticipation of what might happen if Drew made his promised appearance kept my nerves – and Amy's – on edge.

I wanted to get a message out to Paul, but leaving it in the bottle was out – Drew would be on the lookout for that – and with preparations for the ball occupying all our time, I had no opportunity (or good excuse!) to sneak out to the Market House.

'Relax, Hannah,' Amy said as she handed me my petticoat. 'Jud's security people will take care of everything. Nothing bad is going to happen to Paul.'

'I hope you're right,' I said, stepping into the garment and tying it securely around my waist.

'Of course I'm right. In a few hours you'll be dancing the night away, your husband on your arm.'

I was still fretting when Melody entered the room, but for the young teen's benefit, Amy and I pretended everything was normal. Amy helped us both dress and we, in turn, assisted her. After I'd donned my gown and all its associated paraphernalia, only one thing remained – my wig. It had been professionally dressed for the occasion with ribbons and papier-mâché birds. 'It looks like the birds have nested in my wig,' I giggled as I settled it on my head, tucked stray strands of my own hair in with my fingers.

'Cool beans, Mrs Ives. Mine just has flowers,' Melody

complained as she sidled up close to me so we could both share the mirror.

'As befits a maiden,' I said, adjusting one of my birds, a canary, that seemed to be perched on one leg. 'It's birds in my belfry, at least, and not bats, although my husband might beg to differ.'

The gown that Mrs Hamilton had designed for me, based on a Paris original circa 1773, was exquisite. Made of heavy white brocade, it had an elaborately quilted petticoat and matching slippers, all trimmed with gold ribbon and Swarovski crystals. I looked like a superannuated ice maiden.

Melody wore a coral gown in a similar design. My descent into the spring house to look after Alex had ruined the blue gown I'd planned to loan Amy, so Melody and I were lacing her into my blue ruffled gown instead.

I extracted one of the birds, a robin, from the aviary I carried on my head and stuck it into Amy's wig, adjusting it so that it seemed to be peeking out of a curl just over her left ear. 'There, perfect!' And indeed she was. In that gown, and with that flawless face, Amy would send any colonial swain into a deep swoon.

I hoped Paul was immune.

I dusted a little more powder around my shoulders and puffed some into my cleavage. 'Done!'

At four o'clock, the appointed hour, Jeffrey rang a bell summoning us to the entrance hall. All day, I'd been hoping for a message from Founding Father, informing me that Drew Cornell had been found. At first I thought the bell might be heralding a courier, but no. It simply announced that our coach was waiting outside the gate. Amy, Michael and French would have to walk the two short blocks to the State House, but Jack Donovan's socially-prominent family would be transported in style. The other servants – Karen, Dex and Jeffrey – would not be attending the ball at all. Bonfires had been built on the back campus of nearby St John's College for all the slaves, indentured servants and other 'lower classes' where food and an unlimited supply of punch would be provided both before and after a colorful fireworks display.

Our beautiful coach, Jack Donovan informed me as he

escorted me down the walk, had been modeled on one Robert Carter had imported from London for Nomini Hall in 1774. On loan from Colonial Williamsburg, the coach had a black roof, while the doors were painted pea green. It rode on four golden wheels, the rear wheels considerably bigger than the front, and was driven by a liveried groom who sat atop the left hand horse, one of a pair of gorgeous grays. Mist filled my eyes, and I had to blink it away. I was walking into an Arthur Rackham illustration.

As I leaned down to gather up my skirts before climbing into the coach, Jack's eyes drifted to my cleavage.

I was tempted to smack him once upside the head. *Shove those eyes back in your head, buster. These boobs, such as they are, are already spoken for,* but I gritted my teeth, forced a smile, slipped my gloved hand into his, and stepped up into the coach.

Melody scooted in beside me, bouncing on the leather seat. 'This is totally awesome!'

'Awe-some,' echoed her brother.

Jack had one foot on the step and was about to launch himself into the coach when he suddenly reversed direction, planting both silver-buckled shoes firmly on the curb. 'What the hell?'

I stuck my head out the coach window. A rider on horseback was clattering down Prince George Street, heading our way, hell bent for leather. When he reached the coach, the rider pulled his mount up short and leaped from the saddle, leaving the reins to dangle in the dust on the pavement. 'A message for Mrs Ives,' he panted.

'I'll take that.' Jack reached into his waistcoat pocket and pulled out a coin. 'Thank you,' he said, and handed the coin to the breathless messenger who pocketed it, remounted, and rode away at a more leisurely pace.

I climbed over Melody's voluminous skirts and scrambled out of the coach. 'May I have it, sir?'

Jack turned the message over in his hand, studying it curiously. 'It's from Founding Father,' he informed me unnecessarily. I could tell that from the distinctive red seal.

I extended my hand, and Jack laid the message on it. Without hesitation, I tore open the seal and read, 'Drew Cornell taken into custody outside your home. No harm done.' The note was signed simply, 'Jud.'

Hand pressed to my chest to calm my racing heart, I took a deep breath.

'Is everything all right, madam?' Jack inquired with a look of genuine concern.

I folded the note, tucked it into my pocket and smiled. 'Everything is fine, Mr Donovan.' I offered him my hand. 'Shall we proceed to the ball?'

Back inside the carriage, sitting next to Jack and opposite Melody and Gabe, I relaxed against the cushions as the horses clip-clopped up Prince George Street and turned right on Maryland Avenue, heading straight for the State House. As we approached our destination, I noticed that LynxE had provided coaches for some of the other VIPs, too. One after another, the horses clattered around the circle, drew to a halt at the foot of the State House's steep stone staircase, and disgorged their opulently attired passengers. Shortly after we alighted, a golden chariot pulled up carrying the superintendant of the Naval Academy. While the uniformed driver controlled the horses, a footman hopped off the rear to assist the Admiral and his wife. An open landau arrived next, then a small, two-seater chaise. It was a regular *Who's Who* of eighteenth-century modes of transportation, including guests arriving on horseback and on foot.

'Did all the carriages come from Colonial Williamsburg?' I asked Jack as I rested my hand on his forearm and we climbed the staircase that led into the building.

'So they tell me.'

I'd been to the State House on several occasions, but for my companions, who had come to Annapolis from out of town, it was a revelation. 'Ooooh,' said Melody when we stepped into the great hall. Tall columns lined both sides of the shotgun-style hall, and the geometric arrangement of black and white tiles accentuated its length.

'We're in the rotunda,' I told her. 'Look up.'

Steadying our wigs, we gazed up into the dome, still brightly lit by the sun, where a replica of the flag of the Continental Congress was draped.

'Madam?' A liveried slave held his hand out for my cloak. I untied it, and while Jack was lifting it off my shoulders, I moved further into the hall.

The music had already begun, but I couldn't see the musicians. 'Harpsichord, violin and flute, I think, don't you, Jack?' But he had already taken off with Gabe, joining a group of gentleman standing on the side of the hall near the grand staircase over which hung, I knew, the famous portrait of George Washington resigning his commission as commander-in-chief of the Contenental Army, back when Annapolis had actually been the capitol of the United States of America.

Melody executed a pirouette, taking in the view. She pointed. 'Oh, look! The musicians are sitting up in the balcony.' Gliding, as if on wheels, she drifted toward the room immediately on our right where a sumptuous banquet had been prepared.

Formerly the Old Senate Chamber where George Washington had actually resigned that December day in 1783, the room – painted a violent shade of blue – had been undergoing restoration. For the event, construction had been temporarily halted and the room furnished with three long tables, covered with white linen, literally sagging under the weight of an enormous variety of 'cold collations,' including oysters on the half shell, sliced meats of every variety, whole fish, pickled eggs, breads, dumplings, cakes and pies, as well as several dozen dishes that I didn't recognize, at least not from a distance.

Taking pride of place on a raised platform on the other side of the room sat something much more recognizable: a punch bowl, nestled amid a sea of short, squat glasses.

Candelabra stood everywhere: some illuminating the tables; others, tall as coat trees, lined both walls of the hall that would serve as the ballroom for the evening. As we wandered down its length, nodding and smiling at other guests, two slaves appeared with long-necked candle lighters, touching the flame to each of the wicks, even though sunset was well over an hour away.

'This is like a high school dance, isn't it?' Melody observed as I was poking my nose into a room to our left, which had been set up with a half-dozen card tables.

'What do you mean?'

'Girls on one side of the room, boys on the other. How lame.' She rose on tiptoe, waved. 'Look, there's Amy!'

I motioned for Amy to join us. I opened my mouth to tell her what I'd learned from Jud about Drew, but just then, the dancing began and the opportunity passed. A dozen couples took to the floor, and to the strains of Bach's Minuet in G, bowed to the audience and to each other, and began the elegant dance.

The rest of the audience – women on one side and men on the other as Melody had pointed out – simply observed, commenting from time to time on the performance of the dancers as if it were an Olympic event: 'Ooops, she slipped up there. Should have been a right hand turn,' or, 'Who taught him to dance? The football coach?'

As we watched, slaves began making rounds with trays of punch. Amy took a glass when it was offered to her, and I was considering reaching for one, too, when Jack suddenly materialized at my side and snagged one for me as the slave cruised by. He held up a finger to the man – wait! – and snagged a second glass for himself.

'May I have one, too, Papa?' Melody asked with a smile to melt the coldest heart.

Jack considered his daughter, no doubt taking in the dress, the wig, the makeup and the undeniable fact that his little girl was nearly a woman, and handed Melody his glass. When the slave came around again, he got another for himself.

We remained on the sidelines, sipping, watching the dancing, and all the time I was thinking, where the hell is Paul? In the meantime, I couldn't seem to get rid of Jack.

Out on the floor, the dancers took a final bow and drifted off the dance floor, the ladies fanning themselves, the men wiping their brows with lace handkerchiefs, although I couldn't imagine what had been so strenuous about the leisurely dance they had just performed. Almost immediately, another minuet began and Jack asked me to dance. I couldn't graciously refuse, so I nodded, took his hand, and let him lead me out onto the floor, smiling at me all the way in a proprietary way that gave me the willies.

We bowed to the audience and to each other, traced a

Z-pattern on the floor, touched hands, and circled around as Alex had taught us. Jack's face was flushed, as usual, his brow beaded with sweat.

*Paul! I need you!* I longed for my husband to approach, tap Jack on the shoulder and say, 'Excuse me, may I cut in?' but that kind of dance etiquette wasn't invented until the middle of the First World War, so I was out of luck.

At the end of the dance, we bowed to each other and to the audience, then Jack escorted me back to the sidelines where Amy had been watching. 'Not bad, Jack,' Amy said, then clapped her hand to her mouth. 'Sorry, sir.'

'Whew!' I said, snapping open my fan and putting it to good use. 'Who knew a minuet could be so strenuous?' I didn't want Jack to think I was ready for another spin around the floor. Fanning furiously, I looked around for the children. 'Where's Melody? And Gabe?'

Amy pointed with the tip of her fan. Standing with Melody on the sidelines on the other side of the dance floor was a youth I recognized as one of the homeschoolers that augmented Michael's classes at Patriot House. Judging from the hot-eyed looks the teens were exchanging, and the redness of the boy's ears, I thought that Cowboy Tim back in Texas might well be history.

'What's that young man's name?' I asked her.

'That's Jason.'

'Nice lad.' Jack drew himself to attention, pointed out one of his cronies from Middleton Tavern and said, 'Excuse me, Mrs Ives, but I see someone I need to talk to.'

I couldn't imagine what they had to discuss – it was all make-believe, wasn't it? – but I was glad to get rid of him for the moment. Besides, in spite of the reassuring message from Jud, I was getting really worried about Paul. Had something gone wrong?

'Have you seen my husband, Amy?'

'Hannah, I have never met your husband.'

I felt my face redden. 'Of course you haven't. Well, if you see a handsome, elderly-statesman type wandering around looking lost, that's probably Paul. In the meantime, I'm going to take a look around.'

'Don't worry about me, Hannah. Michael and French arrived a few minutes ago. I think they're exploring the card room, so I'll catch up with them there.'

I began my search in the banquet room, selecting a few olives from a bowl on the table, popping them into my mouth, and then wondering what I was going to do with the pits. I began looking around for a receptacle. Sitting in the far corner of the room, almost invisible in the gloom and partially hidden by a curtain, I nearly stumbled over Gabe, head bowed, his knees pulled up to his chest.

'Gabe! What are you doing hiding over there?'

'Why can't I go to the bonfire with Dex?' he whined. 'This place is booooring!'

'As your father probably explained, it's because you are a young gentleman, and Dex is supposed to be a slave boy. Slave boys didn't get to come to dances, unless they were working.'

His lower lip quivered, but he held himself together. 'That totally sucks.'

'I totally agree with you, Gabriel, but that's the way it was back then.'

Gabe had something in his hand. As I drew closer, he tucked it behind his back.

'What do you have there, Gabe?'

His eyes were wide, innocent. 'Nothing.'

'Nothing?'

He stared at me in silence.

I held out my hand. 'Let me see.'

Reluctantly, with exaggerated slowness, Gabe drew out his hand. 'It's an iPod Touch,' he told me. 'I'm playing Angry Birds.'

An iPod. The little devil. 'I thought you turned your iPod in?'

'I did, Mrs Ives, honest. I found this one.'

'You found it? Where did you find it?'

'In a china pot in your room. When you were sick? Remember?'

Truthfully, except for extended conversations with long-dead French philosophers, I had very little recollection of what happened during my extended bout with the dreaded H3N2 virus. I held out my hand. 'Give it to me, please.'

Gabe sucked in his lips, but handed the instrument over. I pushed the button to exit his game and return to the main screen, then turned the phone in his direction. 'What does this say, Gabriel?'

'Amy's iPhone.'

'Exactly. So it isn't an iPod Touch, is it?'

'No, ma'am.'

'And it isn't yours.'

A single tear slid down the boy's cheek. He shook his head.

'Then, why do *you* have it?' I asked, pocketing the phone.

'I kept it because I wanted to talk to my mom, but when I put her number in, it didn't work.' He swiped at his cheek with the back of his hand. 'She writes me letters, but I really, really miss her.'

'Oh, Gabe!' I coaxed the boy to his feet and crushed him against my petticoats. 'I know how hard it must be for you.' I tipped his chin so I could look into his eyes. 'But it wasn't right to take Amy's phone.'

He nodded miserably.

After a moment, I tousled his hair, then marched him back into the ballroom. Although it wasn't the done thing, 1774-wise, I considered turning the boy over to his father for a good tongue-lashing, but fortunately, I spotted several youngsters about Gabe's age clustered at the fringes of the ballroom, attempting to dance but making it look more like a scuffle. 'There are some kids your age, now scoot!' I gave him a whack on the butt to send him on his way.

I rejoined my friends, lined up casually along the wall back where I had left them. I was planning to hand the iPhone back to Amy, but just then, we were joined by Admiral Michael Miller, the Naval Academy superintendent, his ginger hair covered by a powdered wig. Trim, and ramrod straight, Miller wore the uniform of a Continental Admiral of the Revolutionary War which was surprisingly similar to the Navy dinner dress uniform of today – white breeches topped by a dark blue dress coat with tails and a double row of brass buttons marching down the front. The heavily-fringed gold epaulets that decorated his shoulders were a thing of the past, however. The admiral's wife wore a gown of Prussian blue, with tiny yellow bows decorating the sleeves and bodice. Miniature dolphins frolicked through her powdered curls. I had to admire it. 'Navy colors, I see. Blue and gold. I like it! Especially the dolphins.' I pointed at my own elaborate coiffure. 'My theme is birds, as you probably guessed.'

'Where's the good professor?' Admiral Miller wanted to know.

'He should have been here a half-hour ago,' I said. 'Frankly, I'm getting a little worried.'

Mrs Miller touched my arm. 'I'm sure he'll turn up,' she said. 'They've closed downtown streets to vehicles, so traffic has been simply horrendous!'

I didn't point out to her that we lived just two blocks away, so traffic shouldn't have been an issue, but it was just like Paul to get tied up somewhere, with a midshipman needing advice, for example. I fingered Jud's note for reassurance.

Meanwhile, the musicians had moved on to a reel. Melody's friend, Jason, came to fetch her, and when the young couple began dancing, I couldn't take my eyes off her, and neither could anyone else in the room. 'Oh, Alex, you taught that girl well,' I whispered to our dead friend's spirit. 'She is truly the belle of the ball.'

Next to me, Amy said, 'Just listening to that music makes me miss Alex terribly.'

'We all miss him,' Michael said.

After a while, I asked, 'What happened to Alex's violin?'

'Jud packed up all his stuff,' Michael said. 'Sent it home to Alex's parents. We'll miss the funeral service, you know.' He shook his head. 'Doesn't seem right somehow.'

The reel ended, Melody and Jason strolled away to the banquet room. Another reel was announced, and I'd just decided to try and hook up with another glass of punch when a familiar voice said, 'Madam, may I have this dance?'

I pressed a hand to my chest, light-headed with relief. 'Sir, I would be delighted.'

I almost didn't recognize him. I had been expecting the green costume he'd been wearing at our last outing, but Paul

wore a cobalt-blue suit and a gold brocade weskit instead.
Lace spilled out of the ends of his sleeves and over his collar.
His wig was different, too. The silver hair was swept back,
high off his forehead. Two enormous curls, the size of orange
juice cans, trembled over each ear.

'I was *so* worried that something had happened to you!' I
blurted out.

'Not to worry,' Paul said smoothly. 'You got the message
from Jud? That Drew Cornell is in custody?'

I fell back against the wall. 'Yes, thank God! Where did it
happen?'

Paul leaned close. 'Jud's security people picked him up in
Brad Perry's backyard earlier this afternoon. They're not sure
what his plans were.'

Brad Perry is our next-door neighbor. That was way too
close for comfort. 'What happens now?'

'He's being turned over to Navy custody as we speak.'

'I should tell Amy.'

Paul reached for my hand. 'That can wait.' He escorted me
onto the dance floor, my legs feeling as limp as cooked
spaghetti.

We took our place at the head of the line.

*Four steps forward, bow.* 'So, which actor is running around
naked tonight?' I asked in an attempt to lighten the mood.
*Four steps back.*

*Four steps forward, join right hands, turn, turn.* 'Sir Peter
Teazle. That's why I was late. I couldn't find the mid with the
key to the costume room.' *Four steps back.*

*Four steps forward, join both hands, turn, turn.* 'I didn't
really think Cornell would try anything here in a room full
of people, anyway.' Paul sounded confident, but then he didn't
know Drew as well as Amy – and I – did.' *Four steps back.*

It was a fragmented conversation, but between the do-see-
dos, allemande left and rights, and the promenades, I explained
about the note Drew had left in the bottle. 'I wanted to warn
you, call off our plan before somebody got hurt.'

Paul laughed. 'Why do you think I spent all these years
practicing karate?'

'Karate? Ha! Drew's a SEAL. He probably knows Krav

Maga,' I said, naming the terrifying, no-holds barred method of self-defense developed by the Israelis.

The music ended, and Paul escorted me back to where Amy was standing alone, looking around nervously. I introduced her to my husband.

Paul took her hand, raised it to his lips and gave it a gallant kiss. 'Delighted.' He gave Amy the good news/bad news about Drew, and I watched as the tension gradually drained from her face.

'What now?' she asked.

'It's time to enjoy the ball, Miss Cornell.'

'They can't let Drew get away with murdering Alex, Professor. No matter what the medical examiner says, I know he did it.'

Paul tucked Amy's hand under his arm, covered it with his own. 'And there's something else they're going to take into consideration, Amy. Drew's unauthorized action in Swosa may have resulted in the deaths of his ten teammates, plus a well-trained dog named Cody.'

'A dog, too?' Amy blinked back tears.

The music had started again. 'Shall we dance?' my husband asked his young companion, and before she even answered, he whisked Amy away.

I watched from the sidelines.

For the first reel, Paul flirted, Amy was coy. By the second, Paul held on to Amy's hand just a second too long; Amy was a coquette. They called a country dance, and by then, Amy was behaving like a card-carrying colonial vamp and I had found a chair, where I seethed quietly. Paul was a damn good actor, but then, he was wearing actor's clothing.

'Whew!' Amy trilled when the music finally ended, loud enough for me – and for everyone within a ten mile radius – to hear. 'I could certainly use a drink, Professor Ives.'

Paul bowed in my direction – the showoff – and escorted Amy into the banquet room.

Meanwhile, another dance had begun. Michael took pity on me – he must have thought Paul had lost his mind, but was kind enough not to say so – and I danced with the superintendant, too.

After a time, Paul rejoined me, minus Amy.

'What was *that* all about?' I snapped.

Paul leaned close. 'Are you acting,' he whispered, 'or are you really pissed off at me?'

I didn't answer that. 'Where's Amy?'

'In the ladies' room.'

'Oh.' After a moment of silence I said, 'The *superintendant* saw you acting like an asshole, you know.'

Paul snorted softly. 'I'll explain it all to him later.'

'Better you than me.'

'I thought Amy needed cheering up, Hannah. You'd need cheering up, too, if you'd just learned that I'd been arrested.'

'I simply don't get where Drew is coming from,' I said. 'I know he was determined not to leave without Amy, but it would have been a whole lot safer waiting for her while wind-surfing off some beach in Buenos Aires, instead of stirring up trouble here. Look where it got him.'

'Methinks madam could use a drink. Punch?'

'Yes, please.' I felt my makeup crackle, so I suspected I was frowning. But I *could* use a drink. By that time the ballroom was hot, filled to capacity with merry-makers. The great doors on both ends of the long hall stood open, but there was too little breeze passing through them to even begin to cool the room.

In the banquet room, a group of gentlemen, a little worse for wear due to the bottomless characteristic of the punch bowl, could be heard toasting everyone in Christendom in voices loud enough to be picked up by a passing space shuttle. To the king, long may he reign. To the queen. To Barack Obama. To his wife, Michelle. To wives in general, and to girlfriends, past, present and future. To absent friends.

Even the card games were getting rowdy, and I suspected that whist had taken a second seat to poker, although I didn't know what the players would be using for chips.

Somewhere someone began singing, 'Whiskey in the Jar,' only to be drowned out by someone else belting out 'Yankee Doodle' in a drunken baritone.

I was certain that the following day, the *Capital* would report that a good time was had by all.

A jig was called, and somebody said, 'May I?'

The guy was in his mid-thirties, I guessed. Solid, tan, fit. He wore the red and white uniform of a Maryland militiaman. I couldn't tell the color of his hair because it was tucked under a fashionable wig.

'Have we met?' I asked, as I offered him my hand.

My partner smiled enigmatically, his green eyes twinkling in the candlelight as he led me out of the banquet room and onto the dance floor.

The jig began. Using a kind of two-step, we jigged around each other for a bit, until another dancer cut in. I jigged with the newcomer for a while, fearing that the old guy – a long-time senator from the Eastern Shore – might drop dead of a heart attack, until I had the opportunity to jig away and cut in on someone else. Eventually my younger partner found me again. 'I'm Hannah,' I said, my voice bobbly. 'What's yours?'

'Ed,' he said.

'Hello, Ed.' Dancers jigged all around us, whooping and laughing. I was beginning to relax, getting swept up in their merriment, too. Perspiration sheened the faces of every gentleman on the dance floor, ran in rivulets between my breasts, but I didn't care.

At one point I pivoted and noticed Paul watching me, holding two glasses of punch, one in each hand and looking worried. I waved at my husband, grinned, and jigged madly on. What's good for the goose, et cetera, et cetera.

All of a sudden, Ed laughed, grabbed both my hands, and jigged me, bobbing and weaving, through a clot of dancers, toward the enormous bronze doors that led from the twentieth-century annex to the porch on the Lawyer's Mall side of the building. Party-going couples relaxed on benches in the alcoves on either side of the doors, so my partner steered me out onto the porch. 'It's hot, Hannah. Let's get some fresh air.'

I reclaimed my hands and fell back against one of the six massive columns that supported the roof of the porch. 'Whew!' I flipped open my fan. 'What a workout!'

Ed took a step, closing the distance between us. I held out my fan to signal keep-away, but he kept advancing.

Using one arm, he hooked me around the waist and pulled me close. His lips were warm and moist against my ear. 'Let's make Paul jealous, shall we?'

I recognized his voice then. Cold. Bitter. Pitiless.

My heart flopped, flopped again. Drew. 'I heard that you'd been detained. How did you get away?'

He jerked me closer. 'Rent-a-cops. Don't make me laugh.'

He jerked me again.

'Drew, don't.' If it hadn't been for my corset, I think he might have broken my back.

Where the hell was Paul? He'd seen me dancing with Drew, he had to have noticed when Drew dragged me outside. Or had Paul been too distracted, making goo-goo eyes at Amy?

'It's over, Drew. The Navy knows that you're alive,' I hissed.

His forehead was pressed against mine. He shook his head, slowly, dangerously. 'Who told them that? You? Or the imbeciles that tried to arrest me outside your house?'

'They know you murdered Alex Mueller.'

His laugh exploded in my ear. 'That prick.'

As long as I could keep him talking, I figured I was safe. 'It was a mistake to come here, Drew. You've already been spotted. Why don't you leave now, before my husband notices I've vanished and comes looking for me.'

'I don't think so,' he said, his voice glacial.

The hand that wasn't pressing into the small of my back slid over my breast and up my throat, stroking gently at first, like a lover. 'Oh, Hannah.' His fingers closed around my neck, began to squeeze. 'I could snap your neck right now, you know. You wouldn't feel a thing.' His lips touched mine, lightly, then he breathed against my cheek. 'I should have done it that night in Amy's room. Saved myself a lot of trouble.'

Paul, dammit, where was Paul? I tried to scream, but the pressure of Drew's hand was cutting off my air supply.

'Alex was trouble,' Drew muttered. 'And look what happened to him.'

Suddenly, a costumed couple burst through the door and erupted onto the porch, laughing drunkenly, stumbling over one another in their efforts to reach fresh air. Drew mashed his lips down against mine, hard, so hard that my teeth bit into my lower lip.

'Ooops! Excuse us!' the girl giggled.

'Mmmmf,' I tried, but Drew pressed all the harder. He'd dropped his hand, though, so at least I could breathe. I sucked a grateful breath through my nose.

Drew had no weapon, except his hands, but they were deadly. I had no weapon, except my fan. I considered jamming it into his eye.

'Lovebirds,' the young man drawled. 'Sweet.'

'C'mon. Kiss *me*, honey,' she said, clawing at her partner's cravat.

Desperately, I tried to signal one of them with my eyes, but it was too dark for them to see the desperation written in them.

Drew's weight shifted, and something knocked against my hip. Amy's iPhone was still in my pocket. I moaned, fell limp, dead weight in his arms. My head lolled, and I felt my wig begin to slip, tilting, sliding, until it dropped off my head, hitting the floor with a quiet *floof.*

Drew started, giving me the time I needed to reach into my pocket, wrap my fingers around the phone. I pulled it out and jammed it as hard as I could, narrow edge first, into his throat.

He gasped, tried to draw air, but only succeeded in producing an odd squeaking sound. He crumpled at my feet.

I didn't wait to see what damage I had caused. I lifted my petticoats and ran, scrambling down the long flight of stairs that led to the street, hoping to be well away before Drew had time to recover and take off after me.

'We got him!' A woman's voice.

I paused, my heart pounding so hard I thought it would leap right out of my chest. *Who was that?*

'We have him, Mrs Ives,' she yelled again. 'You're safe now.'

The next thing I knew, Paul was running toward me, stumbling down the steps, crossing the street, folding me into his arms.

'How . . . ?' I began.

He held me at arm's length, looked me up and down as if checking for damage. 'I'm sorry, Hannah. We saw Cornell

drag you out . . .' He paused. 'They told me they'd handle
it.'

'They? Who is they?'

'I told you I'd bring back-up. Even though Jud's men got
hold of Drew, until we knew for sure he was in Navy custody,
I thought it better to be safe than sorry. Come with me. I'd
like you to meet them.'

On wobbly legs, supported by Paul, I made it to the top
of the long staircase. The first thing I saw was the drunken
couple looking remarkably sober. He had a cell phone pressed
to his ear and a taser in his other hand. She had a gun. Sitting
at their feet, propped up against the wall with his hands
behind him, was Drew Cornell. His wig, like mine, had
disappeared in the fray and the pale hair underneath was
dirty and matted. His head was bowed, so I couldn't see his
eyes.

'Agent Loftiss, Agent Waldholm, this is my wife.'

I simply stared, too stunned to speak.

'NCIS,' Agent Loftiss explained. She extended her hand.
'Sorry we waited so long to jump in. We were jigging, too,
but lost you for a moment when some rowdy kids blocked
our path.'

*Thank God for whomever invented tasers and the Naval
Criminal Investigative Service.* 'Glad you made it before he
broke my neck. I was scared shitless, if you want to know
the truth.'

Agent Waldholm turned back to his prisoner. 'Up!' He
hoisted Drew to his feet. I could see that Drew's hands were
bound behind his back with flex-cuffs.

Drew glared at me then, face rigid, jaw set, shooting shrapnel
out of his eyes. 'I want to see my wife.'

'Later,' Agent Waldholm barked, propelling Drew ahead of
him, down the stairs. I noticed that his hand never strayed far
from the automatic weapon strapped to his belt, still partially
hidden under his colonial costume.

Loftiss tucked her weapon into her stomacher, adjusted her
hoop, hoisted her skirts and headed down the stairs after
her partner, but paused to speak to Paul. 'Thanks for your
help, Ives.'

'I think it's Hannah you need to thank,' my husband said. 'And Drew's wife, too, of course. Amy Cornell gave up a cool half-million dollars to turn this sonofabitch in.'

'We need more like her, Ives.'

I gave Loftiss a big thumbs up. 'Bravo Zulu, Agent Loftiss.'

'All in a day's work, Mrs Ives.'

When Loftiss had gone, I tugged on Paul's arm. 'Where *is* Amy?'

'Last time I saw her, she was inside, dancing with Mayor Cohen. I think he's smitten.' He stooped, scooped up my wig and helped me settle it back on my head, squinting at it critically, making adjustments. One of the birds had fallen off in the scuffle. He picked it up, too, took careful aim, and jabbed it back into the mound of cotton candy I was wearing on my head.

'Should we tell her . . . ?' My voice trailed off. 'Of course we should,' I said, answering my own question. 'From now on, she won't have to keep looking over her shoulder.'

After the coolness of the evening, the heat in the ballroom hit me like a wall. 'Let's find Amy, then get out of here,' I said.

'What about Founding Father?'

'Screw Founding Father,' I said.

The ladies lounge had a sofa. I took Amy there, told her what happened, and sat with her while she took it all in.

'I should be bawling,' she told me, 'but I ran out of tears for Drew a long time ago.'

'Do you want to go home?'

She stared blindly at the wall. 'Home? Where's home?'

'I meant Patriot House, Amy,' I said gently.

'No, I don't think I want to do that. Not right now.'

I swiveled in my seat, laid a hand on her knee. 'You know what *I'd* really like to do, Amy?'

She shook her head.

'I'd like to go to a bonfire. Would you like to come, too?'

Her face brightened, then, just as suddenly, fell. 'What about the children?'

'Melody can take care of herself.' I leaned closer. 'She's got Jason to keep her company. They're joined at the hip. Tell you what, let's find Gabe, collect Paul and our wraps, and blow this pop stand.'

St John's College had been founded in 1696 on four acres of land. Over the years, the campus had expanded to thirty-two acres, sprawled along the banks of Weems Creek in the heart of Annapolis's historic district.

We strolled leisurely down St John's Street, past the back of the college library, past the state-owned parking garage, heading toward the creek. Several hundred people had gathered along its banks, all dressed in colonial garb. It must have been the price of admission. Somewhere, pork was being barbequed, the aroma permeated the air. A large barrel, or hogshead, was the central attraction. 'What's in that?' Gabe wanted to know as we passed by.

'It's punch,' Amy explained. 'For grown-ups.'

By some miracle, we found Karen and Dex. Karen had spread a quilt out on the lawn, and graciously invited us to share it.

Just as we got settled down, a series of explosions lit up the sky. 'Ooooh,' breathed the crowd. Showers of red and white, fountains of blue, green and yellow, cascaded over our heads. Hot sparks, caught up by the wind, spiraled up, up, and up, then nose-dived, sizzling out harmlessly on the water.

'And the rocket's red glare, the bombs bursting in air,' Paul sang in his gravely baritone.

In the light of a Roman candle, I reached for his hand. 'That's "War of 1812," darling.'

'Whatever,' my husband said, squeezing my fingers.

# TWENTY-FOUR

*'You know, I'm really getting tired of hearing Jeffrey complain about how this isn't right, or that isn't how it should have been. We're not about life as it should have been – without slavery, for example – but how it was! Sure, life sometimes sucked back then, but that's not because people back then were stupid. Does he think people nowadays are smarter? Frankly, I don't think that* American Idol, JetSkis *and high fructose snack foods are evidence that civilization is advancing.'*

Hannah Ives

Although he'd never actually admit it, at least not to me, Paul had managed just fine in my absence. He'd gotten through exam period and turned in his grades. He'd finished *Famous Unsolved Codes and Ciphers* and sent it off to Brent Morris for a tough-love critique. And he'd even helped our son-in-law, Dante, build a teakwood deck on the home he shared with Emily and our three grandchildren in Hillsmere Shores.

Thanksgiving had come and gone, and even if there had been no sprightly renditions of 'Jingle Bells' or 'Walking in a Winter Wonderland' to cram the holiday spirit down our throats, the proliferation of TV ads for perfume, aftershave, diamond jewelry and electric razors was a clue that Christmas was just around the corner.

The promos for *Patriot House, 1774* started on December the third following the NCAA playoffs. Long before then, though – thanks to YouTube – people had started to recognize me on the street: 'Say, aren't you . . . ?' followed by a pregnant pause while they studied every blemish on my face and tried to work it out. At Whole Foods one day, I'm ashamed to say, I confessed to being Susan Sarandon, and autographed the back of the woman's Baltimore Gas and Electric bill.

I'm not much into sports, so I missed the debut of the promo, but nobody else in the world did.

'Mother, did you see . . . ?'

'Grandma, you looked *awesome!*'

'Hannah! I just saw . . .'

I figured there'd been so much hype that when the show finally made its debut, maybe nobody'd even care.

'I can't watch,' I said, shielding my eyes when I finally caught one of the ads on TV.

Paul tugged at my hands. 'Don't be silly. Look at you!' He pointed at the screen. 'You look terrific.'

'I look old.'

'Not old, sweetheart. Vintage.'

'Vintage, huh? Like my clothing.'

They'd let me keep a gown, the blue one with ruffles and little pink ribbons that Melody liked, and all the accessories that went with it. When my daughter, Emily, saw it hanging in the hall closet, sheathed in plastic, she grinned and said, 'So, what are you going to be for Hallowe'en next year?'

'A witch,' I replied.

But I did watch the promo. They were my family, after all.

Melody bent over her embroidery.

Jack draining a pint with his pals.

Amy and Alex, in happier times, playing a duet.

Karen up to her elbows in dough, a dab of flour on her chin.

Dex and Gabe, wrestling on the Paca House lawn with Flash.

And me, with an impish grin, taking off my shoes and stockings so I could run barefoot through the grass.

I wondered if I'd ever see any of them again.

We'd exchanged email addresses, promised to stay in touch, but you know how it is. Melody let me know via Facebook when her mother passed away. I telephoned right away, of course, and we began to chat about once a month after that. I promised to take her on a tour of Eastern colleges when she started the application process the following year.

Amy texts me from Kansas City, Missouri where she teaches music in a private school. I wondered if she moved there so she could be close to Drew, serving fifteen years for multiple violations of the Uniform Code of Military Justice at the United States Disciplinary Barracks – better known as Ft Leavenworth – about thirty-five miles away. Wondered, that is, until an engraved card arrived in the mail announcing her marriage to Philip Henry Graham, III. Amy and I keep in touch playing Scrabble on our iPhones while she awaits the birth of their first child.

When Karen visited Washington, D.C. for a meeting of the American Sociological Association, we finally managed to schedule that lunch that we had promised each other. Once a year at Christmas a card might arrive from Michael or French, but otherwise . . .

I was in our basement office, going through the basket where I keep last year's Christmas cards and updating our address file accordingly, when I came across a plain white business envelope with 'Hannah' written on it in a fancy hand. The envelope was sealed, but it was addressed to me, right? So I stuck my finger under the flap, opened it and looked inside.

I gasped in surprise, as Paul had probably intended. But when I read a little further, I felt like a rat, a bum, the lowest of the low.

Paul was upstairs fixing a broken hinge on a cabinet in the kitchen. He glanced up when I entered the room and smiled crookedly around a screw.

'What's this?' I asked, showing him the envelope.

He spit out the screw, and laid his screwdriver down on the countertop. 'What does it look like, Hannah?'

Tears filled my eyes. 'It looks like tickets for a trans-Atlantic cruise on the Queen Mary Two, but they're dated October the seventh. That was *ages* ago,' I moaned.

'It was for our anniversary,' Paul explained, 'but as you may recall, something came up.'

'You bought tickets for a cruise? We were going to celebrate our anniversary on the Queen Mary Two?'

Paul nodded.

'So, you didn't forget?'

'No, I didn't.'

'I feel like a selfish shit,' I wailed. 'Why didn't you tell me?'

Paul snatched a tissue out of the box on the counter and dabbed at the tears on my cheeks. 'Don't worry, Hannah. I was able to reschedule the cruise. I was planning to give it to you for Christmas.'

'A cruise? On the Queen Mary Two?' I was beginning to sound like a broken record.

He chuckled, kissed the top of my nose. 'Can you be ready to sail by January the third?'

'I can be ready tomorrow.' I tossed the envelope into the air with a whoop and watched it spiral to the floor and scoot under the refrigerator. 'But, wait a minute, Paul. *Patriot House* debuts on January the third!'

'That's why TiVos were invented, my dear.'

He reached for me then, and I came into his arms, grateful that the places I yearned for him to caress were not swathed under yards of silks, laces, braids, whalebones, and furbelows.

Was I flying like Kate Winslet in *Titanic*? Making pottery with Patrick Swayze in *Ghost*? Carried off into the sunset like Debra Winger in *Officer and a Gentleman*?

I'll never tell.

But later, much later, as I lay back on my pillow with the afternoon sun slatting through the plantation shutters and his arm flung lightly over me, I said, 'Do you know what I think?'

'I gave up trying to read your mind a long time ago, Hannah. Is it good, or is it bad?'

'Oh, it's good, it's very good.'

'What, then?' he said.

'I think I've just been flourished.'